PRAISE FOR *DEA*

Kathy Harris takes us on a harrowing ride through the twists and turns of human trafficking. She addresses this very real threat happening under our noses. *Deadly Connection* is a gripping story of how one woman's mistaken identity pulls her into a conspiracy of evil. As Hannah and Jake try to find who was responsible for almost capturing her, they are thrown together to face an enemy who tries to kill them at every turn. If you enjoy a seat-gripping suspense with light romance, you'll love *Deadly Connection*.

~Jane Daly
author of three books including *The Girl in the Cardboard Box*

Deadly Connection grabs you from the first sentence and doesn't let go until The End. Kathy Harris has outdone herself with this page-turner, and I can't wait for the third book.

~Patricia Bradley
author of the Logan Point series, Memphis Cold Case novels and Natchez Trace Park Rangers series

I rarely say this about any book, but once I picked up *Deadly Connection*, I had to finish it. The story raced through a few short days, packing every minute with lots of action, tension, and suspense. Oh, not to mention a growing romantic interest. The introduction of the crazy kidnapper added to the depth of the story, and the reveal of this person's identity was both shocking and satisfying, because enough clues were given to hint at who it is. The ending came at the perfect time, all the loose ends were tied up. I'm looking forward to the next book in the series.

~Leeann Betts
author of *Always a Wedding Planner* and cozy mysteries

Other Books in The Deadly Secrets Series

Deadly Commitment

DEADLY

CONNECTION

The Deadly Secrets Series

KATHY HARRIS

IRON STREAM FICTION

An Imprint of Iron Stream Media
Birmingham, Alabama

Deadly Connection

Iron Stream Media
100 Missionary Ridge
Birmingham, AL 35242
IronStreamMedia.com

Library of Congress Control Number: 2021940374

All Scripture quotations are taken from THE MESSAGE. Copyright © by Eugene H. Peterson 1993, 1994, 1995, 1996, 2000, 2001, 2002. Used by permission of Tyndale House Publishers, Inc.

978-1-56309-534-4 paperback
978-1-56309-535-1 ebook

Printed in the United States of America
1 2 3 4 5—25 24 23 22 21

For all the victims and survivors.

CHAPTER 1

Friday, August 27

Strong arms pulled Hannah Cassidy backward, her heels barely touching the pavement as her captor dragged her across the half-vacant parking lot. The harder she fought, the more the man tightened his grip on her throat, and each breath she drew threatened to be her last. She willed herself not to lose consciousness.

Or hope.

If she could land one, well-placed kick, she would make a run for freedom. Fighting to fill her lungs with air, Hannah summoned the strength to secure her footing. Then, with a twist of her body, she landed a blow, driving her heel into the man's shin.

"O-o-ouch! You little—" He released his hold, enough for her to pull away.

Lunging forward, she calculated her escape. If she could make it to the main street, she could solicit help from a passerby. Her ability to outrun her attacker would either seal her fate—or set her free.

She chose the latter and took off running. Midway to Belcourt Avenue, she heard footsteps falling behind her. And then she heard the shrill scream of a siren.

Could it be that easy?

Turning toward the sound of the siren, she scanned the landscape in front of her in search of her rescuer. But the Metro Nashville police car rolled past on Wedgewood Avenue, lights ablaze, oblivious to her situation. Still, it had been enough to distract the man chasing her, who had stopped to watch the police car. While he was distracted, Hannah ducked behind a nearby vehicle.

Barely breathing, the midday sun beating down on her, she

peered through the window of the SUV that shielded her from her attacker. The man hesitated, glanced over his shoulder to look for her, and then took off running in the opposite direction.

Now taking her breaths in gulps, Hannah watched as her former captor grabbed another woman. The girl, who appeared to be a college student, dropped the books she had been carrying. Papers littered the sidewalk in front of her and scattered into the street.

The young woman's neck jerked backwards as her assailant lifted her feet from the ground and dragged her toward a light-colored sedan. He opened the back left-side passenger door and tossed the girl, her body now limp, into the car. Then he slammed the door. Seconds later he jumped into the driver's seat and sped away, heading up the hill toward Belmont University and, perhaps, the interstate highway just beyond.

Hannah's gut churned as she replayed the last few minutes of her life. *The stranger's arms wrenching her throat, choking, squeezing, dragging her.* How had she managed to escape? And if she hadn't, would her fate have been the same as the young girl who had just been whisked away?

She knew the answer. And it drove her to her knees.

Jake Matheson pulled his dark gray Toyota Tacoma into an empty parking spot on Belcourt Avenue near Twenty-First Avenue South. Glancing into his rearview mirror, he ran his hand through his short-cropped hair and gathered his composure. If this went as usual, he would be on his way home in an hour with zero connection and even more doubt that he could ever find someone special in his life again. Almost two years later, the pain of losing Rylie still stabbed him in the chest.

He switched his phone to mute and tucked his Tennessee Bureau of Investigation Special Agent's badge into his back pocket. His date, whom he only knew as Shannon from her online profile, deserved an uninterrupted conversation. And one without the complications of knowing about his difficult job.

When he stepped out of his truck, a blur of movement caught his attention. Someone, a young woman, had fallen in the parking lot. He slammed his door and ran to her side.

"Are you OK?"

"No—" She appeared to be shaken.

"Are you hurt? Can I help you up?"

"I'm not hurt," the girl said, raising her face to him.

Jake grasped her by the shoulders and lifted her to her feet. After leaning her against a nearby vehicle, he recognized the splotches on her neck as strangulation marks.

"What happened?"

She shook off the question. "I'm the lucky one . . . I managed to get away. But another woman . . ." She pointed toward Wedgewood Avenue. "The man who attacked me. He took her."

Jake scanned the parking lot. "Where? In a car?"

She nodded.

"Can you describe the car for me? And the woman?" He pulled his phone from his pocket preparing to dial 9-1-1. "What about the man?"

"They were in a light blue, or maybe a silver, SUV. A Lexus SUV, I think."

"Could you read the plates?"

"No, not the plates. But the girl was wearing a pink blouse. With ripped jeans. And . . ." She closed her eyes. "She must have been a student because she was carrying books. They fell everywhere."

Jake scanned the parking lot, finally focusing on the pile of books and scattered papers on the sidewalk and in the street. He looked back to the woman in front of him.

"What's your name?"

"Hannah . . . Hannah Cassidy."

"Hannah, my name is Jake. I'm with the TBI. Do you remember anything about the man who attacked you?"

Her eyes clouded. "No . . . I'm sorry. I didn't see his face. He was dragging me backwards." She put her hands to her neck. "I couldn't breathe."

"I understand." Jake dialed 9-1-1.

"I remember he was tall." Hannah said. "He towered over me. And he was dressed in a light-colored polo shirt, maybe even silk. And khakis." She shook her head. "It all happened so fast."

"You're doing a great job, Hannah. Hold on while I—"

"9-1-1. How can I help you?"

"Yes. This is Jake Matheson. I'm a Special Agent with the TBI. A woman has reportedly been abducted. I have the witness with me. We're in the parking lot behind The Pancake Pantry, at the corner of Twenty-First and Wedgewood. You're looking for a sil-ver or light blue Lexus SUV with two passengers. The victim is—" He gestured to his hair.

"Blonde," Hannah said. "Long blonde hair. About the length and color of mine."

"The victim is blonde," Jake repeated. "She's wearing a pink blouse and torn blue jeans. The suspect is tall. Medium build?" He looked to Hannah again. She nodded. "He's wearing a polo shirt and khaki pants."

"We're sending a car, Agent Matheson. Will you be on the scene?"

"I'll be here. With the witness."

Jake hung up the phone. "Hannah, are you OK to stay here by yourself for a minute? I want to secure the evidence."

"Yes."

Hannah was either a woman of few words, or she was in shock. Jake guessed the latter considering the unfocused look in her eyes. He ran to his truck, pulled gloves and an evidence bag from his trunk, and then slammed the hatch door closed.

After checking on the girl again, he sprinted across the parking lot where he found three books lying on the sidewalk. He snapped a photo to document their position and then stepped into the street to retrieve a notebook that had landed in a lane of traffic.

Jake froze when he read the name on the cover.

Shannon Bridges. It was the woman he had planned to meet for lunch.

CHAPTER 2

A Metro Nashville police cruiser rolled to a stop beside Jake, blue lights flashing on top of the car.

"TBI." Jake held up his hands, along with his badge.

The female police officer, who was driving the vehicle, powered down her window. "What's going on?"

"Jake Matheson, TBI." He motioned to the blonde woman standing several yards across the parking lot ahead of them. "We have an assault victim. Her assailant got away, but not without taking another woman with him."

The officer nodded. "We have a detective and an ambulance on the way."

"Good. I think she may need medical care. She's bruised up. She has strangulation marks on her neck, and I'm guessing she's in shock."

The female officer redirected her gaze to the notebook in Jake's left hand. "What's that?"

Jake could feel the heat rising to his face. Either the mid-morning sun was starting to get to him, or the realization of what had just happened to Shannon had hit him.

"This belonged to the alleged kidnapping victim." He gestured to the other items, strewn across the parking lot behind him. "I was in the process of securing the evidence."

"I'll help with that." The sandy-haired, clean-shaven man speaking was sitting in the passenger seat to the right of the female officer.

Jake thanked him, but before the officer could even open his car door, a dark gray, unmarked sedan pulled into the parking lot beside him. Almost immediately, a dark, gruff-looking man with graying hair at his temples jumped out of the car and walked toward them.

"Lieutenant." The policewoman acknowledged her superior with a nod.

"Good morning, Officer Sykes." He peered into the window of the cruiser. "What's going on?"

"We have both an alleged assault and a kidnapping." The female officer motioned toward Hannah, who was now walking back and forth across the far side of the parking lot. "That's the assault victim."

"You take care of her." The lieutenant tapped the cruiser on the hood. "I'll assist with this."

"Yes, sir." The driver engaged the gear lever, and the cruiser lunged straight ahead toward Hannah, who now appeared to be weaving as she walked.

"Hurry." Jake's words hung in the air as the car drove away. *It looks like she's about to pass out.*

A brusque voice interrupted his concern. "Lieutenant Dan Browne with the Metro Nashville Police, Investigative Services Division. And you are?"

"Jake Matheson, TBI."

"Nice to meet you, Jake. Whose is all of this?"

Jake turned his attention to the paper-strewn parking lot behind him. "Apparently her name is Shannon Bridges." He held the notebook upright so Browne could read the name written on its cover.

"She's the alleged kidnapping victim. Our witness saw her drop her books when she was grabbed."

"I have evidence bags in my vehicle. Give me a second." He held an index finger in the air. "We'll get all of this secured."

After about ten minutes, Browne and Jake had bagged and tagged every piece of paper and book the victim had dropped. Notations on two or three of the items further ID'd the victim as Shannon Bridges.

"At least anecdotally, we know who we're looking for." Browne slammed the trunk lid of his Chevrolet sedan after stowing the evidence.

"I'm certain it was her, Lieutenant."

The older man gave him an inquisitive look. "Because . . . ?"

"It's a long story." Jake hesitated. "But I was meeting a woman named Shannon here for lunch."

Browne cocked an eyebrow. "So you knew her?"

"Sort of." Jake wasn't sure how to say it, so he just blurted it out. "I was supposed to see her today for the first time. We met online, and I'd asked her to have lunch with me this morning."

"So you happened along at the right time." It wasn't a question. It was more of a pronouncement.

"I'd say I was a few minutes too late, wouldn't you, Lieutenant?"

The older man clapped his hand on Jake's shoulder. "Don't beat yourself up, son. Let's see what our witness has to say." Browne motioned toward the blonde, who was now being assessed by a crew of paramedics.

"I'm OK." Hannah pushed the paramedic away. "I was just nauseous, that's all." She straightened her shoulders. "I'm better now . . . really."

The paramedic didn't seem to agree, but he took a step back, just as two men approached, the younger man who had come to her rescue and another man, who was dressed in a sports jacket and khakis.

"May we have a few words with her?" The older man flashed a badge.

"Of course, sir. We'll be here if you need us." The paramedic stepped farther back.

"Ms. . . . ?" The older man asked.

"Cassidy."

"Ms. Cassidy, I'm Lieutenant Daniel Browne with the Metro Nashville Police, Investigative Services Division." He flashed his badge and then motioned toward Jake. "I believe you've already met Detective Matheson with the TBI?"

Hannah nodded, shifting her attention to the younger man

and then back.

"What can you tell us about the other woman?"

Hannah closed her eyes, trying to remember every detail. "She was about my height. Longish blonde hair. And she was carrying books, or something, that she dropped when he—he grabbed her." She shuddered.

The police officer waited a few seconds and then encouraged her to continue. "What was she wearing?"

"A pink blouse and light-colored blue jeans." Hannah visualized the other woman walking across the sidewalk.

"Was she coming toward you?"

"Not exactly. But she was walking from the Belmont area to Twenty-First behind us." It was then that Hannah realized the older man was taking notes.

"Go on," he said.

"I don't know what else to tell you. He gr-grabbed her." Hannah grimaced. "And she didn't fight back. Not enough. He forced her into the backseat of his car . . . and—"

"And?" the policeman asked.

"I'm not sure she's still alive, Lieutenant Browne."

"What do you mean?" the TBI detective asked.

Hannah closed her eyes again and shook her head. "He hurt her. He hurt her bad . . . before he shoved her into the backseat of his car, he jerked her neck hard. Too hard."

"Tell me what you saw, Hannah." The older man's voice softened.

"She went limp. Her neck was wrenched, and then her whole body went limp." Hannah's voice cracked. "It didn't look good. It didn't look good at all."

Jake watched Hannah sway back and forth, her fists clenched as she replayed Shannon's abduction in her memory. He motioned to the paramedic standing closest to her.

"Do we need to get you to the hospital—"

"Excuse me, Lieutenant," Officer Sykes interrupted. "I'm sorry to bother you, but . . ." She whispered something into his ear.

He nodded. And she stepped away.

"What's going on?" Hannah winced. "What did she tell you?"

"It's not good news." Lieutenant Browne shook his head. "A body matching the description you gave us has been found in Williamson County."

Hannah gasped, and the paramedic took a step closer to her.

Lieutenant Browne turned to Jake. "I'm sorry, Detective Matheson. I wish I had better news."

"You knew her?" Hannah turned to Jake.

He nodded. "We'd never met, but I knew her from online. I was planning to have an early lunch with her this morning." He thought about the messages they had exchanged. Shannon had seemed like a nice girl. "I just wish—"

"Wish what?" Hannah blinked moisture from her eyes.

Could he really say it out loud?

"I wish this wasn't my fault. If I hadn't asked her to meet me for lunch, she wouldn't have been here today." He glanced over his shoulder to the far side of the parking lot, which was now crisscrossed with yellow police tape. It would remain an active crime scene for quite a while. At least until the proper authorities had combed every inch of the pavement searching for a clue. Car tire marks. Cigarette butts. Discarded debris. Anything that might provide them with clues. Especially DNA. And video surveillance footage from nearby businesses.

Unfortunately, this crime scene was now the scene of a homicide. Shannon Bridges had been murdered, while on her way to meet him. A family would live forever without their daughter, sister, grandchild. Shannon's friends would come here every year—on what used to be an ordinary date on the calendar—to grieve and remember.

He understood it all too well, how they would grieve. Grief had become personal for him when he lost Rylie. She had been his best friend since the second grade. The girl he had loved to tease in high school. And the woman he knew he wanted to marry by the time they reached college.

Rylie, on the other hand, had taken some convincing. He smiled, reliving the memory. But when she finally fell, she fell hard. He had been one lucky guy, marrying his best friend. Or, at least, that's what they had planned—until the cancer had taken her away shortly before her twenty-ninth birthday.

Jake knotted his fists. It didn't seem right. And it certainly wasn't fair.

"Jake?"

He snapped back to the moment.

"Jake? Is that you?"

He turned to the sound of the woman's voice.

"I'm sorry." She looked at her watch. "I was running late, and then I waited for you . . ." She moved her gaze from Jake to the Metro officer beside him, and then to the paramedics and Hannah.

"Shannon?" He wasn't sure he could believe his eyes. But he knew it was her. She looked exactly like her photos.

"Yes. What's going on here?"

"How is that possible?" Lieutenant Browne turned to Jake.

"It's her," he assured the officer.

"If that's true . . . then . . ." The police lieutenant took two steps toward Shannon. "If you're Shannon Bridges, then who was the other woman?"

CHAPTER 3

Jake looked from the Lieutenant to Shannon, and then back again, waiting for an answer.

"I'm Shannon. Shannon Bridges." The petite blonde's smile wavered.

"Ms. Bridges, I'm Lieutenant Daniel Browne with the Metro Nashville Police Department. There was an abduction nearby, and we were afraid it was you who had been taken."

"Abduction? Why me? I don't understand."

"We found your books, ma'am. And papers with your name written on them. Across the parking lot."

Shannon's hand flew to her mouth. "Nooo! Nooo! Oh, no . . ."

"What's wrong?" Jake placed his arm around her shoulders. "You're OK. That's the important thing."

Shannon backed away. "Nooo. It's not!" She wiped her eyes. "They must have taken Ginny."

"Ginny?" the lieutenant asked.

"Yes! She's one of my students. I—I'm her instructor at Belmont." She pointed down the street. "I'd asked her to meet me for coffee this morning, before my lunch with Jake. And . . ."

Shannon's face contorted, and she paused. "I'm sorry. Give me a minute." She rubbed her eyes with the back of her hand and took a deep breath. "After we met, I asked Ginny if she would mind carrying my books back to the office and giving them to my assistant. Ginny is such a good student, responsible and reliable—"

"Ms. Bridges," the lieutenant interrupted. "Can you give us a physical description of Ginny?"

Shannon looked away and then back again. "Of course. She's eighteen. A beautiful young woman—like all the girls I teach. But she's quieter than most. That's one reason I try to meet with her outside of class. To draw her out." She glanced to Hannah. "She has long blonde hair. About the same length and color as yours."

Hannah nodded and mouthed, "Yes."

"What was she wearing when you last saw her?" Jake asked.

"Let me think . . ." Shannon closed her eyes momentarily. "A pink blouse. One of those baby-doll cuts that are so in style right now. And blue jeans. Distressed jeans."

"Yes, that's who I saw," Hannah spoke up.

"What do you mean?" Shannon turned to her.

"You're describing the girl I saw abducted." Hannah's voice cracked. "Ginny was taken by the same man who attacked me."

Shannon's expression softened. "That must have been awful." She studied Hannah. "You look a lot like her. It's not just your hair. The two of you could be sisters."

Hannah nodded and wiped her eyes. "I'm so sorry you've lost your friend."

"What do you mean? You're looking for her? You're not going to stop looking, right?" Shannon turned to the lieutenant.

"Ms. Bridges, If Ginny was the woman who was abducted, we have found her and, unfortunately, she was killed by her abductor."

"No!" Shannon cried out. "No! That can't be true." She wrung her hands. "I just saw her, and she—she was fine." She searched Jake's face for reassurance. "Is he right?"

Jake nodded. "I'm sorry."

"Ms. Bridges, we need your assistance. My officers will need to gather some information from you. Ginny's last name. Any identifying marks . . ."

He motioned to Officer Sykes.

"We also need a contact and phone number at Belmont so we can obtain Ginny's family's contact information." He hesitated. "Unfortunately, we'll need to notify Ginny's next of kin of her death."

Hannah sat quietly at a corner table at The Pancake Pantry, waiting for the police officer to interview her. A few minutes earlier, she had finally convinced the paramedics that she didn't need to—or, more distinctly, *would not*—go to the hospital, promising that she would go to the emergency room if her headache or other symptoms worsened. Besides, what was a little pain? She could rest better at home. And she would sleep better in her own bed.

Even though her pain tolerance had always been high, her temples throbbed and her neck hurt. But that, too, would pass. The pain of what she had just witnessed would not. She steeled herself for what would be an emotional battle. What had seemed like an ordinary day when she left her apartment three hours ago had turned into a nightmare. One she knew she would have to relive over and over.

Surviving a brutal attack. Watching Ginny's kidnapping and ultimate murder. And now . . . wondering what would happen next.

Today, she had survived only by sheer determination and the grace of God. How else would a five-foot-five, one hundred-fifteen-pound skinny girl best a six-foot-tall strong man?

She shuddered, then willfully settled her nerves. Taking a sip from the glass of water in front of her, she tried to focus on the conversation two tables away. Shannon Bridges spoke quietly, in what appeared to be short, mostly inaudible responses to the police officer's questions. The college professor looked to be in her late twenties. And remarkably composed for the circumstances. But Hannah knew from personal experience that losing someone had long-lasting implications and that Shannon would have a rough road ahead. She had not only lost a friend and student but, just like Hannah, she would have the guilt of being spared.

Why Ginny and not us? It didn't seem fair.

Almost a decade ago, Hannah had become all too familiar with survivor's guilt when she lost her childhood friend Casey. A song, a fragrance, or even the first chill of the fall air could remind her of her childhood friend and ambush her joy. At the most unexpected time, an old memory would steal today's happiness. And holidays, weddings, and the birth of babies would forever leave an empty place because Casey was gone.

Grief was especially good at a gut punch when she celebrated even life's little successes. Casey had missed their high school graduation and Hannah's success as a Nashville songwriter. But Hannah had learned years ago to celebrate anyway. Casey had taught her that every day was a gift. This was one of those times when she was especially grateful for the moment, even if what was happening right now didn't make sense.

She glanced again at Shannon. They had only met this morning. But there was now a connection between them. Between them and Ginny . . .

Ginny. What was her last name?

A tear slid down Hannah's cheek. She brushed it aside and breathed a prayer for the young girl's family, promising herself—and them—that somehow something good would come of this.

She would do everything she could to help bring Ginny's murderer to justice. Even if it meant putting herself in harm's way. It was the least she could do.

After all, Ginny might still be alive if Hannah had not been the one to survive.

Jake sat alone at a table across the Pancake Pantry dining room, watching Metro Officer Pati Sykes debrief Shannon Bridges. Hannah Cassidy was seated a few tables away.

Although he believed the danger had passed, a little extra precaution couldn't hurt. And, besides, he needed a few minutes with Shannon. If he hadn't asked her to lunch, none of this might have happened. And her student, and mentee, might still be alive.

Shannon sat stoically watching the policewoman sort through papers. Paperwork was the bane—and occasionally the blessing—of a law officer's existence. Documentation could sometimes cost you your job. It could also save your life. But he still hated it. If he had wanted to be a secretary when he grew up, he would have learned to type better. But the way it was, he had barely mastered the tiny keyboard of the smartphone resting on the table in front of him.

Hopefully, he would hear from his supervisor soon. That call would determine if Jake had his own hoops to jump through. Ginny Williams's body had been found over the county line. If there was any evidence pointing to human trafficking, he would be brought into the investigation as more than just a bystander.

His gaze returned to the three women across the room. A vicious killer had become their common enemy, no matter what his motivation had been. The expressions on their faces were somber. Jake also saw resilience.

The truth was . . . no one made it through this world without it.

Officer Sykes and Shannon stood and shook hands. The policewoman gave the college professor a business card, pointed toward Jake, and then offered a final salutation before walking toward Hannah's table.

Jake rose from his seat, caught Shannon's attention, and beckoned her to his table. She avoided his eyes but walked in his direction.

This wasn't going to be easy.

"May I buy you another cup of coffee? Or the lunch I promised?" Jake helped with her chair and then returned to his seat.

"I've lost my appetite." Shannon glanced at her phone and then slid it into her handbag. "Maybe some other time."

He nodded. "I understand."

"I can't think about a relationship. Not even lunch. Not knowing that Ginny . . ." She dotted her eyes with her hand.

He didn't speak.

"Please don't take this personally." Her dark eyes finally engaged his. "But I'd prefer we not see each other again." She looked away again. "I would always think about today. About Ginny."

He thought about reaching out to her but reconsidered. Their relationship was professional now. "No offense taken. I'm sorry to have put you through this. Perhaps, if I hadn't—"

"Stop." She shook her head. "It's not your fault. No more than it's mine." She winced. "Or Ginny's."

Jake pulled two business cards from his pocket and held them out to her. "It's not quite that easy. I will need your address." He hesitated. "And your phone number."

"I don't—"

"I can get the information from Officer Sykes, if you prefer. But I may need to follow up about the case." He studied her face. "Business only."

"OK." She took the cards and retrieved a pen from her purse.

She wrote her address and phone number on one of the cards and gave it back to him, tucking the other card into her purse.

"Thank you."

"May I leave now?" She stood.

"Of course." He rose from his chair. "Do you need someone to escort you home?"

"No!" Her expression softened. "But thank you."

He nodded, and she turned to walk out the door.

CHAPTER 4

Jake snapped a photo of the information Shannon had given him and then placed the business card inside his wallet before retaking his seat. Nothing about this morning had turned out the way he expected.

Shannon Bridges was the spitting image of her pictures online, something you didn't often see on social media. And she was a beautiful woman, just as he had expected. But something about her unsettled him. Maybe she was just more mature than her twenty-eight years. Or maybe he had read her wrong from their brief messages.

Twenty minutes later, he glanced across the room and saw Officer Sykes walking toward him.

"Agent Matheson, I've finished with Hannah's interview. I assume you'll want to speak with her too?"

Before he could respond, his phone rang. It was Frank Tolman at the Bureau. Jake held a finger in the air. "I need to get this. It's my supervisor."

Officer Sykes nodded and took a seat nearby.

"Yes, sir."

"You've had an interesting morning, Matheson."

"So, you heard my voicemail?"

"Yes. And it was followed by a call from Dan Browne at Metro. He wants us to come on board with the investigation. I'm putting you in charge."

Jake turned to Officer Sykes and gave her a thumbs up. "I'm on it, Frank. I'll talk to you more when I see you on Monday."

"Have a good weekend, Jake."

Jake ended the call and laid his phone on the table.

Officer Sykes stood and walked to his table. "I take it that the

TBI is on the case."

He nodded.

"So, we're suspecting that this was trafficking?"

"It's a possibility, don't you think?"

Sykes rapped the table with her knuckles. "Let's do it." She pulled a business card from her pocket and gave it to Jake. "Here's what you'll need if you want to reach me."

He stood, took the card, and placed it in his wallet alongside Shannon's information. "I'll probably be talking to you soon."

She swiveled to walk away and then turned back. "I'm sorry today didn't turn out like you'd expected."

Word had evidently gotten around that he had been meeting Shannon for a date. "I just wish I'd been here a few minutes earlier." He walked with her across the room to Hannah's table.

"Ms. Cassidy," Officer Sykes said. "I'm finished with my interview. Agent Matheson would like to ask you a few questions now."

"OK." The young woman paled.

"Do you have anything you would like to ask before I leave?"

Hannah shook her head. "Nothing I can think of." She frowned. "I'm sorry. There are probably a lot of things I should ask, aren't there? I'm a little bit shaken up right now."

"Agent Matheson can help if you think of something else. In the meantime, here's my card." Sykes handed her a business card. "Please call if you think of anything you forgot to tell me." The officer paused. "Or if you just need to talk."

Hannah smiled. "I will. Thank you."

"You take care of yourself."

"Yes, ma'am."

"You too, Agent Matheson," Officer Sykes said to Jake, before turning for the door.

Hannah watched as Special Agent Jake Matheson lowered himself into a seat across the table from her.

"This will only take a few minutes."

"I'm happy to help any way I can, Agent Matheson." She took in a long breath. "After all, I'm the lucky one. I'm still alive."

"This has to be difficult for you." He motioned to the server and then turned back to Hannah. "May I buy you a coffee?"

"No, thank you. Caffeine is the last thing I need right now." The pain in her temples surged, and she winced.

"Is your head hurting?"

"You don't miss anything, do you?" She did her best to fake a smile. "My head and about everything else in my body is hurting. But I'll be all right."

He studied her.

"Really," she reassured him. "I'm OK."

"You should have gone to the—

"—hospital." She finished his sentence for him. "I know. You've told me that a few times this morning. But I'm OK."

"You're either a strong woman or you have a high pain tolerance."

She smiled, for real, this time. "Probably a little of both."

He leaned back in his chair. "Then let's get this done so you can go home and get some rest."

"That sounds like a plan!"

It was the first time she had seen him smile.

He pulled out his phone and started typing, one finger at a time. "I need your contact information," he said. "I'm sure you gave it to Officer Sykes, but for the sake of expediency I might as well take it too."

Hannah slowly recited her address and phone number and watched him enter it into his phone. As soon as he'd finished, she asked, "What's next?"

When he looked up, Hannah saw a flash of sadness in his eyes. He quickly recovered and cleared his throat. "For starters, because you are the only witness to Ginny's kidnapping, we will need you to work with a composite sketch artist."

"I don't think—"

"How can I help you, sir?" It was the server.

"Are you sure you don't want anything?" He looked to Hannah.

She nodded.

"I'd like a coffee," he told the young woman.

"Weren't you just sitting over there?" she asked, pointing over her shoulder.

"Yes."

"I'll bring you a fresh cup. No charge." She turned to walk away.

"Wait." He reached in his pocket and pulled out two bills. "Cream, no sugar, please." The lines around his eyes softened.

The server thanked him and walked away.

Agent Matheson returned his attention to Hannah. "I'm not sure how much I can help you. I only saw him from a distance. When he was close to me, I had my back to him."

His eyes searched her face. "Can you remember the fragrance he was wearing. His voice. Even . . ." He hesitated. "The touch of his hands on your skin."

Hannah shuddered. "I'm not sure how much of that I want to remember."

"I'm sorry," he said. "It's not easy being victim of a violent crime. If you'd rather—"

"Oh, no. Like I said earlier, I'm the lucky one." She thought about her attacker. "Give me a minute."

Hannah took a long breath and released it slowly. *Please God, help me.* She thought about the way the man had reached around her shoulders. "He was tall. Probably more than six feet."

"Good," Agent Matheson said, typing notes into his phone.

Hannah closed her eyes, doing her best to recall more . . . *anything* she could about her attacker. "His voice was deep, and . . ." She stopped and opened her eyes.

"You're doing great," Jake Matheson reassured her.

"I'm a singer. I pay attention to voices, and his was shaky. You know, like he was nervous. I remember thinking that was odd. It was like . . . he didn't really want to do what he was doing."

Jake continued to type, while she spoke.

"And . . . his hands were soft. Not rough. Or callused. They were not the hands of a working man. You know, a farmer or a construction worker. They were the hands of a . . . businessman."

The server approached and set a steaming cup of coffee and two cartons of cream on the table in front of them.

Jake thanked her, opened one of the cream cartons, poured it into his cup, and stirred.

"A businessman." Hannah continued. "Isn't that odd? Why would a businessman want to murder a college student?"

Jake looked up from his cup of coffee. "If I've learned anything in this business, it's that motive is not always rational. Killers don't necessarily think rationally."

Hannah nodded, processing that idea.

"Can you remember anything else about his physical presence?"

Hannah slumped back in her chair. She was exhausted. Her head was hurting, and she just couldn't think anymore. "I don't think I can. I hope what I've told you will help."

He gave her a sympathetic smile. "What you've told me will help a lot. You may recall other things when you meet with our sketch artist. She has a way of helping with that."

One of the first things an interrogator learns is when to stop. Jake knew he had reached that point with Hannah this morning. She looked exhausted and emotionally spent. Anything she told him at this point might not be trustworthy. The mind has a way of creating an unrealistic reality when tired. Anyone who had endured a sleepless, worrisome night knew the truth in that. There was something about the light that chased away fear. Something about the light that revealed the truth.

Jake opened the front door of the restaurant for Hannah, and they stepped into the midday sun. A glance at his watch revealed a predicted high today in the mid-eighties and the humidity was unseasonably low. Not bad for a post-dog-days-of-summer Saturday in Nashville. He escorted the pretty blonde around the Belcourt and Twenty-First Avenue side of the restaurant, engaging her in light conversation and hoping to keep her mind from returning to the scene that had brought them here.

"Which way to your car?" he asked.

"It's in the back." Hannah pointed to the far-right side of the parking lot. "I was going to pick up a snack at the convenience store and then changed my mind. I thought I might get lucky and find a short line at the Pantry." She shrugged. "I wish I hadn't changed plans. If I had gone the other way . . ."

"It might have been worse."

"Than being attacked?" Hannah turned to stare at him. "Or watching another woman be kidnapped?"

He winced, having just failed miserably at keeping the conversation light.

"This is it." Hannah stopped next to a blue Honda Civic. "Thank you for walking me to my car."

He opened the door for her. "I'd like to follow you home, if you don't mind. I'm concerned about your safety, Hannah."

"Agent Matheson, I'll be just fine."

"Humor me?"

She studied him for a matter of seconds and then said, "OK."

A few minutes later, Jake pulled his Tacoma behind her Civic and followed Hannah out of the parking lot. She made a right onto Wedgewood Avenue, and then took off like a bolt of lightning. Jake had to step on his accelerator to keep up with her.

This woman was no shrinking violet. She was lucky he wasn't a traffic cop.

They drove past Belmont University, where Ginny had been a student and Shannon taught. The campus on the right, with its large antebellum and red brick buildings, stretched for acres behind and around Freeman Hall, one of several structures on the campus that dated back two centuries. Beyond the university, the Civic slowed, two of its three right brake lights illuminating. Her turn signal flashed, and Hannah took a right onto Twelfth Avenue South.

Jake could only hope she was as vigilant as she was courageous. So far today, she had fought off an attacker, narrowly escaped kidnapping—and possibly death——and witnessed the brutal kidnapping of a young woman not quite her age.

He had been in law enforcement long enough to question everything. And motive was one of his primary concerns right now. It was quite possible that Hannah could still be in danger. Had she been the intended target? Or had she just been in the wrong place at the right time? Once he knew if her attack had been intentional, accidental, or only convenient, he could better understand motive. And that would help him protect her.

But right now, he feared for her life.

CHAPTER 5

Jake followed Hannah down Lawrence Avenue, then took a right onto Tenth Avenue South. A few blocks later, the blue Civic slowed to a stop in front of a small stucco cottage. The modest home nestled between two larger houses. Many of the homes in the neighborhood had been built in the 1940s and '50s and recycled through several decades and many different lifestyles. Now the Gulch and several blocks of Twelfth Avenue South north of Sevier Park had become tourist destinations. Jake and Rylie had often driven through Twelve South, as the area was known locally, on their way to and from hiking excursions at Radnor Lake State Park, which was only a few miles from there.

Hannah parked on the concrete drive in front of the cottage, stepped out of the car, and hurried up to Jake's truck before he could turn off the ignition. He powered down the window.

"Thank you. As you can see, I live in a quiet neighborhood. I appreciate your—"

An older woman who had been working in the front flower bed turned, held her hand to her eyes, and watched them. Jake responded with a wave to the older woman.

Hannah turned to address her. "I'll be right there, Dixie."

"Your mother?" Jake asked.

"No. My landlady. I live in the upstairs apartment."

Dixie started walking toward the truck. "Hi, Hannah. What are you doing home so early? I thought you were away for the day."

"I—I had something come up . . ."

The silver-haired woman greeted Jake. "Hi, I'm Dixie Grace Carmichael."

"Jake Matheson, ma'am. Nice to meet you."

She grinned. "Would you like a glass of fruit tea? I have a

secret recipe."

Jake chuckled. "I need to be going, ma'am. But I would appreciate it if you would take good care of Hannah."

Dixie put her arm about Hannah's shoulder. "She's special, isn't she? How do you know her?"

"Dixie, I'll tell you more when we go inside."

There was no doubt, Hannah was trying to get rid of him. "I'm with the Tennessee Bureau of Investigation, ma'am." Jake passed a business card out the window.

Dixie took it and gasped when she looked at the card. "Criminal Investigation Division?"

"Yes, ma'am. Actually, I just happened onto a crime scene this morning. But I'm glad I was there. Hannah is all right, but she's had a rough morning."

Dixie's mouth flew open, and her hand went to her chest. "Hannah? What happened?"

"I'm all right, Dixie. Really. I had a bit of a problem. It—it's just that I was attacked by a man who—" She glanced to Jake and then back to the older woman. "It was . . . a mistake or something. I'm OK now."

"Is she really all right?" The older woman looked to Jake.

"She's shaken up," he said. "But she's obviously a strong woman. She fought the guy off."

"I'm OK." Hannah sighed. "I'm sore and tired. And I need to rest and process everything. But I'm OK."

"I can't tell you how much this worries me." Dixie studied Hannah closely and then turned to Jake. "Mr. Matheson, are you sure you don't want to come in?"

Hannah started to protest but shrugged.

"I will for a few minutes, Ms. Carmichael."

"Dixie."

"I'm Jake. Let me close up my truck, and I'll take you up on that tea."

Hannah and Dixie walked to the house while Jake secured his badge and gun. Then he exited and locked the truck. Hannah was waiting for him at the front steps. Dixie opened the front door, and they stepped into a small living area with a fireplace, sofa, and chairs to the left and a dining room to the right. An office with a rolltop desk and a grandfather clock occupied the area between the living room and the kitchen bar. Beyond that, Jake could see a long hall leading to the outside. To the right of the kitchen, an open staircase covered in carpet led to the second floor, presumably Hannah's apartment.

"You have a beautiful home, Dixie."

"Thank you, Jake. Please have a seat. I'll be right back with the tea."

Jake lowered himself onto the white sofa, while Hannah settled into one of two gray side chairs and closed her eyes, giving him time to assess the security of their surroundings. Looking out the window directly in front of him, he could see the bottom of a metal staircase, which most likely provided an outside entrance to the upstairs apartment.

There was a second window on the same wall between the large fireplace and the office area. The kitchen, where Dixie stood pouring drinks, lay toward the back of the house. From where he sat, Jake could see a back door down a short hall beyond the kitchen.

A few minutes later, Dixie returned to the living room and handed Jake a glass of iced tea. She placed a second glass on the coffee table in front of Hannah, who had apparently drifted off to sleep.

"She must be exhausted," Dixie whispered.

Jake nodded and took a sip of tea.

"Do you know who attacked her?" the older woman asked, lowering herself into the other side chair.

"We're not sure yet, but we will find out. In the meantime, please convince Hannah to be careful. We want her to stay safe while we're looking for the guy."

"Of course. Hannah is like a second daughter to me. We will make sure she is safe."

We? Jake looked around. "Does anyone live here besides you and Hannah?"

As if on cue, a dog—a brindle-and-white dog—trotted into the room, took a seat in front of Jake, and stared at him.

"Hey . . . what's your name?" Jake reached to pet the dog and then stopped himself. He glanced to Dixie. "Is he friendly?"

Dixie laughed. "*She* is very friendly. In fact, she'll be in your lap if you don't watch her. Isn't that right, Ophelia?" Dixie looked back to Jake. "She's an American Staffordshire Terrier."

Jake held out his hand, and the dog sniffed it. But instead of waiting to be petted, Ophelia walked over to Hannah and nudged her.

Hannah awoke with a start. "Oh . . ." Her face flushed. "I'm so sorry. I may have fallen asleep."

"We hadn't noticed, dear." Dixie winked at Jake and then responded to his last question. "It's just Hannah and me living in the house, but my friend Roland is here a lot."

Jake took a final drink of tea before setting his glass on the coffee table and standing. "I hope you will both be extra cautious until we can find Hannah's attacker."

"I can assure you we will." Dixie eyed Hannah. "Won't we, Hannah?"

Jake turned to Hannah. "You probably need to stay close for a couple of days until you're in better shape physically."

She nodded and stood.

"Thank you for the tea, Dixie. It was delicious. It was also nice to meet you." He turned to Hannah. "You're fortunate to have Dixie and Ophelia to look after you."

"Yes, I am," Hannah agreed.

"We help each other," Dixie said. "We're all family here."

Hannah walked with him to the door and onto the front porch, pulling the door closed behind them. "Thank you for not mentioning Ginny."

"I would like to think that Dixie will be vigilant without being scared."

Hannah studied him. "Do you think I should be scared?"

He shook his head. "No. I think you should be cautious until we know who the original target was."

"Do you think it was me?" she asked, walking with him down the concrete steps.

"It could have been you or Shannon." Jake clenched his jaw. "Or he might not have had a specific target. You could have been picked at random."

Hannah stopped walking. "What are you suggesting?"

"It's possible that he's working for a trafficking ring. That he was looking for any pretty girl he could find," Jake said. "We just don't have enough evidence yet to support a specific motive. The best-case scenario is that we catch him soon, so he can't hurt anyone else."

"For Ginny's sake," Hannah said.

"And for yours," he cautioned her. "Keep your doors locked. And stay home as much as you can."

"I'm not going to let him run my life, Mr. Matheson."

Jake opened his mouth to respond but held back.

Her expression softened. "But I will stay around the house this weekend if that makes you feel better."

"Thank you," Jake said as he opened the driver's side door of his truck. "And, in case you were wondering, I wanted to confirm where you live, because there's a good chance that our agents and Metro patrol cars will be keeping an eye on your house on a regular basis for a while."

Hannah hurried into the house and closed and locked the front door behind her. Dixie was waiting when she turned around.

"So what are you hiding from me?"

"What?" Hannah could feel her face warm. "What do you mean?"

"I wasn't born yesterday, child." Her motherly landlady's wry smile turned to a frown. "I know there's more to this story, Hannah. What happened this morning? You're not telling me everything."

"Have a seat." Hannah settled into the spot on the sofa that Jake had just vacated. Dixie returned to her chair and remained silent.

Taking a few seconds to think about her response, Hannah continued. "There was also a kidnapping."

"No!" The word came out in a squeal, and Dixie's hands flew to her mouth.

"After I was able to fight him off, the man who attacked me ran and grabbed another girl." Hannah closed her eyes, reliving the awful scene. "He kidnapped her."

"Oh, honey."

"I was a witness to it, and . . ." Hannah hesitated. "The girl was found later. She was dead."

"Are you sure?"

"Yes." Hannah nodded.

"Hannah, I can't even imagine how you . . ." Dixie's voice trailed off. "I'm so glad you're all right. Did you know the other girl?" Moisture gathered in Dixie's eyes.

"I had never seen her before." Hannah found it difficult to get the words out without crying. "She was a college student, not even twenty years old."

Dixie stood, walked into her kitchen, and then returned with a napkin for Hannah. Hannah wiped her eyes and continued. "Dixie . . . I saw the whole thing. The man snapped the girl's neck backwards and then stuffed her into the backseat of his SUV." She was once more reliving those terrible moments. "I'm not sure he meant to kill her, but . . ." She wiped her eyes again. "But the girl fought back . . . and he pushed too hard. And . . . she went limp."

Dixie crossed the small room and sat down next to her, putting her arms around Hannah's shoulders and pulling her close. "Hannah, you'll get through this. I'm right here with you. Let's pray for the other girl's family."

CHAPTER 6

Monday, August 30

Hannah promised Dixie that she would be downstairs for supper at six and then raced up the interior staircase to her apartment. Dixie had been one her mother's best friends since elementary school, but she had now taken on another role, mothering Hannah since her parents had moved to Montana.

Dixie had been pampering her for the past two days. "If you're not here on time, I'll be checking on you," Dixie shouted from the bottom of the stairs.

"It wouldn't hurt for me to miss a meal." Hannah laughed. "Your cooking is too hard to resist." She tugged at her jeans. "And I haven't done anything but lie around the house for two days."

"You need more meat on those skinny bones," the older woman teased and then grew serious. "You need to rest too. Now . . . go on up there and take a nap or something."

"I appreciate you, Dixie," Hannah shouted down before stepping onto the landing of her apartment.

But instead of turning right into her bedroom, she took a left and headed straight to her office nook. She needed to do something more productive than taking a nap. She hadn't picked up a guitar since last week.

Plucking the Taylor Sweetwater acoustic from its stand, Hannah took a seat in the nearby chair. She strummed, tweaked, and tuned until the tone of the instrument was just right. Having a perfect sense of pitch had always been a curse as well as a blessing.

She took a deep breath. Could she do this? Could she write a song about her assault? Or even harder, could she write about watching another woman be carried away to her death? Music had always been a balm for her. A way to decompress and to heal. A way to deal with the good, the bad, and the injustice.

She focused on the seven BMI songwriter medallions hanging on the wall in her kitchen across the room. She could do this.

Hannah's apartment kitchen consisted of no more than a cabinet and a sink under an eave window, and a smaller cabinet on an adjacent wall to the left. The smaller cabinet had been built around a dorm-size fridge and had an apartment-size microwave occupying most of the space on the laminate countertop. It was all she needed. She never cooked. Even if she'd had a full set of kitchen appliances, she wouldn't have used them. Music had always been her focus. After Casey died, Hannah had vowed to follow her dream. Just as her best friend had urged her to do.

Now, songwriting and recording occupied almost every moment of her time and almost every aspect of her life. Instead of pots and pans, she had stored packages of guitar strings and boxes of picks in her pantry next to a few jars of sunflower butter and sleeves of grain-free crackers. Her BMI medallions hung from a kitchen tool utility rack.

Hannah swiped at a small speck of dust on the side table next to her chair. She couldn't let her attacker defeat her. She had fought back and survived to tell her story. Actually, Ginny's story. But how did you set a nightmare to music?

The truth was her life had been almost perfect until last Friday. She had been writing—and succeeding. She was respected by her peers and climbing the ranks in a competitive industry. She strummed a minor seventh. She could do this. Music was the perfect healer. She would write to heal those who remained. Those who needed healing. There was nothing more cathartic than writing your troubles down.

Her mom had once told her that. She had told her to write her problems on a piece of paper, and then rip up the paper. Or even better, set it on fire, and watch the smoke and ashes floating upwards to heaven. Hannah had always thought of that as giving your problems to God. He was big enough to handle them. She just had to be careful not to try to take them back.

A ringing phone interrupted her reflection. It was Dixie's daughter, Audrey. "Hi, Hannah! Are you planning to go to the academy tomorrow?" Audrey waited a beat. "If you are, could Brandon ride with you?"

"He's welcome to ride with me," Hannah said. "I'll need to leave Dixie's house about one o'clock. Is that OK?"

"Perfect!" Audrey said. "It will be a treat for him to ride with you. He loves you so much."

Hannah lowered her phone to the table. Taking Audrey's special needs son, Brandon, to the riding academy might not please Jake Matheson, but she knew it was one of the best things she could do for herself. She needed to get back to normalcy, and spending time with Brandon at the riding academy was the perfect start.

Her phone buzzed again. This time the caller ID read *Tennessee Bureau . . .* Hannah sighed.

"Hey, it's Jake Matheson. How are you feeling today?"

"A lot better."

"You sound better. I've just talked with our composite sketch artist, Special Agent Amy Force, and she can be at your place tomorrow at eleven thirty. Will that work for you?"

"Absolutely." Hannah made a note on her music pad.

"Do you want her to come to the front door or would that be an inconvenience for Dixie?"

"The front door is fine." Hannah laughed. "Trust me. Dixie is keeping me on a short leash. I'm sure she will require your agent to show ID."

He chuckled. "I knew I liked her."

"Of course you do." Hannah laughed. It felt good to break out of the funk she had been in for a few days. But she had to ask. "Do you have any more information about the attacker?"

"We've picked up a few leads, some underground information. We're following up on everything and, unfortunately, that takes time."

"OK."

"I promise, Hannah. We'll get this guy soon."

Jake hung up the phone, put the cap back on his fountain pen, and tossed it across his desk. Apparently too hard. The pen knocked over a plastic paper clip cube, sending the clips skittering across his desk and the dispenser rattling to the floor. He shook his head. Sometimes the dominoes fell in his favor. Sometimes they didn't. He reached down to pick up the dispenser, and then gathered up the clips, dropping them into the plastic dispenser one at a time.

Solving a crime was a lot like gathering paper clips. It took a lot of time to fit everything into the box. But then somebody or something would come along and scatter everything you had done. If that happened with Hannah's case, he would start over again. He hoped he would not have to, but he had a feeling this case had a lot of twists and turns. He just hoped there were no more deadly ones.

His gut had rarely steered him wrong, but it did happen. Just like it had when Rylie had been diagnosed with her cancer. That had turned out all wrong. He picked up the pen she had given him and rolled it between his fingers. Rylie had gifted it to him five years ago, just before their engagement—and just before he had taken the oath of service for the TBI. He had used it to sign his official paperwork. And he had kept it on his desk since his first day in this office.

Rylie had known him long before he had dreamed of becoming an officer of the law. But after he made his decision, she had encouraged him to stay steady in his course. To never give up. And she had been right. It had been the best decision of his life. He had learned more in the last five years serving at the Bureau than he had learned during his initial training or his four years in college, while studying for his bachelor's degree in Criminal Justice Administration. Book learning taught you the law. But, as an agent, he had learned how to think like a criminal.

A great football coach studied his competition, spending hours watching game tapes, poring over plays, and gauging their effectiveness against his team and his coaching philosophy, so he could best counter their moves. Likewise, a good actor will get to know his or her character. Ideally, they will "become" that character, looking at the world from his or her point of view.

Like a good coach or an award-winning actor, Jake had learned how to put himself into the mind of the bad guy. He would unravel their process, figured out what motivated them—and then what they feared. There were common elements to most criminal minds. Many of them were brilliant. But there was always some kind of unique quirk that set them apart. A good investigator might be able to find them because of their commonalities, but he would catch them because of their quirks.

Jake had always been fascinated by bad guys, and he had become passionate about stopping them. It was what kept him going when his job was challenging and his salary was small. It was what kept him going after Rylie died.

He pulled himself back into the moment. To this case.

Right now, he was seeing only a small part of the puzzle, not the big picture. And there were a lot of possibilities. The man who killed Ginny may have been working for an organized gang or a human trafficking organization, or both. He might also be a lone wolf. Or a hybrid, somewhere between the two. Whatever his affiliation, he was dangerous. Not only to Hannah, but to the other women whose paths might cross his.

At this point, Jake knew he had to focus on Hannah. She had been the only witness, although from a long distance and under duress. He hoped her recall would be better today. It had been his experience that, for whatever reason, people would often remember additional details after they had time to process an event. Perhaps they unblocked them. That process could take hours. Sometimes it could take days. It could also take weeks. Jake hoped against the latter. Every minute was critical right now. There was a kidnapper and killer on the street.

So far, the police department had come up empty-handed. None of the surveillance cameras in the parking lot, or in nearby buildings, had captured a clear image of his face. They had only substantiated the basic details. The man's build and clothing were almost exactly how Hannah had described them. One camera had captured with brutal detail the moment that Ginny's neck had been snapped backwards, ending her life.

Hannah had witnessed a murder. And even if she had or hadn't been the intended target on Friday morning, the guy would still be looking for her. He had no way of knowing how much she remembered.

All of that was a given, but too many unanswered questions remained. If Hannah hadn't been the original target, how did Ginny fit in? Had it been a simple case of mistaken identity? Or had the guy chosen his victims at random? The two girls had little in common except their physical appearance. Young, slender blondes. Both in the wrong place at the wrong time. Or were they?

It was the unknown that bothered Jake.

He picked up the phone and dialed Hannah.

"It's Jake again. I'm sorry to bother you, but I'd like to talk to you. Are you free in about an hour?"

"I'll be here all day," she said. "Come over any time."

Jake picked up his keys and grabbed his cell phone. He had enough time to stop for lunch on the way. Or he could pick up a single red rose and take it to Rylie's grave, just as he'd done once a month since he had lost her.

On the way to the florist, his phone rang. It was Frank Tolman, his supervisor.

"Yes, sir."

"Matheson, we have a problem."

Jake clenched his jaws in anticipation of the bad news.

Tolman waited a beat and then said, "Shannon Bridges has disappeared."

CHAPTER 7

"Disappeared? What do you mean?"

"Exactly what I said. Shannon Bridges has disappeared," Tolman repeated. "Vanished into thin air."

Jake's heart took a dive to his stomach. "Is there a chance she was kidnapped?"

"We don't know. She didn't show up for work this morning, so one of her coworkers called her. When she didn't answer, they became worried and called Metro."

"Did Metro check her home?" Jake swerved to miss a half-filled garbage bag and a piece of an old tire in the middle of the two southbound lanes of Ellington Parkway.

"Her landlord let them in. There was no sign of forced entry, and almost nothing was missing."

"Could she have just stepped out?"

"Not likely. The last time anyone saw her was last night. And her purse was on the coffee table with a wallet full of cash inside."

"That rules out robbery. Any security cameras?"

"None."

"Any forensics?"

"Nothing so far. Forensics is doing a sweep now. I'll keep you posted."

Jake thought for a minute. "What do you think happened?"

"Whatever the reason, she left in a hurry. And there is one interesting twist."

"What's that?"

"Her cat is missing too." Tolman waited a beat. "Where are you?"

"On my way to Hannah Cassidy's house."

"Good. We need to wrap some extra security around her. I'm

going to head over to Shannon Bridges's house. Do you want to meet me there in about an hour?"

"Can do. If anything breaks, keep me posted."

"Will do."

Jake hit the end button on his phone and pressed the accelerator closer to the floor.

Markham parked his truck in his three-car garage, grabbed a paper sack full of cat food, and walked quickly across the concrete to his back door. Opening it slowly, he stepped inside and was immediately surrounded by a half-dozen cats.

"Hey, little babies," he said. Trying not to dump the contents of the grocery bag, the big man bent down to stroke the heads of as many of the creatures as he could.

Straightening, he felt along the wall to locate the nearby light switch. Successfully toggling it upward, he was rewarded with an electrical pop as the light bulb blew out. He cursed and then stumbled forward toward the kitchen doing his best not to step on any of the two dozen feet now in his path. Turning left, he made his way toward the center of the kitchen. He set the sack of food on the marble countertop and toggled the switch above his cast iron farmhouse sink, illuminating the room and sending a posse of small black roaches scrambling for cover.

He cursed again. He would take care of those later. For now, his work was done for the day. His babies had food, and he could rest for a while.

"Come in, Jake." Dixie greeted Jake at the front door. "Hannah will be right down." She gestured toward the living room seating area. "You know your way around. Please make yourself comfortable."

"Thank you, ma'am."

"I'll be right back with a glass of tea."

Before Jake could decline the offer, Dixie took off for the kitchen. He settled into a corner of the sofa where he could watch the back of the house. A few minutes later, Hannah bounded down the stairway. She wore a red shirt and blue jeans. Her long blonde hair was pulled back in a ponytail.

Jake stood. "You look like you're feeling better."

"I am." She smiled. "And I'm ready for your good news. It's why you're here, right?"

"I do have news," he said, retaking his seat. "But it's not good."

Hannah's blue eyes clouded, and she sat in one of the two gray side chairs, never losing focus on him. "What is it?"

"Shannon Bridges has disappeared."

Hannah gasped.

"What's wrong?" Dixie returned to the room with a glass in her hand.

"Have a seat with us, Dixie." Jake motioned to the older woman. She handed him the glass and then settled onto the other end of the sofa.

"I'm afraid to ask. Has there been another kidnapping?"

"We don't know yet, ma'am." Jake looked from Dixie to Hannah, who was now staring in the other direction. He saw her wipe her eyes with the back of her hand.

Jake returned his attention to Dixie. "Shannon, the other woman who was at the scene on Friday morning, has disappeared. There may be a good explanation, but . . ." He thought about the impact of his words. "We're even more concerned now about Hannah's safety."

"Hannah!" Dixie's hand flew to her mouth, and she turned to Hannah, who was looking down at the floor. "I don't want you to go to the riding academy tomorrow. It's just not smart."

"Of course, I'll go." Hannah stood and paced across the room. "It's what I need to do . . . to get all of this off my mind. Besides . . ." She paused. "Oh, no . . . Dixie—"

Neither Dixie nor Jake spoke, waiting for what Hannah had to say.

"Brandon is supposed to ride with me to the academy

tomorrow. I can't . . . I need to call Audrey right away. I can't let that happen."

Dixie leaned forward in her seat. "Brandon is going with you?"

"I assumed you knew." Hannah paced. "Audrey called me yesterday and asked if I would drive him. Apparently, she has a conflict."

"Oh, Hannah. That doesn't seem like a good idea," Dixie said.

Jake held his right hand in midair. "Somebody please fill me in. Who is Brandon?"

Dixie turned to him. "Brandon is my grandson."

"He's six." Hannah stopped pacing and stared at Jake.

"Hannah volunteers at the special needs riding academy in Franklin where Brandon attends twice a week."

"He's autistic," Hannah said.

Jake nodded with understanding. "Would it hurt if Brandon misses his class this week?"

"It's better that he doesn't. He needs the routine." Hannah took a seat. "But he can't go with me. It could be dangerous."

"You don't need to go either, my dear. You need to stay here for a while."

"No, I'm going. Can you call Audrey?" When Dixie nodded, Hannah went on. "I have to do this, Dixie." She hesitated. "And it may be best for you too."

"What do you mean, honey?"

"You're probably safer without me here. If he gets to me, I don't want him to hurt you too." She looked down at her hands. "I should probably find another place to live for the next few weeks. I can rent a hotel room some—"

"Hannah! That sounds too dangerous." Dixie turned to Jake. "What do you think, Jake?"

"Hannah, as of this morning, the Bureau has assigned a twenty-four-hour security detail to watch Dixie's house. We're doing our best to keep *both* you and Dixie safe."

Neither Hannah nor Dixie spoke, and he continued. "We don't know enough yet to say with certainty that you're still in danger. But Shannon's disappearance is an indication that this is not over."

He took a breath and addressed Dixie. "If it's not, and if Hannah was the original target, the truth is . . . this guy may already know where she lives, as well as her routine. He may also know about Brandon's riding schedule and her involvement."

Dixie folded her hands in her lap. Hannah's were knotted together. Jake could see resilience, as well as fear, in both women's eyes.

"I'm only concerned about Hannah and my grandson," Dixie said. "I'm not worried about myself."

"There's nothing wrong with well-placed fear," Jake agreed. "It's God's gift to help keep us out of trouble. But," he said, looking to Hannah, "we can't let fear chase us in the wrong direction. Or make rash decisions."

He turned to Dixie again. "You asked what I thought, so I'll tell you. I would rather keep the two of you together as much as possible. You're easier to watch when you're together. At the same time, and within reason, I think you should go about your lives."

He turned to Hannah again. "When I spoke to my agent-in-charge on Saturday, he asked me to take the lead on this investigation. Hannah, that means that I will be your new best friend for a few days, a few weeks . . . however long it takes to catch this guy."

"But who will watch over Dixie?"

He resisted the urge to smile. "Don't worry about that. I promise you, our agents and Metro are already outside, patrolling this house."

"Oh, my . . ." Dixie sighed. "My neighbors will be wondering what's going on."

"Don't worry. We're discreet when we need to be."

He pointed out the window. "Look, right there."

Dixie and Hannah stood and walked to the front window of the house.

"Do you see that man walking his dog?"

"Yes . . ." Dixie stretched out the word.

"That's one of our men. He will be here, along with others, to watch Dixie tomorrow when we go to the riding academy."

"We?" Hannah turned and stared at him.

He smiled. "I'm going with you."

CHAPTER 8

Tuesday, August 31

At eleven thirty sharp the next morning, Hannah opened the front door to greet Special Agent Amy Force, a slender brunette, probably in her forties, who was wearing stylish khaki pants and a linen jacket.

"Hi, Hannah. I'm Amy." She held a badge in front of her to confirm her identity.

"Nice to meet you. Come in." Hannah stepped aside, while holding the door open. "Where do you prefer to work?"

The woman looked around. "Is the dining room table all right with you?"

"Of course." Hannah led the way to Dixie's dining room table that, along with the large Amish-constructed buffet, completely filled the small room. "Would you like a drink? I have water, fruit tea, and coffee," Hannah asked after the agent had taken a seat on the far side of the table.

"No, but thank you. I'm having lunch with a friend after we're finished here."

Hannah settled into a chair on the opposite side of the table. Amy Force made her life sound like it was completely normal. Hannah had always envisioned special agents as superheroes. "I have to admit, your job fascinates me," she said.

Agent Force looked up at her, smiling. "Why is that?"

"I don't know. You're just different than the rest of us."

"That's what my husband says." The woman laughed, putting Hannah at ease. Except for the ten- or fifteen-year's age difference between them—and the seriousness of their meeting——they might well have been girlfriends enjoying a morning together. "I'm ready to start! How about you?"

"I'll do my best. I hope I can help. I didn't see him close up."
Her mind drifted back to the day of her attack. "I would be better
at describing the feel of having his arms around my neck, than . . ."
She stopped, sensing the other woman staring at her.

"You've been through a lot," she said. "Don't expect too much
of yourself."

Hannah nodded.

"And remember," Agent Force smiled. "This isn't rocket science. We're just putting pieces of a puzzle together."

"Thank you."

"So what can you tell me about him?"

Hannah closed her eyes. "He's at least six feet tall. And he's
strong, maybe even muscular."

Hannah remembered how the man had ambushed her. He had
come from out of nowhere and grabbed her from behind. "I had
this feeling of being . . . you know, helpless."

Agent Force nodded and waited for Hannah to continue.

"I didn't see him until later. He was dragging me backwards
across the parking lot, and I was kicking and clawing. And . . ."
Hannah's neck muscles tensed. She sensed the beginning of a headache, something she had struggled with since her attack.

"Somehow . . . and I don't know how. . . I was able to break
free of him."

The woman was making notes.

"The next few seconds are missing in my memory. I must have
been in shock. I probably saw his face at one point, but I just can't
remember. I can only remember being happy to have broken his
hold on me. To be free. I was afraid he would catch me again."

She shuddered and continued.

"I hid behind a car. An SUV, as I remember."

"What happened then?" Amy Force studied Hannah's face.

"I saw him running away. I was so happy! I thought he was
leaving." She lowered her voice to a whisper. "Wouldn't that have
been nice?"

"Yes," Agent Force said softly.

Hannah moistened her lips. "Instead . . . when he got to the other end of the parking lot, he grabbed another girl. She was walking down the sidewalk, and she didn't see him coming."

Hannah looked at Agent Force for the first time in a few minutes. The other woman's eyes were kind and caring.

"It was awful." Hannah continued. "The way he threw her into his car . . ."

Hannah stopped to breathe. She had to breathe—

"You're doing great. Tell me what you remember most about his physical appearance. What stood out about him? Was it his height? His hair color? His stature? How about the manner in which he ran?"

Hannah put herself back into the moment. "He was dressed more like a computer geek than a tough guy, and he ran the same way. He ran like a man who sits behind a desk all day, not an athlete."

She thought about his facial features. "He had darkish hair. I didn't see his eyes. The only time he looked at me was fleeting, and over his shoulder, when I was watching him through the windows of a nearby car. I didn't see him all that clearly . . . And I just can't remember."

"How was he dressed?"

"In a polo shirt and khaki pants. I'm sure of it. His shirt may have been silk."

"Why do you say that?"

"Because it fit him so perfectly. And I remember the touch of it on the back of my arm." A shiver ran down her spine.

"Keep going, Hannah," Agent Force said. "What else do you remember about his physical characteristics?"

Hannah slumped in her chair. "Not much. I'm sorry."

"What about his nose?"

"It was average. Nothing remarkable. I only saw him from the side, except from a long distance."

"Did he have facial hair?"

Hannah shook her head. "Not that I remember."

"Zoom in on his face, Hannah. Was there anything unique about his face? Maybe a mole? A scar?"

Hannah closed her eyes. "No . . . not really. He was just too far away at that point—oh—wait! I do remember something interesting. He had a tattoo on the back of his forearm. It would have been his left arm. It was in the shape of a square with squiggly lines running inside and out of it."

"Good! Any idea what it was?"

Hannah opened her eyes. "I have no idea. There wasn't much to it. It was a kind of artistic rendering. It reminded me of something you would see in a computer geek magazine."

Agent Force was keeping busy at her computer screen while Hannah talked.

"OK." The TBI agent clicked her mouse for a final time. "We have a start. I want to show you a few different face types. Can you step over here?"

Hannah stood and walked to the other side of the table. She watched over Agent Force's shoulder as she pulled up six drawings, two rows of three.

"Which one of these would you say is right?"

Hannah pointed to the second sketch on the bottom row. "There, that one."

"Good." Agent Force hit enter and another screen appeared. This time it was three rows of a dozen noses.

"I had no idea there were so many different types of noses." Hannah sighed. "I'd say it's this one. Small." She pointed to the sketch in the middle of the page. "And strong."

"OK." Agent Force hit enter again. "Let's take a look at lips."

After running through sketches of eyes, ears, brows, and hairlines, Agent Force sent the computer into processing mode. When the color wheel stopped spinning, a single image appeared on the screen.

Hannah sucked in her breath. The composite looked a lot like the man who had attacked her.

"This is rough, but from your reaction I'm guessing it's close."

"Yes." Hannah said. "That looks somewhat like him. At least what I can remember." Hannah hesitated. "At least overall. I just can't visualize his face as a whole."

CHAPTER 9

Agent Force had just finished packing her computer away when Jake Matheson and Dixie Grace walked in the front door, one behind the other. Jake carried a bag of groceries in each arm.

"What are the two of you doing together?" Hannah asked.

"He drove up just as I was unloading the car. How lucky can a girl be?" Dixie grinned.

"Agent Matheson." Agent Force acknowledged her coworker as she stepped up to him.

"Hi, Amy." Jake raised his arms to show off the bags. "Official duties."

"I'm guessing you were a good Boy Scout."

"Eagle Scout, actually." Jake Matheson laughed and then refocused on Hannah. "I hope you and Amy were able to come up with a good sketch of our guy."

Agent Force nodded in Hannah's direction. "She did great. We have a good start. I'll be servicing copies midafternoon."

"Hi, I'm Dixie Grace Carmichael." Dixie extended her hand.

"Special Agent Amy Force. Nice to meet you, ma'am." She shook Dixie's hand. "You have a beautiful home."

"Did Hannah offer you anything to drink?"

She smiled. "Oh, yes, ma'am. But I'm on my way to lunch."

Hannah held the door open for Agent Force, while Jake followed Dixie into the kitchen.

"Thank you so much for your help," Hannah said.

"You take care of yourself, OK?"

"Thank you. I will." Hannah closed the door behind them as they stepped onto the porch for Agent Force to leave.

"He's one of our best," Agent Force reassured her, before walking down the front steps to the sidewalk. "You're in good hands."

"I appreciate your encouragement," Hannah smiled. "And your help."

She waited for the agent to drive away before going back inside the house.

"Please take good care of her!" Dixie pleaded. "I'm just so—"

"Dixie," Hannah interrupted. "Stop worrying about me!"

"I'll take good care of her, Dixie, I promise. We'll see you back here in a few hours." He turned to Hannah. "Are you ready to go?"

"Yes, give me one minute," Hannah said. "I need to run upstairs and grab my work boots."

Jake followed Hannah to her blue Civic and opened the door. She took a seat, and he handed her the boots he had carried to the car for her.

"Thank you." She took them and set them on the passenger -side floorboard, then reached into her pocket and pulled out a piece of paper. She handed it to him.

"What's this?"

"Directions to the riding academy in case I lose you." Her blue eyes twinkled.

He shook his head. "Don't you want to ride with me?"

"Why would I do that?"

"Don't you think you can keep up with me?"

"Ms. Cassidy, you need to slow down. I followed you here last Friday, and you're lucky I'm not a traffic cop."

"I can do that," she said. "See you there."

He hid a smile—and a lot of frustration—and walked back to his truck. He had barely turned on the ignition, and she took off.

Jake Matheson, you're in for a wild ride.

Hannah turned right on Caruthers Avenue and worked her way to Interstate 65 South, which she followed all the way to Franklin.

Traffic wasn't bad, and she throttled her Civic, never breaking the speed limit. Once she passed Old Hickory Boulevard, she wound her way toward Natchez Trace Parkway.

St. Francis Therapeutic Riding Academy sat in the middle of some of the prettiest land in Middle Tennessee. The indoor riding arena covered nearly an acre, including the surrounding stables and tack room. Hannah volunteered one day a week, doing mostly dirty work, which included mucking out the stalls.

It was she who had introduced Audrey and Brandon to St. Francis three years ago. Brandon had been three years old and nonverbal. But the horses had become the catalyst that had changed that. It had taken a few months, but it was during one of his sessions at St. Francis that Brandon spoke his first words.

"I love you," he had said, leaning down from the saddle and hugging the horse's neck.

Hannah had been with him at the time, and it had reinforced the bond between her and the young boy. He had made steady progress with his speech since that day, and St. Francis had become his favorite place to spend time. It was one of hers too.

She parked the Civic near the front of the building next to a pristine white fence. Jake pulled into the place beside her. She was changing into her boots when he walked to the driver's side of her car.

"How much do you know about horses?" she asked.

He grinned. "I know the front end from the back. That's about it."

She studied him. "Well, if that's true, just remember that both sides can be dangerous, so keep your distance."

"Got it," he said, taking hold of her arm to help her across the gravel-covered lot.

"Something tells me you're dangerous too, Mr. Matheson."

Jake stopped and looked at her. "What does that mean?"

She felt heat rise to her cheeks. "Just that you're a gentleman. Girls like that."

Was he also blushing, or was it the midday sun that warmed his face?

"Even the independent ones?" he asked.

She smiled and started walking.

He took her arm again, this time with a lighter touch. "By the way," he said, "we need to get our stories straight. I'd rather not let anyone here know that I'm with the TBI. Or that I'm here to protect you."

"You think?" She grinned, looked straight ahead, and kept walking.

"Maybe just tell them I'm your friend visiting from out of town. And remember to call me by my first name."

She stopped and swiveled toward him. "No worries, Jake. I've got this. I'm not going to break your cover. I'll just tell them we're dating." She laughed and walked into the riding arena ahead of him.

You'd better watch your mouth, girl. How many times had her mother said those words? Maybe it was in her DNA to say what she thought. And to live life to its fullest. Or maybe it was losing her best friend so young to a dreadful disease that reminded her to live every day to the fullest. Before she died, Casey had told her as much.

"Live your life for both of us, Hannah," she'd said. "I'll be with you."

That had been Hannah's last conversation with her best friend since second grade. It had taken Hannah almost a year to embrace those words. But when she finally had, she had found freedom in them. Since then, she had often felt Casey with her, urging her on when things got tough.

Each day is a blessing, she had heard Casey say, day after day for more than a year after her leukemia diagnosis. Looking back, they had been.

She punched her code into the time clock on the wall and motioned for Jake to follow her to the front desk. "Hi, Lindy. How are you today?"

"I'm good, thanks. Looks like you have a guest with you today."

"Yes . . . this is my friend, Jake." Hannah turned to Jake. "Jake, this is Lindy."

"Nice to meet you, ma'am."

"Nice to meet you too, Jake." She handed him a clipboard. "We'll need you to sign this waiver. Please list Hannah as your supervisor. And we'll also need your phone number."

Jake gave Hannah a sideways glance at the word *supervisor*.

"We appreciate you checking us out. Are you interested in becoming a volunteer?"

"You never know," Jake said. "I've heard a lot about your place. I'm sure you do good work."

"Thank you," Lindy said, retrieving the clipboard. "We owe it to people like Hannah. She not only volunteers, she also holds fundraisers for us."

"She's something else," Jake said and then winked at Hannah. She could feel herself blushing.

"Hope you two have a good day." Lindy waved as they walked away.

"So you host fundraisers?" he asked as they walked through the arena doors.

"It's not a big deal. I host a songwriter night in town once a year and it helps raise money for the facility. They operate 100 percent on grants and donations." She looked around. "They have state-of-the-art equipment here." She turned to Jake. "And they're always wanting to add more kids to their program."

"When is your next event?" Jake asked.

"Next week."

He stopped walking. "I'm not sure that's a good idea, Hannah. Remember, we're trying to keep you below the radar as much as we can right now."

She thought about it for a minute. "I understand," she said. "But . . . we could also use the event to lure the killer to us."

"Hannah. I don't think—"

She held her right palm in the air. "And that's only if he's actually after me." She started walking again. "There's a really good chance I was just in the wrong place at the wrong time." She turned to Jake again. "He probably has no idea who I am."

CHAPTER 10

Hannah Cassidy had grit. There was no doubt about it. But she also had no idea about the danger she could be in.

Jake followed her through the glass exhibition door to the periphery of the riding area. The vast dirt track reminded him of a Little League baseball field. Something he knew well. He had played Little League until he was fourteen. It was his baseball prowess that had earned him a ticket to Vanderbilt University in Nashville, a place that would have been completely unaffordable to him without a scholarship. It was at Vanderbilt that he had earned his Criminal Justice Degree.

"Hey . . . where'd you go?" Hannah interrupted his thoughts. By this time, they were standing in the back hall of the stable and grooming area. "What do you think?"

"I think it smells like . . . horses."

She laughed. "The best smell in the world. Well, almost. It's hard to beat Dixie Grace's apple pandowdy just out of the oven." She gave him a sideways grin.

Jake looked past Hannah to the rough-hewn wood stalls and the bales of straw stacked in a corner and realized how well she fit this place with her plaid shirt, blue jeans, work boots, and ponytail. If she'd only had freckles, it would have been the perfect picture of the girl next door. She was a breath of fresh air, although he wasn't sure he would say the same about his surroundings.

"I guess it takes getting used to, the smell of a stable that is," he said, looking around. "So . . . what do you do here all afternoon?"

Hannah led him to a small room about ten feet from where they had been standing and opened the door. "This is the equipment room."

Jake saw rows of shovels, pitchforks, buckets of all sizes, and wheelbarrows.

"The first thing I do is clean out stables." She stepped backwards two paces. "See this chart?" she said, pointing to a printed schedule of chores that had been posted on the wall next to the door.

He nodded.

"This is my to-do list and today I will be cleaning stables two, three, four, five, and six. Want to help?"

"Sure," he said. "But no pictures on social media. You might ruin my GQ image."

Hannah laughed. "I don't think of you like that at all. You look right at home here."

He took the shovel and pitchfork she handed him.

She pointed to the wheelbarrows. "You'll need a few buckets and one of those too."

"What's my first assignment, boss?" Jake asked, piling all of his equipment into a wheelbarrow.

"You take two and three. I'll take four, five, and six."

She glanced at his feet. "Wait here." She disappeared into the equipment room. A few minutes later she reemerged with disposable shoe covers and a pair of gloves. "Put these on first. We don't want to take any chances."

Twenty minutes later, Jake had finished the first stall. "Now I know why you wore your work boots," he said.

"It can get messy." Hannah peeked inside to inspect his work. "You did a great job. How much longer before you have the second one finished?"

"I'll be done before you're done with your other two."

"Really? OK. Well, you'd better get busy."

After he had finished his work, he found Hannah sitting on the bench outside. "Are you finished with both of yours already?"

"I am," she said. "But, then again, I was finished when you started on your second stall."

Jake opened his mouth to protest, but she stopped him. "No worries. It's an acquired skill." She jumped to her feet. "Let's finish the job!"

They made several trips with their wheelbarrows and buckets to recycle the bedding on the manure pile behind the barn. After they were finished, Hannah pointed to the fresh bales of straw stacked against the wall.

"Now we can put down clean bedding."

In less than thirty minutes, they had completed everything.

"Now comes the best part of the day," Hannah told him.

"I'm almost afraid to ask what that is." Jake laughed. He took a seat on the wooden bench Hannah had vacated earlier.

"I'll be right back," Hannah said. A few minutes later she returned with a big black horse on a lead. She tethered the horse to the pole in the grooming area.

Jake watched as she meticulously groomed the animal. It was obvious that she loved what she was doing.

"How did you become interested in equine therapy?" he asked.

She stopped working and studied him. "Do you really want to know?"

He nodded.

"Years ago," she said, starting to work again, "my best friend Casey's little brother was attending a similar academy on the north side of Nashville. When Casey and I were old enough to drive, we would take him to his classes.

"It was a much smaller facility than this and run by a man who had been a journalist in the music business. He retired to manage the riding facility. Delaney taught me everything I know about horses. He was a cowboy. A real one. Not the urban kind you see so much on Music Row."

Jake could tell she was enjoying the reminiscing.

"Delaney was a wonderful storyteller and a talented song-writer." Hannah glanced back at him as she worked. "He had a big influence on my songwriting too. But from the beginning I was hooked on horses, along with the work the riding academy was doing. Seeing the effect it could have on kids moved something inside me." She untethered the mare she had been grooming and walked her to a nearby stall.

"How about your friend Casey? Does she still volunteer too?"

Hannah's face clouded. "No," she said. "Casey passed way when we were seventeen."

"I'm sorry." He regretted asking the question.

"Saying goodbye to her was the hardest thing I've ever had to do. We were inseparable."

He understood more than she knew.

Hannah pulled a cube of sugar from her pocket and gave it to the big, black mare, rubbing her affectionately on the top of the muzzle as the horse chewed. Then she turned to Jake. "Casey will always have an impact on my life. In the midst of her dying, she truly taught me how to live."

"What do you mean?" he asked.

She looked so intently at him, he felt she could almost see through him. "She taught me to cherish every day. To not take it for granted." She smiled. "And to never consider a day wasted if I have done what I wanted to do."

She sat down next to him. "We need to enjoy each day for what it is."

Jake nodded.

Her phone rang, and she pulled it out of her pocket.

"Hey, Dixie, what's going—?"

He watched the smile fade from her face.

"Really?" She paled and glanced toward him. "OK. I understand. Yes, we'll be careful."

She lowered the phone to her lap.

"What did she tell you?" he asked.

She shook her head in disbelief. "Dixie's friend Roland was walking Ophelia this afternoon, and Ophelia led him to the outside staircase that goes up to my apartment. While she was sniffing around, Roland looked up and saw something unusual at the top of the stairs. He walked up the stairs and found a screwdriver and a crowbar."

She stopped talking.

"Go on . . ." he prompted.

"Dixie said it looked like someone had been trying to break into the apartment."

CHAPTER 11

Jake dug his phone from his pocket and dialed his office. "Hannah, please call Dixie back and ask her to be sure that Roland doesn't touch anything. I'm sending someone over now to dust for fingerprints." He shifted his attention back to his phone. "Forensics, please."

Hannah nodded, picked up her phone, and paced the length of the stables while she talked to Dixie. As soon as she had finished the call, she returned, slipped her phone back into her pocket, and took a seat next to him, waiting for him to get off the phone. Once he did, she said, "I need to finish my work so we can leave."

"Can't someone else do it?"

She frowned. "Why do we need to hurry? It's not going to change what just happened."

"You're right." He stood. "But let me help you so we can get it done faster."

An hour later, he walked her to her car. "Stand over there," he said, pointing to a spot about thirty yards from the vehicle. Then he walked around the Civic, looked under the wheel guards, and walked back to her. "Now, hit your lock release."

She gave him a panicked look.

"It never hurts to be careful."

Hannah pressed the door release button on her fob, and they heard the familiar click of the security system.

Jake walked her the rest of the way and opened the door for her. "Keep me in your rearview window," he cautioned. "I don't want to lose you in traffic."

Hannah refrained from speeding on the way home, and they were back in Nashville within thirty minutes. When they arrived at Dixie's house, a tall, thin man about Dixie's age was standing on the front porch to greet them.

"Roland Davis," he said and reached to shake Jake's hand.

"Nice to meet you, sir. I'm TBI Special Agent Jake Matheson. Do you know if my forensic team has been here yet to dust for fingerprints?"

"They just left." Roland opened the front door. "Come on inside. Dixie has at least a half-dozen questions for you. She's in the kitchen."

The smell of fried chicken met them at the door, and as soon as Dixie saw them, she rushed to Hannah and gave her a hug. "Are you OK?" she asked.

"I'm fine, Dixie. You need to stop worrying so much."

"I keep telling her that." Roland shook his head. "But I'm glad we installed those deadbolts on your apartment door. That gives me a lot more peace of mind." He turned to Jake. "It's a good neighborhood, but you can't be too careful."

"When is the last time you used that entrance?" Jake asked Hannah.

She paused to think. "It has probably been a week. I usually come and go through the front door because Dixie likes to know when I'm here and when I leave."

"You two are making me sound like a worrywart and a busybody," Dixie complained. "When will you know about the fingerprints, Jake?"

"We should know soon if we were able to lift anything worthwhile. I don't suppose you have security cameras installed?"

Dixie shook her head. "I wish I did."

"There's a chance the attempted break-in was unrelated to Hannah's assault last week," Jake said.

"That's what I told Dixie," Roland said. "There are several schools around here. In fact, there's one right up the street. It could have been some kids just messing around."

Jake's phone rang, and he picked it up. "Matheson."

"Jake, it's Barrett in forensics. We found one good set of prints and a partial print. And we have a match. His name is Anthony Albert Smith. Ring any bells?"

"None that I'm aware. I'll see if the family knows. When you have more info on him, let me know."

Jake pressed the end button on his phone and slipped it into his pocket. "They have a match on the fingerprints."

Everyone in the room took a collective breath.

"What's his name?" Hannah asked.

"Anthony Smith. Anthony Albert Smith. Ever heard of him?"

Hannah shook her head.

"I don't know him." Dixie wrung her hands.

"I've never heard the name," Roland said, shaking his head.

"We have his home address. If he still lives there, Metro will be paying him a visit soon." Jake turned to Hannah. "In the meantime, we wait."

"At least you have a lead," she said. "I'm ready to get this all behind me."

"When do you think you'll know something more?" Dixie asked.

"It could be soon if he's still living at the same address."

"Would you like to stay for supper, Jake?" Dixie asked. "It's almost ready now."

"No, but thank you, Dixie. I want to meet Metro at Smith's house, but first I want to check Hannah's apartment for any sign of breaches or another security issue."

"We're having fried chicken," Roland urged. "And if you don't mind staying, I have an idea I'd like to share with you."

"Maybe you'll know more by the time supper is over." Dixie was already walking toward the kitchen.

"You're welcome to stay," Hannah added. "I'm sure Dixie would be thrilled to have you."

Jake' stomach growled. "That's a gracious offer, but—"

Someone knocked at the front door and then it opened. "Hey, Mom. I'm sorry if I'm interrupting but—" The woman and boy stopped, staring at everyone.

"Audrey, honey." Dixie rushed to the entry. "Oh, and there he is. My grandbaby. Hi, Brandon sweetheart." She closed the door behind them and urged them into the living room. "I want you to meet someone. Jake, this is my daughter, Audrey—"

"Jake?"

Jake couldn't believe he was seeing correctly. It was Audrey Carmichael, one of Rylie's college friends. *Why hadn't he put the names together?*

"It's great seeing you again, Audrey." He stepped toward her. "I don't think I've seen you since . . ." He hesitated. "The funeral."

"I hope you've been—" She stopped midsentence, realizing that he was completely out of place in her mother's house. "What are you doing here? In Mom's house? Is everything OK?" She turned to Dixie who shook her head.

"I'm here on business," Jake said.

"I thought you were with the TBI." Audrey turned to her mother again. "What's going on?"

"Honey." Dixie paled. "Hannah was attacked by someone. Jake—Agent Matheson—is working on the case."

"Oh, my goodness. Hannah, I'm so sorry." Audrey's hand flew to her mouth.

"It's been interesting to say the least." Hannah gave Audrey a weak smile.

"Miss Hannah!" The young boy broke loose of his mother's arms and ran to Hannah. "I missed you today! Did you see Knickers?"

"I did, Brandon. And she missed you." She gave the boy a quick hug. "I missed you too."

Brandon smiled. "But I'll see you next week, right?"

"You sure will!" Hannah brushed the hair off his forehead and then turned to Jake. "Right now, I want you to meet Jake. He's an agent with the Tennessee Bureau of Investigation. How about that?"

"Wow! That's cool!" The boy, his eyes wide with excitement, turned to Jake. "I want to be in the Tennessee Borough of Investimation when I grow up."

Jake smiled at the six-year-old. "That sounds great. We can work together. What do you think about that?"

"I'll be your boss." Brandon grinned.

They all laughed.

"Speaking of growing up." Audrey checked her watch. "We need to get home, Brandon, so I can cook your supper. Daddy will be waiting."

"OK." Brandon didn't appear convinced. "I'll see you next time, Jake!"

"You got it, pal," Jake said.

"By the way, he never forgets a name," Audrey said, before turning to leave. "He will be talking about you all evening and probably into tomorrow."

Jake nodded and smiled.

"Jake." Her expression changed. "Please take good care of these people. They're very special to me."

"I will. It's good to see you again, Audrey."

"How do you know her?" Hannah asked Jake after Audrey left.

"It's a long story," he said. "I—"

"I have an idea," Dixie interrupted. "Why don't you tell us everything over supper. It will be ready in fifteen minutes."

Jake nodded. "You've talked me into it, Dixie. I can't pass up fried chicken that smells that good."

"Smart man," Roland mused.

"Great." Dixie clapped her hands together. "Roland, would you please set the table?"

"Absolutely." Roland took off for the dining room, and Jake turned to Hannah.

"While we're waiting, I'd like to take a look at the breached entrance in your apartment."

"Let's go this way." Hannah led him toward the staircase. "But you get what you get. I didn't tidy up before I left."

Jake laughed. "I won't judge. I promise."

When they reached the landing at the top of the stairs, Hannah stopped. "To the right is my bedroom. To the left is my living area."

"Let's take a left. I'm especially concerned about windows and your outside entrance."

Hannah stepped aside and let him pass her so he could look

around. The apartment was small, but efficient. "Have you ever had any break-ins?" he asked, while inspecting the window above her office nook.

Hannah shook her head. "Not since I've lived here. I don't think Dixie has ever had a problem either. It's a quiet neighborhood."

"Everything looks good here." He took several steps to the right to what appeared to be a closet. "May I open this door?"

"Of course. It's a storage closet."

He opened the door to a small room that was filled with a big box of cables and various pieces of sound equipment. Speakers, amplifiers, an electronic keyboard, and a small mixing console. "Do you use all of this?" he asked, looking over his shoulder.

She nodded. "I sure do. Tools of my trade."

"Impressive," he said, closing the door and walking toward her small kitchen. He inspected the windows over the sink, checking the seals and the locks, and then noticed a number of medallions hanging from the wall.

"What are these?"

Hannah stepped up beside him. "Just some awards."

"May I?"

She nodded.

Jake lifted one of the medallions from the small hook that secured it to the wall and read the words embossed into it: BMI Award Winner.

"Nice," he said, returning the medallion to its place and moving his focus to the framed certificate hanging on the wall to the right. A magazine clipping taped to the front read: Songwriter Hannah Cassidy Wins BMI Millionaire Award.

He turned to Hannah. "Millionaire?"

She laughed. "It doesn't mean dollars. It's for a million air plays achieved by one of my songs."

"Congratulations . . . seriously!"

"Thanks." She blushed and changed the subject, pointing to the door across the room. "That's the outside entrance."

He returned to inspection mode and walked to the other side of the room. He looked closely at the doorjambs and scanned the framework of the door. Then he checked the locks. "Roland was right. This all looks good."

Completing his inspection of the apartment, he looked at each of the two windows on either side of the door. "Also, good here."

He hesitated. "May I check your bedroom?"

"Of course," she said. "I'll be right here if you need me."

Jake stepped around Hannah and walked across the landing area into her light-filled bedroom. There were two big windows on the far wall, but just as the others, they appeared to be intact.

"Let's go downstairs," he said. "I think I can smell Dixie's fried chicken from all the way up here."

Twenty minutes later they were gathered around the dining room table, with Ophelia lying at Jake's feet. Hannah watched as Jake unfolded his napkin and laid it in his lap. He was about to take a sip of his iced tea when Dixie asked Roland if he would say grace.

"Let's all join hands," Roland said, before bowing his head. "Heavenly Father, we thank you for your mercy and for everything you give us each day. We ask you to keep us safe and direct us in your path. We thank you for this food, and we ask you to bless it to our bodies. In name Jesus', amen."

"Amen," Dixie said. "Hannah, would you please pass the chicken to Agent Matheson? He looks hungry."

Jake took a piece of chicken and gave the platter back to Hannah. He then helped himself to a scoop of Dixie's green beans, before passing that bowl on to Hannah.

"A good-looking meal, as always," Roland said. "Jake, do you want some gravy for your potatoes?"

"Sounds good." Jake poured gravy over his mashed potatoes, and then helped himself to the slaw Dixie had made from cabbage she had grown in her garden. He filled the rest of his plate with sliced tomatoes. When he took a bite of the chicken, he sighed. "Dixie, this chicken is the best," he said. "You need to write a cookbook."

Hannah laughed. "She is. She's a food blogger. She has forty thousand followers on Instagram."

"She grows most of her own vegetables too," Roland added.

Jake shook his head in disbelief and then turned to Dixie. "You're a woman of many talents."

"I enjoy myself." She blushed. "I love to cook for people. You need to come back again soon." She took a bite of her potatoes. "So I have to ask. How do you know my daughter?"

Jake dabbed his mouth with his napkin and leaned on the edge of the table.

"Audrey went to college with my fiancée. They were good friends. After college, Rylie and I stayed in touch with Audrey for a while, but I had no idea she had a six-year-old son."

"Isn't he precious?" Dixie gushed. "He's a blessing. Smart as a whip too. People underestimate him, and it's usually to their detriment. He has quite the knack for remembering things." Dixie paused. "I'm sorry. I can get carried away talking about him." She reached out to Jake. "Tell us about your fiancée. When is your wedding?"

Jake seemed to be surprised by her question. "Oh, I'm sorry. I didn't explain. Rylie passed away almost two years ago."

"Jake, I'm so sorry." Hannah clutched her napkin to her chest.

"Dixie and I have both been there." Roland reached for Dixie's hand. "It's not easy. I'm sorry you're going through it."

"It's a process," Jake said, then looked to Hannah. "Hannah and I were talking earlier about the good we can find in our losses. I'm a better man because of having had Rylie in my life."

"I had no idea when I was talking to you earlier that you had lost somebody so close to you. Forgive me for my self-indulgence." Hannah could feel herself blushing.

"No . . ." He shook his head. "You helped me see another side of it. Really," he told her. Then he turned to Dixie. "Ma'am, this is the best meal I've had in, well . . . I'm not sure how long. Thank you for your hospitality."

"You're very welcome." Dixie smiled. "I hope you saved room for dessert. I made a fresh peach pie."

"Oh, no. . . ." Jake held his stomach. "That's probably my favorite."

"That's what I love to hear!" A few minutes later, she jumped up and started grabbing plates.

"I'll help." Hannah stacked Jake's plate on top of hers.

While the women were in the kitchen, Jake asked Roland about his family.

"I have a son and a daughter," he said. "My daughter is married. She and her husband have two boys. They stay busy, as you can imagine. My son-in-law works for the TVA, and Rebecca is a marketing executive with Amazon."

"I'm sure you're proud of her," Jake said, taking a drink of his tea. "What about your son?"

"R. J.?" Roland smiled. "I'm proud of him too. He's done very well considering the unfortunate start he had."

"I'm sorry to hear that."

"My wife left when he was young. Rebecca, my daughter, was older and she did OK. But R. J. resented his mother, and in the end, I think he came to resent all women because of it." Roland leaned back in his chair. "I was in the military, serving overseas at the time."

"It's a shame that one event in his life led to that."

"I'm glad you understand that." Roland studied him.

"What do you mean?"

"I hope you won't let one event, one loss, ruin the rest of your life."

Jake nodded.

"Did your son ever marry?"

"Not so far." Roland said. "I've had to rely on my daughter to give me grandchildren." He laughed. "And I've got two special ones."

"I'll look forward to meeting them," Jake said, wondering if he would have the opportunity.

"Fortunately, R. J. has been successful in business."

"What does he do?"

"He's an engineer for the railroad."

"That's interesting. I've always wondered what it would be like to drive a train."

Roland chuckled. "He doesn't drive them. He designs railroad tracks and crossings. In fact, he's working on a project about twenty miles north of Nashville."

Dixie and Hannah walked into the room carrying the dessert plates. Dixie set one in front of Jake.

"Oh, I didn't think to ask you," she said. "Would you like to have ice cream on your pie?"

"No, ma'am. I will enjoy the pie on its own. But thank you."

A few minutes later, the conversation lulled while everyone was eating pie. Roland broke the silence. "Jake, I have an idea I want to share with you." He put down his fork. "This is just something you may want to consider, and I suppose it depends on what happens with the suspect your men have a lead on right now, but I own an old house, actually a small ranch home on the lake near Hendersonville. It's where I grew up and was vacated when my mother moved to assisted living. The place is completely furnished, and no one is living there right now."

Roland looked to Dixie and then to Hannah.

"I would be happy for the girls to move out there for a while if you feel they are in danger staying here."

Jake dabbed his mouth with his napkin. "That's an interesting idea, Mr. Davis. Thank you. May I think about it?"

"Absolutely." Roland picked up his fork and took a bite of pie. "I just wanted you to know it's an option."

CHAPTER 12

Wednesday, September 1

Jake opened the door to his house in Germantown, a quaint neighborhood not far from downtown Nashville, and was greeted by an empty room. The quiet darkness was quite the contrast to what he had enjoyed last night. His supper with Hannah and her piecemeal family, Dixie and Roland, had taken his mind off his own troubles. And Ophelia's antics had kept them all entertained.

Maybe he should get a dog. He had thought about it all day at the office. Rylie had wanted them to get a Labradoodle as soon as they were married and were living together here on Monroe Street. But her schedule had been as busy as his. It wouldn't be fair to an animal to leave it alone all day, and he wasn't crazy about hiring a dog walker. Not in his line of work. The fewer people with a key to his house the better.

Hannah was fortunate to have such a supportive environment. The fellowship of friends, almost family really, sitting around the dinner table, eating and laughing despite their problems, had cheered him last night. Hannah, Dixie, and Roland were pulling together for each other, just like he and Rylie used to do.

Jake stepped around the sofa and stood in front of the framed photo of Rylie sitting on the mantel. It was the only picture of her he had on display in the house. He had taken the others down. Not because she had disappeared from his life. Quite to the contrary. Of course she hadn't. She was with him, on the inside, where her memory could warm him.

Hannah had been right. Just as her friend Casey had left a lasting influence on her, Rylie had left a legacy of love with him that he would always treasure. He may have removed the other photos from the house but not from his memories. The photo of them at the beach with friends on spring break more than ten years ago. The photo of the two of them at Rylie's graduation—he had been so proud of her graduating with a master's degree in viral research from Vanderbilt. And the photo of them the night he had proposed.

Jake could recall each of those special moments without seeing a picture in a frame. But removing their physical presence in his home did help him deal with well-meaning friends and family, who showed up at his house looking for signs of his inability to move on. Once he had removed the photos, they had, for the most part, stopped reminding him to get on with his life and to accept the reality that Rylie was gone. But what they had meant for good had actually been a cruel punch in the gut.

If they only knew. He *had* accepted reality. He accepted it every night when he was lying in bed alone, knowing that he would never have the chance to marry his best friend. Jake's stomach rumbled, reminding him that it was time to eat. He walked into the kitchen and opened the refrigerator. There wasn't much inside. A carton of milk, a loaf of bread, a few jars of condiments, and a big jar of his favorite strawberry jam.

Supper would be a peanut butter and jelly sandwich. He didn't feel like going back out to pick up food, even though Monell's, one of the oldest and best restaurants in the city, was less than a block away.

Jake had just popped two slices of whole wheat into the toaster when his phone rang. It was his office.

"Matheson, it's Tolman. We caught up with our boy Smith. He had moved, but we found him in another apartment across town. He admitted to the attempted break-in at the Cassidy girl's house."

"That's great." Jake took a seat at his kitchen table.

"He confessed to about a dozen other break-ins, or attempted break-ins, in that same part of town. But . . ." Tolman waited before continuing. "He has a solid alibi for the morning of the assault and kidnapping. He was at work in a grocery store in Bellevue. We were able to verify that with video footage from the store owner."

Jake's heart sank. He stood and placed the phone back inside his pocket. They were back to square one in trying to find out why they had one girl murdered and one who had disappeared.

He walked to the pantry and reached for a jar of peanut butter. He had talked to Tolman about Shannon before leaving the office today. At this point, they had no credible theory as to her whereabouts. Jake had a bad feeling about that one. But, until they dug up a good lead, there was little more they could do to find her. He was confident his team was doing everything they could.

His job right now was to protect Hannah Cassidy. If his hunch was right, this had been no random murder. The victims were young and pretty. If he were a betting man, he would place his money on the idea that Ginny's murder, and Hannah's attack, had been the work of a human trafficking ring.

Hannah offered to help Dixie with the supper dishes, but the older woman waved her off.

"I'll be just fine on my own, honey. I have a new recipe idea brewing in my head, and I need time to think about it. You go on upstairs—or stay down here and watch TV."

Dixie was always creating. Her new taco casserole recipe had been tasty tonight.

Hannah thanked her again for the meal and turned toward the apartment staircase. Until last week, Hannah had eaten with Dixie only one or two times a week. She had relied on her small pantry of items to stave off her hunger. But all that had changed last Friday. Since then, Dixie had been watching over her like a mother hen watches her chicks.

Yet having only the two of them around the dining table tonight had brought on a feeling of loneliness. Maybe it was just that she had been in the house too long. But then she was certain that Dixie had noticed it too. They had both talked about how much they had enjoyed having Roland and Jake with them. Hannah was beginning to get attached to the handsome TBI agent.

Keep it business, Hannah. He's not here to see you. He's here to protect you. Once this crazy nightmare is over, he will be moving on to his next job.

She tugged at the waistband of her jeans as she climbed the stairs up to her apartment. Going up and down the stairs was the only exercise she'd had this last week. Jake had suggested she not go on her daily run around the neighborhood. But that request had been easier to oblige for the first day or two. She had now been cooped up for the better part of five days.

Hannah had a three-mile run through the neighborhood mapped out that included a sprint through Sevier Park, plus a circuit up and down Twelve South. Half of her route was scenic; the other half was entertaining as she passed by tourists wearing their bridesmaid sashes and locals walking their dogs on a leash. The shops and restaurants that lined part of the two-lane thoroughfare between downtown Nashville and Franklin Road occupied about a mile of that distance, and Dixie's cottage was only about four blocks from the primary retail area.

This part of Nashville, with its quaint little boutiques and neighborhood restaurants, from Epice to Urban Grub to Taqueria del Sol, was still a remarkably quiet neighborhood and a convenient place to live. During all but the coldest months of the year, there were tourists walking up and down the sidewalks day and night. Even when the out-of-towners weren't around, you would see young couples and college students. It was mostly a younger crowd because of the proximity of Vanderbilt, Peabody, and especially Belmont. But older couples lived here too, many in houses they had owned or occupied for decades, long before the area had experienced a resurgence in popularity. Dixie had told Hannah she remembered a time when she had been afraid to drive through the area.

Much of the same could be said about Hillsboro Village, except that it had always been considered a safe part of town. Ironically, that was where Hannah and Ginny had been accosted last week. Walking distance from Belmont University, Hillsboro Village had been a popular shopping and eating area for locals and college students since the early 1970s. The Pancake Pantry, where Hannah had been going for food on that Friday morning, had been one of the mainstay attractions. The food was good, but tourists often visited the iconic eatery for the possibility of seeing a country music superstar. Music Row legend had it that Garth Brooks used to eat there regularly, as did Minnie Pearl, Roy Acuff, Porter Wagoner, and Vince Gill.

Just as Hannah had walked Twenty-First Avenue South and Wedgewood Avenue countless times, Ginny had likely done so too and never dreamed that something so awful would happen to her. Only the grace of God had kept Hannah safe that morning. Now she owed Ginny's family a debt. A promise to do whatever it took to bring Ginny's killer to justice. He was a man she had hoped never to see again. But if she were going to help bring him to justice, it just might be inevitable.

Markham pulled thirteen cans of cat food from three rows of symmetrically stacked cartons on top of his blue marble countertop. There was no reason to store the cans in the cupboard when he would go through his stock every few days. With more than a dozen cats—now a baker's dozen—he fed them a lot of fish 'n' gravy. Of course, his babies were worth the expense.

So had his house been. It afforded him a lot of privacy and security. The blue-gray-and-white variegated marble in the kitchen had pleased him the first time he saw it. The kitchen had been one of the main reasons he bought the house, which sat on a hill in a cul-de-sac not far from Green Hills Mall. His massive pantry and industrial-sized refrigerator were virtually void of contents, except for the daily essentials of milk, apple juice, and ready-to-eat dinners that he purchased in every conceivable variety.

He opened the glass-fronted door of the cabinet directly in front of him and counted out thirteen white porcelain bowls. After opening the same number of cans, he spooned food into each bowl, and then set twelve bowls on the two yoga mats he had bought at Walmart as kitty placemats. He ran through the same routine twice a day, along with filling the six or seven water bowls he had placed strategically around the house.

Markham reserved the final bowl of food for the new kitty in the house, a beautiful gray tabby. Then he walked to the refrigerator to pick out a dinner entrée for himself and his guest.

CHAPTER 13

Thursday, September 2

Hannah was still in her pajamas and robe when her phone rang the next morning. *Tennessee Bureau* . . . flashed in her caller ID. It had to be Jake Matheson.

"Dixie's Kitchen," she answered with a smile in her voice.

He laughed. "How did you know it was me?"

"Interesting," she teased. "I would have thought that the TBI knew about caller ID."

"So I'm the only TBI agent who calls you?"

She laughed. "Usually . . . and I hope you're calling with good news?"

"Not completely, but I do have some information."

"I'll take it." Hannah sat down on the window seat that overlooked the backyard.

"We have the man in custody who tried to break into your apartment." Jake hesitated. "But he's not the man who attacked you. This guy has a solid alibi for last Friday morning."

Hannah sighed. "I can't say I'm not disappointed." She had been hoping for this to be over.

"We're working as fast as we can."

"I know," she said. "And I'm grateful. Have you heard anything from Shannon?"

"Nothing yet. I'd like to think she slipped off on her own and is hiding somewhere until all of this settles down."

"What are the chances of that?" Hannah watched Dixie and Ophelia walking toward the garden. Dixie carried a basket to collect ripe tomatoes, while the dog sniffed the ground for evidence of rabbits, squirrels, and neighborhood cats.

"There was no sign that she was taken by force, so it's possible," he said. "But we're not ruling anything out."

Hannah's heart dropped to her stomach. Despite their good efforts, the TBI hadn't come up with much in the way of answers in the past five days. Everything Jake Matheson said had been qualified with "We're following up on every lead" or "We're not ruling anything out."

"Jake, I made a decision last night. I'm going to perform at the St. Francis fundraiser on Saturday. It's too late for me to cancel."

"I'd hoped you would change your mind."

"I thought about it. I really did. But I need to do this. Not just for the academy, but for me. I need to start living my life again. I can't just sit around the house forever."

"You realize it's possible that the man who attacked you could have been targeting you and not Ginny, right?"

Hannah thought about it for a minute. "If that's the case, then I'm making the right decision."

"And how's that?"

"Why should I wait for him to attack me when I'm at home or out for a run and, perhaps, the most vulnerable? Why not set up the right circumstances to catch him?"

She waited for Jake to respond but his silence told her that she was right.

"What time do I need to meet you at your house?"

"What do you mean?"

"I'm here to protect you, remember?"

"Rehearsal is tomorrow at five o'clock."

"I'll see you at your place at four thirty."

"Thank you."

Hannah hit the end button on her phone and tucked it into the pocket of her robe. She had a lot to do today, and very little of it could be accomplished at home. If the man who had attempted to break into her apartment had nothing to do with her attack, then chances were good that her attack had also been random. If that were the case, what did she have to fear? She hadn't even seen the man well enough to identify him clearly.

She would be careful, but she was going out this morning. She couldn't waste another day when she had three new song demos to mix and pitch to Tim McGraw's producer. She would be able to finish those in two hours in her Hillsboro Village studio, one she shared with two other songwriter friends. They had dubbed the small thirty-by-thirty-foot space "the Gold Mine" after writing their first successful song there a few years ago. The space was divided into two rooms, one for the sound board and workstation, and the other for the musicians and singers to perform. They used the second room, when it was not being used for recording, as their songwriting area.

The Gold Mine was tucked into the back corner of a commercial building in Hillsboro Village and wasn't much more than a hole in the wall, an unused warehouse space they had managed to lease for a great price. Hannah had been walking from the studio to The Pancake Pantry the morning of her attack.

If she worked quickly today, she would have enough time to record the final song for her new recording project . . .

"Hannah!" Dixie called from the bottom of the stairs. "Do you mind helping me in the garden?"

Hannah looked at the clock on her wall above the bar. Hopefully, Dixie's request wouldn't delay her too long. She had to get to the studio.

"Give me a few minutes, Dixie," Hannah said, before hurrying to her bedroom to pull on a t-shirt and a pair of running shorts. Maybe she would even go out for a run after she finished her recording.

A few minutes later, Dixie was explaining to Hannah how to inspect a garden for bean beetles. Hannah shrugged her shoulders. "They look harmless to me, like yellow ladybugs."

"They're more destructive than they look." Dixie plucked one of the tiny hard-shelled insects off the underside of a leaf and deposited it into a Mason jar. She had given Hannah a jar too.

Dixie snapped a bean from its stem and held it in the air for Hannah to see. "See the black spots on this bean? They also eat holes in the leaves and can eventually kill a young plant. If we don't take care of them now, we'll have even more of them next spring."

"OK," Hannah said somewhat unenthusiastically. "I'll start over here." She walked to the far side of the garden, which was about ten feet wide and stretched the length of the privacy fence that encompassed Dixie's backyard. Almost immediately she spotted a stray beetle crawling across the leaf of a squash plant that was still ripe with fruit—a crookneck yellow variety almost the same color as the beetles she was hunting.

Hannah used her index finger to knock the insect into her jar, then shouted to Dixie, who was working more than twenty feet away. "This reminds me of catching lightning bugs and putting them in a jar when I was a little girl."

Dixie laughed. "It's not quite as much fun, but it helps to have company." Her wide smile conveyed even more than her words. "I would be out here all day if I had to do this by myself." She stopped working and turned to Hannah. "Did I interrupt anything important?"

Hannah shook her head. "Not really, but after we finish, I'm planning to drive to my studio to work on a few song mixes."

"I don't think Jake would like that." The older woman frowned as she disposed of another beetle.

"He's not the boss of me, Dixie. I've already given up my volunteer work for St. Francis tomorrow. How much more do I have to give up?" Hannah regretted the words as soon as they left her mouth. Her frustration had gotten the best of her.

Dixie stopped working. "He's only trying to help you, honey. We're all trying to help."

"I know, and I'm sorry," Hannah apologized. "I didn't mean for that to come out like it did. I'm just frustrated. I do appreciate him. And I especially appreciate you, Dixie."

"We're all in this together, and we'll get through it," the older woman reminded her. "Remember how hard it was to get through the COVID-19 lockdowns? That took a year. Jake Matheson is only asking for a few days."

"At least I could go out for a run during COVID." Hannah wiped perspiration from her forehead and looked up at the midday sun.

The dog days of summer had apparently decided to hang around through Labor Day. She would need a shower before going out this afternoon.

"You can do that soon, honey." Dixie gave her a warm smile. "And, as soon as we finish here, I'll stir up a batch of fresh lemonade. Have I ever made you my lemonade with mint and basil?"

"No, you haven't." Hannah perked up. "That sounds wonderful."

Markham carried the tray of food up the stairs and down the hall past three bedrooms, one on the right and two on the left, walked down three short steps, and into his media room, where eight theater chairs, four rows of two seats each, were positioned for watching a large theater screen on the back wall of the house. To his left, a long span of floor-to-ceiling windows equipped with electric, light-blocking blinds looked out onto his front yard. The fourth and far wall of the media room had been decorated with a display of oversized posters from iconic movies of the 1970s— *American Graffiti, Animal House, Saturday Night Fever, Rocky,* and *Nashville.* The five movies had all been popular when his father was in his teens and early twenties. None of them had significance to Markham, but they had been permanently mounted to the wall by the home's previous owners, and he had decided to leave them. Not only because they provided ambience. But because they obscured the entrance to the secret room.

Markham transferred the weight of the food tray to his left hand and released the hidden latch behind the Nashville poster. A full-size door swung open, and he entered the room. Although he had never expected to use this room when he bought the house, it now provided the perfect place for his temporary guests, Shannon Bridges and her cat Miss Phoebe.

"I'm sorry to bother you, Miss Shannon, but I have your lunch." He nodded toward the tabby lying on the bed beside her. "I have Miss Phoebe's lunch too."

Markham set the tray on the table at the foot of the twin bed, which all but filled the small room. With its lack of windows and abundance of sound proofing, the tiny space was a perfect hidden guest suite. It even had a half bathroom at one end, so his visitor had everything she needed.

"You're in bed late this morning," he said. "I hope you'll enjoy the lemon chicken and rice I warmed up for you. It's one of my favorites. I brought you a bottle of sweet tea too." He adjusted the lampshade next to one of the only two chairs in the room. "Do you need anything else?"

"I need to get out of here," she growled at him.

"I can't do that. You know too much, and I'm afraid you won't keep it to yourself."

He reached down, scooped up Miss Phoebe, and set her on the floor beside the freshly prepared dish he had just put down.

"You're a good kitty," he said, rubbing her around the scruff of her neck.

"I promise. I won't say anything." Shannon pulled the covers closer to her.

Markham shook his head. "You can leave in good time. But first I have to get the girl."

CHAPTER 14

Jake glanced at the clock on his office wall. He had time for a call before heading upstairs to his late-morning meeting. Although he hadn't committed Poe's number to memory, he probably should have.

Poe was one of his best informants. Of course, Poe wasn't his real name—no one trying to stay alive on the street would take that chance—but it was appropriately descriptive of the dark, seedy-looking man. His parents had given him the unfortunate first name of Edgar, which when paired with his family name, Allan, had likely brought a lot of teasing from his classmates, along with the nickname of Poe. By some strange twist of fate, Poe had also grown into a thin, sharp-featured man, who physically resembled the famous poet.

What Poe lacked in personality, he made up for in smarts. Street smarts. His nondescript physical attributes allowed him to infiltrate the depths of Nashville's street crime syndicate without rousing suspicion.

Hanging out with unsavory characters usually reaped unsavory information. And, in Poe's case, quite a bit of financial reward. A good street informant could earn enough—and legally—to eke out a meager living for himself, as long as that person didn't have a penchant for drugs or alcohol, which Poe didn't.

Poe's area of expertise was trafficking, both drugs and human, but he was especially connected to the underground world of sex trafficking in Nashville.

Jake picked up his phone and dialed the snitch.

"Yeah." Poe had mastered the art of one-word responses.

"It's Payday. What's the word on the street?"

"There's a lot of rumble about a girl who was killed."

"Do you know who did it?"

"I don't know his name."

"Can you find out?"

"I'll try. I don't know that he works for an organization, but he's a mess-up. Not the best at what he does. Everyone else is trying to lay low for a while until the heat dies down."

"Anything else?"

"That's all I know. I'll work on getting the guy's name."

Jake hung up his phone. He had his answer. Ginny's death and Hannah's assault were tied to a human trafficking ring, whether intentional or accidental.

He looked at the clock again. It was time for his staff meeting. Afterward, he had another call to make. He grabbed his badge and took off for the elevator, locking his office door behind him.

About twelve thirty, Hannah and Dixie finished their garden work and went inside for lunch and lemonade. Hannah watched from a seat behind the kitchen bar as Dixie hand-squeezed lemons from a white basket on her black granite countertop. Dixie's kitchen looked like a vignette from a Southern ladies' magazine. Her entire house was the same way. Decorated with touches of black, blue, and lemon yellow against a white palette, it had the feel of femininity but not overpoweringly so. Dixie's style, including the apartment upstairs, exuded contemporary cottage charm.

Hannah could envision the magazine layout now, maybe even a cover shot, which would feature a photo of Dixie's living room taken from the front entrance. The huge white fireplace, which had been surrounded by a wall of mahogany wood planks, anchored the room. In the winter, a fire would be flickering around the gas logs. In the summer, Dixie's pure-white, contemporary-styled sofa with its splashes of color and texture, from lemon yellow throw pillows to the fake fur ottoman and throw, would generate the main focal point of the room.

The camera's eye would be drawn next to mahogany beams

running perpendicular to the home's outside walls and leading from Dixie's kitchen office to the kitchen itself, with its white cabinetry, stainless steel appliances, stainless steel hardware, and black granite countertops.

But it wasn't a show kitchen. Dixie was serious about her cooking. She had retired from a successful journalism career to pursue her passion for avant-garde Southern cuisine. After twenty years as the anchor of a local midday television show, Dixie had a built-in following for her food blog, but she had doubled that number in the past few years and was now working on her first cookbook. Hannah was fortunate to be a taste tester for many of Dixie's revitalized throwback recipes from her Southern heritage.

"So after you squeeze your lemons—being careful not to let any seeds slip by you—you pour the juice into a glass pitcher and add an equal amount of water, plus an equal amount of simple syrup." Dixie worked as she spoke. "I made the simple syrup with fresh basil, fresh mint, sugar, and water earlier this morning, so all I have to do now is pop it out of the refrigerator and into the pitcher."

"That's looking good, Dixie," Hannah said.

Dixie added ice to her pitcher and stirred the lemony-colored mixture with a long spoon. She topped it with a sprig of mint, and then poured two glasses. She gave one glass to Hannah.

Hannah took a sip. The flavor took her by surprise. "It's great. Tangy, savory, and sweet at the same time." Hannah let the taste linger momentarily. "It's fresh tasting . . . and thirst quenching."

Dixie laughed. "You're an expert food reviewer, my dear. I need to put you on staff."

"I think I'm already on your benefactor list. You're too good to me, Dixie."

"We all need help from time to time, Hannah," Dixie said, setting a plate of cold cuts and carrot sticks in front of Hannah. "In this life we need to learn to give and receive. Both are equally valuable when we commit to the cycle." She wiped moisture off her countertop with a dish towel. "One day you will be on the giving end, as I know you already have been many times in your young life."

"I'm not all that young anymore, Dixie." Hannah laughed.

"Oh, honey. You're just getting started at . . . how old are you now?"

"Twenty-seven! That's not young in my business." Hannah shook her head. "By thirty, a musician has usually gone past his or her opportunity to succeed as a performer. I have a lot to do in the next year if I'm going to live my dream."

Dixie smiled. "Well, it won't hurt to give yourself another few days or a few weeks to return to your—" The older woman stopped mid-sentence, as if struck by a new idea. "If you have time today, I have an idea for you."

Hannah set down her glass, which was now empty, and picked up a carrot stick.

"Why don't you go with Roland and me to visit his mother's assisted living community. You can take your guitar and sing a few songs for the residents. I know they would love it!"

"I would enjoy that, but I really need to—" She was interrupted by her phone.

It was Jake.

"What are y'all up to this afternoon?"

"We just finished working in the backyard, and I was thinking about going to my studio for a few hours."

"Oh . . ."

Hannah could tell that her last comment had taken Jake Matheson by surprise.

"Well, I have another suggestion, if you're interested."

"Tell me."

"I'm leaving the office around four o'clock today, and I haven't had my run yet. Would you like to join me?"

"Oh . . . well. Yes! That would be great." She couldn't wait to stretch her legs again. "Where will I meet you?"

"I'll just meet you at your place about four thirty, if that's OK. We can run your neighborhood. You can give me a tour." He hesitated. "Does that work for you?"

"Yes. Sounds good. See you then."

Hannah hit end on her phone and didn't even try to hide the

smile that had ambushed her face. She looked to Dixie. "What time are you and Roland leaving?"

"Probably about one thirty."

"I'll go with you," Hannah said. "That was Agent Matheson, and he's coming here at four thirty to take me for a run."

"How nice of him!" Dixie said.

"That doesn't leave me time to work at the studio, so I'll take you up on your invitation. It sounds like fun."

"Great! Roland and I will enjoy it too."

Hannah got up from her seat. "May I help you with the glasses?" she asked.

"No, dear. I've got them."

"OK." She picked up her plate of food. "Thanks for lunch, Dixie. I'm going to run upstairs and take a shower before we leave."

CHAPTER 15

Jake took a seat at the conference room table a few minutes before his afternoon briefing was set to begin. His boss, Agent-in-Charge Frank Tolman, was seated at the head of the table. Special Agent Beau Gardner took a seat beside Jake. And within a few minutes, Special Agent Andy Mann and Criminal Intelligence Unit team member Randall Mays took seats across the table.

After a few minutes of small talk, at two o'clock sharp, Tolman said, "Let's get started." Tolman turned to his right. "Andy, what can you tell us about the pathology of the Genevieve 'Ginny' Williams case?"

Mann cleared his throat. "Ginny Williams, nineteen years of age, died on the morning of August 28, of a cervical fracture resulting from blunt force trauma. Based on the medical examiner's report and a witness statement, Ms. Williams most likely died instantly at the hands of a yet to be identified man."

Mann rifled through paperwork.

"At this time, we haven't found any significant DNA evidence from the body or in the area where Ms. Williams's body was found by two teenage boys who were fishing in the Harpeth River. They made the discovery at approximately twelve hundred hours, which was shortly after the reported kidnapping and murder. The body was found in a wooded area just off Old Hillsboro Road in Brentwood."

"What are the chances of finding video evidence of the body being dropped?" Tolman asked.

"None at all. It was an isolated area."

"Tire tracks?"

"Nothing, sir. Nor have we had any suspicious sightings of someone driving a silver Lexus. As you can imagine, there are a lot of Lexus SUVs on that side of town."

Tolman nodded.

"Randall, what do we know about Williams?"

"Her family gave us full access to her computer and her phone, and we're going through them. So far, nothing stands out except that she had been playing around on a few online dating apps."

Jake took a quick breath and waited for his turn to speak.

"I'll keep you posted as we learn more," Randall said.

"OK." Tolman rubbed the back of his neck. "What connection are you seeing between Williams and Shannon Bridges? Are there any emails or texts to indicate that Bridges had plans to go out of town?"

"No, sir. The only emails and texts I have seen, at least so far, have given us very little. They're indicative of a typical teacher-student relationship. Not much personal information was shared between them."

"Do we have access to Professor Bridges's computer?"

"At this point, sir, we haven't located her computer. According to her assistant, she worked on a laptop and carried it back and forth between her work and her home. She must have taken it with her when she left her home."

"That's not helpful."

"No, sir. We'll keep looking."

"OK, Agent Gardner. What are you seeing in the Cassidy girl's neighborhood?"

"Everything looks normal, sir. My guys and Metro have been watching the house for several days, and we've seen nothing of concern."

"Great." Tolman nodded. "Let's hope it stays that way." He turned to Jake.

"Jake, you've been on the inside. What's going on with Ms. Cassidy personally? Any suspect phone calls or other communication? How is she doing physically?"

"No suspect communication that I'm aware of," Jake said. "Physically and emotionally, I believe she is doing as well as could be expected. To my knowledge, she hasn't complained of any lingering physical issues, and she appears to be handling everything OK, with the exception of being stir-crazy.

"I've had a difficult time convincing her to stay out of the public eye. As you know," he said as he looked to Tolman, "my main consideration has been whether or not Hannah was the original target of the kidnapper, or if that was Ginny Williams, making Hannah the unfortunate bystander. From a distance, or to someone who didn't know either of them well, they shared a lot of physical characteristics. Long blonde hair, slender build, roughly the same age. Although Ginny was several years younger."

Frank nodded, and Jake continued. "Of course, the next question is *why were the two girls attacked?* Was it random and spontaneous? Was it planned? If it was the latter, it makes sense that one of the girls was most likely the target. But which one? It's a case of which came first, the chicken or the egg. Until we know which girl was the target, we may not understand the reason for the crime. But if we don't know the reason for the crime, how do we decide which girl was the intended target?"

He took a breath.

"Sex trafficking," Mays said.

Mann, who had been absentmindedly tapping his pen on the table, nodded in agreement.

"Exactly what I think," Jake said. "That's why I called my source in that area, and he seemed to confirm that idea. He said the word on the street is about a 'mess-up' that brought on the unintended death of a new girl, and that the underground is laying low right now."

"Does he know what organization is responsible?"

Jake shook his head. "No. But he has an ear to the ground, trying get a name for the guy who did it."

Tolman nodded. "Good work, everyone. We can—" He stopped mid-sentence. "By the way, Matheson, can you please explain how you ended up on the scene right after the kidnapping?"

Heat rushed to Jake's face. "I was meeting someone at The Pancake Pantry."

Tolman nodded. He was already aware because Jake had told

him. Evidently, he wanted to get it on the table for all involved.

"And who were you meeting?" Tolman asked.

"I was meeting Shannon Bridges, sir."

There was a collective intake of breath and then silence. Jake made eye contact with each of the men. "I met her online, asked her to meet me for something to eat, and you know the rest of the story."

"Not good," Mann said.

"Very interesting," Gardner added.

"Believe me, I know. I've thought about it almost nonstop. And now, with Shannon's disappearance, it keeps getting worse."

"Any idea how it all fits together?" Tolman asked.

"I wish I knew." Jake turned to his supervisor. "Even being that close, it still doesn't make sense."

Tolman nodded. "Well . . . that's it for now, gentlemen. We'll reconvene Monday, if not before." He looked around the table. "Good work from all—"

"Wait." Randall Mays held his right hand in the air, palm out, as he read something on the screen of his cell phone. He frowned and laid his phone on the table.

"I just got word from forensics," he said. "They have a partial DNA sample on a disposable latex glove that was found about six feet from the body." He reread the message. "They have also found a potential match."

The room stilled.

"Please, understand, this is not definitive, but the tentative match is a former Marine and a retired schoolteacher. His name is Roland Davis."

CHAPTER 16

Roland was sitting on the sofa playing tug-of-war with Ophelia when Hannah came down the stairs carrying her guitar case.

"How's your day?" she asked as she stepped into the great room and leaned her guitar against the sofa.

Roland stood. "My day has been good," he said. "But then again, all of my days are basically the same since I'm retired."

Hannah laughed and took a seat on the other end of the sofa.

"That's not a lot different than life at twenty-seven when you've been told to stay close to home," Hannah said, looking around the room. "Are we waiting on Dixie?"

He grinned, a twinkle in his eyes. "Yes, we are. That's how I spend most of my days."

Dixie entered the room in time to hear the final part of Roland's comment. "How did you say you spend your days?"

"Never mind, dear." Roland winked at Hannah. "Hannah and I were just having a private conversation."

Dixie swatted him playfully with the palm of her hand. "I'm sure you're talking about me, but that's OK. I can take it." She laughed.

Roland stood. "Are we ready, girls?"

Hannah jumped up, grabbed her guitar, and started out the door.

Roland stopped her. "Let me carry that for you."

"Thanks." Hannah opened the front door for them. "Do you want me to drive separately?" she asked.

"Oh, no, honey. You can ride with Roland and me."

Roland opened the front passenger side door for Dixie and the rear passenger side door for Hannah, closing the doors behind them after they were seated. He popped the trunk and stowed the guitar, and then stepped around to the driver side of the car and got in.

"Where are we going?" Hannah asked as Roland engaged the ignition.

"Mother lives in an assisted living facility in Hendersonville." He glanced over his shoulder to Hannah. "I hope you don't mind going that far."

Hannah looked at her watch. "That should be fine, and you're just ahead of rush hour so we should be back in time. I need to be here to meet Jake at four thirty."

"We won't stay long," Roland said. "Just a half hour or so."

"How old is your mom?" Hannah asked.

"She's ninety-two." Roland backed the vehicle onto the street and headed north on Tenth Avenue South. "She's as sharp as a tack, but arthritis took away her mobility a few years ago."

Within thirty minutes, Roland was pulling into the parking lot of a nice-looking brick building on the east side of Hendersonville.

"It doesn't take too long in light traffic," he said. "Vietnam Veterans Parkway helps with getting through Hendersonville. I remember when Gallatin Road was our only option."

"Hendersonville has grown a lot in the past ten years," Hannah said. "I remember coming here when I was a young girl growing up nearby. We always loved the bowling alley."

Roland laughed. "Our favorite sport back in the day was the Sumner County Drive-In."

"Roland!" Dixie chuckled. "Mind your manners."

Hannah laughed. "You two are hilarious."

Roland stepped out of the car and hurried to the passenger side to open the women's doors. Then he grabbed Hannah's guitar from the trunk.

"This looks like a nice place," Hannah said.

"It's very nice." Dixie nodded. "And the staff is wonderful."

"I feel good about my mother being here," Roland said. "They offer quite a few activities." He blushed. "By the way, I forgot to mention. I told the recreational director that you were going to perform for all the residents. I hope you don't mind."

Hannah stopped walking. "Oh!" She considered what she was wearing, a pink eyelet blouse, blue jeans, and pink sneakers. "Am I dressed all right for that?"

"You look fine, dear," Dixie said, urging her along.

"At least I'm clean." Hannah laughed.

Roland opened the front door, and they stepped inside a large reception area that resembled a family living room, complete with a fireplace and comfortable-looking sofas. "This place is lovely," Hannah said.

A few minutes later, they were escorted into another large room with two rows of chairs placed in half circles near a grand piano. Some of the chairs had been replaced by residents in wheelchairs. Many of the elders, mostly women, smiled—some laughed and clapped their hands—as they walked into the room. Hannah noticed that a few had almost expressionless faces. Those were the ones who stole her heart.

Roland took Hannah's arm and led her to where a beautiful, older woman was sitting in a wheelchair. "Mother, this is Hannah. Hannah, this is Harriet Davis."

The woman's striking sea green eyes drew Hannah in. She took a seat in the empty chair next to the woman and took her hand, which was milky white and frail. The woman lightly squeezed Hannah's hand.

"I'm so glad to meet you, Ms. Davis," she said. "Your son Roland is one of my favorite people."

"I'm glad to meet you too, dear." Harriet Davis smiled. "Thank you for coming to see us. I understand that you play music. I used to be a music teacher."

"How wonderful!" Hannah said. "I wasn't aware of that. Now I'm going to be nervous about hitting a wrong note."

Harriet patted her on the hand. "We've all hit wrong notes in our lives, honey. It's just part of our unchained melody."

Hannah leaned back. "I remember that song! Would you like for me to sing it for you?"

Harriet leaned back in her chair. "Oh, my goodness, honey. You weren't even born when that song was popular."

"I love the old classics, Ms. Harriet." Hannah smiled. "I used to sing it on my show."

"I would love it if you would sing it! It was my husband's and my favorite song."

"Just for you then!" Hannah stood, and Roland gave her the guitar case. She walked to a chair in the middle of the half circle, took the guitar out of the case, and took a seat. After a minute or two of tuning, she strummed a G chord. Then she scanned the beautiful faces in front of her.

"I'm so honored to be here today," she said. "Thank you to Harriet Davis and her son, and my friend Dixie Grace, who brought me here to sing a few songs for you." Hannah smiled at Harriet. "If my new friend Harriet doesn't mind, I'm going to start with this one, and then I'd like to dedicate a song to her in a little bit. But first of all—" Hannah took a deep breath and looked around the room. "Does anyone have a birthday today? This week? Or even this month?"

A few of the residents held up their hands. One of them laughed and waved.

"OK! Let's begin with everyone singing 'Happy Birthday'!"

By the end of the first song, Hannah had many of them laughing and singing along with her. She decided to keep the show upbeat, and a little bit nostalgic for the elders, by performing a few classics they would remember. Songs such as "You Are My Sunshine" and "Red River Valley."

"I think that last song is one of country music's oldest classics," she said with a laugh. "So classic my fingers almost didn't remember the notes." She looked at Harriet. "Ms. Harriet, I'm sure I hit a few wrong ones. Thank you for reminding me that's OK."

Harriet smiled and nodded. Hannah took a deep breath, hoping she had the chops to pull this one off.

"I would like to dedicate this classic to you, Ms. Harriet. 'Unchained Melody.'"

Hannah stood and took a seat at the piano. She ran her fingers up and down the keys to acclimate and said a little prayer that she wouldn't mess up. The vocal detail and intimacy of the Righteous

Brothers' classic, one that had later been recorded by expert vocalists like Elvis, the Drifters, Andy Williams, and even the cast of *Glee*. Her favorite cover version was sung by LeAnn Rimes.

Hannah closed her eyes, took a long breath, and sang the familiar and beloved lyrics that so poignantly captured the longing of an absent love. When she had finished, she looked out to the audience. There may not have been a dry eye in the room, including her own. The residents were clapping and smiling, but there was one loud clapper in the back of the room.

Jake Matheson! *Why was he here?*

CHAPTER 17

Jake had positioned himself in the back of the room so he could watch Roland Davis. He had made sure that Roland knew he was here. The older man's reaction had been one of surprise but certainly not guilt. Jake considered himself a good judge of people after only a quick assessment. It was a necessary skill in his business. And Roland had never struck him as someone who had something to hide. Especially something as heinous as kidnapping or murder.

Preliminary DNA was sometimes wrong. Or, at the very least, it didn't tell the complete story. Not because it was an inexact science. There was little doubt that DNA was one of the better ways to exonerate an innocent man or woman who had been wrongly accused of a crime. However, the reverse wasn't always true. At least, not according to some of the forensic studies that had been published recently. It had created quite a debate in the forensics business.

Only in the past decade or so had the theory of DNA migration been studied, and the results could be far-reaching in the world of crime investigation and court proceedings. DNA could be transferred indirectly and, when that happened, the facts could be misleading.

Jake watched and listened as Hannah sang. He'd had no idea that she was so talented. And her ability to connect with the audience was on par with her talent. She was a pretty girl, with a pretty voice, who loved people. If he could keep her alive, she was most likely destined for success.

As soon as she finished her set, Hannah walked around the room to greet each of the residents, taking their hands or kneeling in front of their chairs and introducing herself. She chatted with each of them for a few minutes, asking them about their personal stories. One woman was a nurse who had worked in a military hospital. Another was a retired schoolteacher. Several smiled but spoke very little, while others were effusive.

Hannah went to Roland's mother last. "How did I do?" she asked, eager to have pleased.

"You were wonderful, dear. I'm so grateful you came to see us today." She reached for Hannah's hand. "I hope you will come back."

"I will. I promise," Hannah said. "I enjoyed it so much."

"Roland." Harriet reached for her son's arm. "Please be sure and bring Hannah back to see us."

"I will, Mom," he said, smiling. "But I'd better be getting her home now." He looked at his watch. "She has a special appointment."

Jake stepped up beside them.

"Well, hello there, Agent Matheson."

"Roland." Jake nodded.

"What are you doing here?" Hannah asked.

"I was in the neighborhood," he said.

She somehow didn't believe that. "How did you know where I was?"

"It was easy," he said. "When I couldn't reach you on your cell phone, I called Dixie. She told me."

Dixie, who was standing beside them, nodded and smiled.

"Is everything OK?" Hannah asked. "Do you have bad news about the case?"

"Everything's fine. I just need to talk to you about a few things and thought you could ride back to Nashville with me."

"Really?" Hannah couldn't think of a reason not to agree. She turned to Dixie. "I'll see you and Roland back at the house."

"That's fine, honey. We'll be there in a little while. I'm hoping to convince Roland to take me out for an early supper, so I don't have to cook tonight."

Hannah laughed. "You go, girl." Then she remembered. "Jake,

I want to introduce you to someone before we leave."

She leaned down to Harriet, who had been talking with the woman beside her. "Ms. Davis, before I go, I would like to introduce you to a friend of mine. This is Jake Matheson."

"Mr. Matheson, I'm Harriet Davis. It's a pleasure to meet you."

Jake took the elderly woman's hand. "It's very nice meeting you, ma'am."

"Ms. Davis, I will see you soon, OK?" Hannah said.

"That's fine, dear. You two have a good time."

Hannah winked at Jake. He smiled, took her arm, and they left through the side door. A few minutes later, they were riding in a government-issue black SUV and on their way to Nashville.

"Please tell me what's going on. I know you didn't just happen to be in the neighborhood." She was beginning to feel somewhat intimidated.

"I've been doing some research," Jake said, glancing toward her. "And while nothing is for sure, I'm concerned that your assault and Ginny's murder may be the work of a human trafficking organization."

Hannah gasped. "You really think so?"

"I'm more convinced after today."

"Why?"

"Hannah, I have my sources. But those can't be revealed."

"I understand," she said, her mind racing with possibilities. She stared out the side window of the SUV. "I'm not sure why, but that just seems like the worst of all scenarios." She turned to look at him. "I could have been whisked off to some third-world country or something. So could Ginny if she hadn't . . ."

Jake merged into traffic on Interstate 65.

"How is that even possible?" Hannah asked, almost under her breath.

"Unfortunately, Nashville isn't immune to such a thing. In fact, no place is. It's more prevalent than most people think."

"They just snatch people off the street at random?"

"It's not usually like that," he said. "More often than not, the victims are younger, and they know their traffickers. It can even be family. Mothers and fathers sometimes traffic their own children."

"We all know cases of abuse. I mean, I went to school with a girl who, I found out later, was subjected to that kind of thing without her parents' knowledge. Awful," Hannah said quietly. "But trafficking your own child? How could someone do that?"

"It happens." Jake shrugged. "I'm wondering if, perhaps, Ginny was a victim of something similar to that."

"No! You don't think . . ."

"It could make sense. She may have been trying to get away from it, so they sent a thug to bring her back."

He turned to her.

"You could have been the unfortunate victim of mistaken identity. Your attacker may have realized he had messed up when he saw Ginny, the girl he was really after."

"But . . ." Hannah gave it some thought. "How would he have known that Ginny was at The Pancake Pantry that day if he wasn't following her?"

"We still have a lot of questions to answer. Everything is supposition right now, but we're learning more every day."

"I guess it has only been a week."

"Yes." He glanced in his rearview mirror. "Hey, it looks like Dixie and Roland are behind us, and they started after us." He chuckled. "He must drive like you do."

"Very funny." Hannah was glad to change the subject.

"How well do you know Roland Davis?" Jake asked.

"He's been seeing Dixie for about a year now, I would guess," Hannah said. "He's a nice man. Why?"

"Just wondering." It appeared he wanted to say more, but he didn't continue.

"No, seriously," she insisted. "Why did you ask me that?"

Jake slowed to exit the interstate on Rosa L. Parks Boulevard. "Jake?"

He stopped at the red light and turned to look at her. "Please don't jump to any conclusions when I tell you this. I shouldn't even tell you while we're still investigating all angles . . ."

"And . . ."

"Roland's DNA is a partial match for the man who strangled you."

"No!" Hannah shook her head. "It wasn't him!"

Jake shook his head. "I told you not to jump to conclusions."

"How can I not? You're trying to tell me that Roland Davis was my attacker." She crossed her arms and looked out the passenger side window.

"Not necessarily."

Hannah turned to him. "Then what are you trying to tell me?"

He appeared to be miffed. Perhaps she had overreacted. But, he had all but accused Roland of something she *knew* he hadn't done. She was there, wasn't she?

Jake took a left onto Rosa Parks, heading toward downtown Nashville.

"I will explain, but I have a question for you first."

"What?"

"Are you still open to going for a run?"

"Yes. Of course."

He took a left on Monroe Street and a few blocks later pulled to a stop. "Then relax in the car for a minute, while I run inside and change clothes."

"You live in this house?" He had parked in front of one of the older homes near Monell's on Sixth.

"Yes. Why do you find that amusing?" He gave her a crooked smile.

"I don't know. For some reason you seem like a condo guy."

"Hannah, apparently you don't know me like you think you do." He powered down the windows and turned off the ignition, taking the keys. "TBI protocol. I can't leave you in a government vehicle with the keys inside."

"You mean you're afraid I'll drive off and leave you."

"Well, you are mad at me."

Mischief flashed in his dark brown eyes. *Why did he have to be so handsome?*

"Not mad enough to break a law. I'm assuming that would be a felony."

He chuckled. "You're not only a great singer, but you're also smart."

She crossed her arms. "Get out of the car and change your clothes, Agent Matheson. I'll be here when you return."

She would have preferred to have delivered her last words without a smile, but she found him too amusing. And attractive. Her face was flushed when he stepped out of the car and shut the door. But, before walking up the sidewalk, he turned and leaned on the open driver's side window, looking in at her. "Do you have my mobile phone number in case you need me?"

She raised empty hands. "It doesn't matter. I forgot to bring my phone. That's why you had to call Dixie to find out where I was."

He looked around. "OK. Stay put. I'll be right back."

CHAPTER 18

Jake jogged up his sidewalk, put the key in the lock, and opened his front door. Stepping inside, he disengaged the alarm and hurried to his bedroom to change clothes. Within a few minutes he was headed back out the door.

But Hannah wasn't in the car.

He pulled the door closed and ran down the sidewalk, looking right, then left. His heart racing, angry with himself. Why had he left her alone?

"Hannah?" he shouted, looking up and down the street.

"Yes."

He spun around. She was walking toward him from the direction of his backyard.

"What are you doing?"

"What do you mean?"

"I mean, why did you leave the car? You knew I would be right back."

"Exactly," she said with a slight smile on her face.

He paced to the passenger side of the vehicle and opened the door for her.

"You have a beautiful backyard," she said. "But I noticed that you have some kind of beetle on your hydrangea."

"What?"

She stepped past him and got into the SUV. "Dixie had me plucking beetles in her garden this morning. Yours are different, though."

Jake shook his head and closed her door. She was, perhaps, the most intriguing woman he had ever met.

And that scared him.

He walked to the other side of the SUV, stepped inside, and

switched on the ignition.

"Are you going to tell me now why you're concerned about Roland?" Hannah asked.

"Because his DNA is a partial match. But . . ." He emphasized the last word. "My guess is that it's a case of DNA transfer. Do you know what that is?"

She shook her head. "I don't."

"DNA transfer is a relatively new way of thinking that has broad implications for criminal investigations and court proceedings. It has been studied for a decade or so, and studies are proving that a person's DNA can appear in places that person has never been by way of indirect transfer."

He glanced at Hannah to gauge her reaction. She nodded.

"In your case specifically, it's possible that Roland could have touched a shopping cart at the grocery store, and the next person to use that cart was the man who assaulted you. Hypothetically, your attacker could have picked up some of Roland's DNA that morning and then driven to The Pancake Pantry and assaulted you, stolen a car, and then left Roland's DNA."

Hannah looked at him, her blue eyes wide with interest. Jake could also see fear.

"Are you OK?" he asked.

She nodded. "Yes, please keep going."

"OK." He leaned back in his seat and continued. "Theoretically, DNA is an exact science. The problem is that new technology is improving faster than our ability to analyze results. Our equipment has become so sensitive we can detect minuscule samples of DNA, handfuls of cells, and identify people. That's great! But the problem is that we can't yet determine how those cells were deposited. Whether they were left directly by that person or indirectly through DNA transfer. Do you see now why I asked you not to jump to conclusions?"

"Thank you," she said softly.

"For what?"

"For believing that Roland didn't do it."

Jake pulled the SUV into Dixie's driveway next to Roland's car and turned off the ignition. "Don't thank me yet. There's still a lot to be done."

She nodded.

He turned to her. "Hannah, you might as well know now. My colleagues will need to talk to him. In fact, they're on their way here now."

"Why?"

"Because he can help us determine his innocence. Do you understand?"

She nodded.

"He can also help us find out how and where he may have crossed paths with the killer." He watched her reaction. "Do you think you can go in the house and act normal, change into your running clothes, and come back out?"

"I can do that."

"OK." He opened his door. "Let's do it."

Hannah used her key to open the front door and saw Dixie and Roland sitting at the kitchen bar, takeout boxes scattered on the countertop in front of them. Jake walked in behind her and closed the door.

"What did you pick up to eat? That smells so good," she said.

Dixie laughed. "I talked him into Chinese even though he wanted pizza from Amerigo's."

"Way to go, Roland," Hannah teased.

"I'm no fool," he said. "I'm saving my credits for a trip to the Loveless Cafe next time. Dixie hates that place, but she loves me enough to eat there."

Dixie swatted him on the shoulder. "I don't hate it. I just like my biscuits better than theirs."

"Oh my, Dixie." Jake laughed. "Those are fightin' words around this town."

"I'll tell you what, young man. I'll take you up on that challenge." She bristled in jest. "The next time you're here for supper."

"Don't bet too much, Jake," Hannah cautioned. "I promise, you're going to lose your money."

"I'll be easy on him." Dixie laughed. "Are you two getting ready for your run?"

"Yes." Hannah took off for the stairs. "I can't wait!"

"She's been looking forward to this all day," Dixie said.

Hannah ran up the stairs, rifled through her chest of drawers for a clean pair of shorts, and pulled an aqua vintage Taylor Guitar t-shirt from the closet. She checked her makeup, pulled her hair into two quick braids, and picked up her running shoes before running back downstairs.

"I'm ready," she said. She stopped at the bottom of the staircase to put on her shoes.

"That was fast. I'm impressed," Jake said.

"I was afraid you'd change your mind." She waved to Dixie and Roland. "See you two later. Enjoy your Chinese."

Jake opened the door for her, and they hurried down the sidewalk to the street. "Which way do you want to go?"

"This way." Hannah nodded to the right. "I'll show you my regular route."

"Let's do it!" Jake took off at an easy gait. "Want to speed it up?"

"Absolutely." A few minutes later they had relaxed into a comfortable pace.

They continued on Tenth Avenue North, past Waverly-Belmont Elementary School, past Caruthers Avenue, Montrose Avenue, Gilmore Avenue, and finally Halcyon Avenue before reaching Sevier Park. "I always run up this way," she said, pointing to the right. "Then I take a right at Granny White Pike and run the perimeter of the park before turning into the park entrance and making a circuit back to Granny White."

It took another ten minutes to return to the entrance on Granny White Pike. "Ready to head for Twelve South?" Hannah asked.

He nodded in agreement, and they took a right toward downtown Nashville. About a half mile up the street, Jake asked about a stop for coffee.

"Sure," she said.

"Is the White Bison OK with you?"

"Sounds great."

They ran past Burger Up on the left, Edley's Barbecue and Christie Cookies on the right, and then stopped to stretch and walk up and down the sidewalk at Montrose Avenue, near Bar-Taco. Jake took Hannah's arm and escorted her across the street as they walked toward the combination coffee shop and convenience store.

The White Bison, with its gigantic white buffalo statue in the front, was a bit off the beaten track from the more touristy attractions of the Twelfth South District. It was also usually less busy. "Upstairs or outside?" Jake asked as they walked inside and up to the coffee bar.

"I'm good with outside. We can people watch."

"Sure. What would you like to drink?"

"An iced coffee would be great," Hannah said and then walked around the store while Jake ordered their drinks. A few minutes later they were sitting at a table near the sidewalk and savoring their coffees.

"How long have you lived with Dixie?" he asked.

"It's been almost two years now." Hannah set her cup on the table. "Aspiring singer-songwriters don't earn a lot, and I needed a place to live without a lot of overhead. What I have earned, I've invested in my studio.

"Dixie has been much more than a landlord to me. She's an encourager and a good friend. I've known her as long as I can remember. She and my mom were always doing things together until my parents moved to Montana two years ago."

"Why did they move?"

"Dad had always wanted to live there. They visited a couple of times and both of them fell in love with it." She looked at him. "I'm happy for them. It's not everyone who gets to follow their dream."

He nodded.

"How long have you been at the TBI?"

"Almost six years now. It was my dream. Or, at least, it has been since college. Rylie encouraged me to pursue it."

"You were lucky to have her, Jake. I'm sorry you had to lose her so soon."

His expression clouded, and she saw a fleeting glimpse of bitterness in his eyes. It was time to change the subject. "I would never have guessed you for a horticulturist," she teased.

"Rylie and I bought the house together right after we were engaged, and she lived there until she died. They were her project. She loved hydrangeas." He shrugged and took a drink from his cup. "I've made it a point to try to keep them alive."

"You've done a good job."

"How do you manage to stay so positive?" He turned the tables on her.

"I don't know." She took time to think about her answer. "I'm not sure I'm all that positive. I'm just thankful." She hesitated. "I'm alive, even after a near-disastrous attempt to kidnap me and do who knows what else . . ."

He studied her. "Are you handling all of that OK? Are you having flashbacks, bad dreams, anything you need help with? Because I can get that for you."

She shook her head. "No. Not really. I'll admit that I've thought about it a lot. But I've not had panic attacks or nightmares or anything like that." She looked up at him. "I think I'm doing OK. To tell you the truth, I've been focusing on my escape more than the attack. And I've been thinking a lot about Ginny's family."

"It can't be easy for them right now."

"I've been praying for them."

"That's good."

"The way you said that didn't convince me that you think it matters."

"What do you mean?"

She could feel the wall go up between them. "Did losing your fiancée draw you closer to God? Losing Casey did for me."

"Not at all." He toyed with his cup. "Why would it? He let her die."

Hannah swallowed a sip of coffee. "I'm sorry. That was personal. I need to learn to keep my mouth shut."

"You don't need to apologize. I don't mind talking about it. I used to talk a lot about my faith. And I did my best to live it." He looked up at her. "I tried to do everything right. Church every Sunday. No bad language." He shrugged. "Not that I use a lot of bad language now. But I don't go to church anymore."

"Why not?" She dared to push again.

"Because God let me down. I would be a hypocrite if I didn't acknowledge how I feel about that." He coughed out an uneasy laugh. "Those were the people who made me angry when I was a regular churchgoer. You know, the ones who were all about Sunday school and maybe Wednesday Bible study, but come Monday, they were living more like the world, paying no attention to God in their lives."

"At least they were making the attempt, I guess. I'm not going to judge them."

"There you go being positive again." He shook his head. "I can't agree with you on that one."

"I get it . . . really. Nobody likes that kind of thing, but—"

"Hey, they do what they have to do. I just don't have a desire to go to church and be a hypocrite."

She thought for a minute. "You would go with me, right?"

"What?"

"Aren't you supposed to go with me when I go out right now? To protect me."

"That's not fair."

She smiled wryly.

He folded his arms. "If you must know the truth, I did go to church with a client several times last year. But that was work too."

"Really?" Curiosity got the best of her. "And who was that?"

"I can't go into details. I'll just say that we were working on bringing down a major drug cartel."

"You worked on *that* case? Wow . . ." She sat back in her seat. "Everybody in Nashville knows about that case. In fact, one of my friends worked with Danielle Samuels at Amorè."

He nodded. "I work with Caleb."

She slapped herself on the forehead. "Of course you would

know Caleb Samuels. What was I thinking?"

"He and Danielle are both hardworking people. It's a shame the restaurant was destroyed in the Christmas Day bombing."

"Somehow everything that happens works to the good."

He stood, smiling. "Thank you, Positive Polly."

Hannah took a final sip of her coffee and got up from her seat. "Sorry. It's just my nature."

"It's refreshing. Never apologize for that." He took the cup from her hand and tossed it, along with his, into a nearby trash can. "Are you ready to finish the run?"

She tugged on her shorts. "Want to race?"

He grinned. "You'll regret that challenge."

"Why?"

"I was the sprinting champ in my high school class."

"Really? We'll see how well you do with endurance. I won a few medals myself." She took off running.

Jake faltered at the start but caught up with her in a few steps. "I'll be waiting for you at the Frothy Monkey." He laughed. "I might even have a snack before you get there."

He had no problem beating her to the goal and eased up after he reached it so she could catch him. For the rest of their run up Twelfth Avenue South, they kept an easy pace, redirecting occasionally to avoid sightseers taking in the ambience.

"This area always reminds me of a seaside community with its small shops and quaint little restaurants," Hannah said.

"Maybe in the summer," he said with another laugh. "Remember the six inches of snow we had last winter?"

"You're right. I hadn't seen anything like that in my lifetime. Not in Nashville."

"Which way?" he asked her as they approached Caruthers Avenue.

"Let's keep straight. We'll cut over at Caldwell." She gestured with her right hand. "We can get in another mile."

He nodded, and they settled back into an easy pace, jogging past MAFIAoza's Pizza, Taqueria del Sol, and Jenni's Ice Cream. The smells of sage and cumin enticed, but they kept running, dodging tourists and locals walking their dogs until they had passed the shopping district.

"That was fun," Hannah said as they slowed to a stop in front of Dixie's cottage on Tenth Avenue North. After they had stretched, Hannah said, "I guess we need to see how it went."

Jake walked her up to the porch and held the door for her. Dixie was standing in the kitchen, working at the sink, when they stepped inside. As soon as she saw them, she hurried across the room, not even acknowledging Hannah.

"Jake, tell me what's going on. The TBI just took Roland in for questioning."

CHAPTER 19

"Jake, you didn't tell me this would happen!"

"You knew?" Dixie stared at her.

Hannah looked to Jake for help, but he was dialing his phone. She looked back at Dixie. "Jake told me a little about it while we were out. But I had no idea this was going to happen."

Both women stared at Jake. He nodded, acknowledged someone on the other end of the line, and walked into the dining room.

"Dixie, let's sit over here." Hannah directed the older woman to the sofa. "Jake will work this out. He told me earlier that they found some of Roland's DNA, but he explained how it's not a big deal."

"Then why would they take him in for questioning?" Dixie wrung her hands. "Hannah! You know Roland couldn't . . . he wouldn't do anything like that."

"I know." Hannah tapped her foot on the floor. "If anyone knows it wasn't Roland, believe me, it's me."

Jake joined them in the living room, slipping his phone into his pocket. "I just talked to a friend on the interrogation team. He said they have verified Roland's alibi for that morning." Jake sat down next to Hannah on the sofa. "It just so happened he ran into a friend, who we were able to call for confirmation."

"So that's the end of it?" Hannah asked.

"Yes. But they will want to talk to him a bit more. They need to find out how a transfer of his DNA could have happened. Where else he had been that morning, who he might have seen. That kind of thing. Roland may be able to help us find the best lead so far."

"Praise God," Dixie said. "I'm so grateful we have you, Jake. Audrey told me you were a good man, and I know now why God put you in that parking lot to rescue Hannah last week. You're rescuing all of us."

Jake shook his head. "You're too kind, Dixie. I'm just doing my job."

Jake settled onto the sofa next to Hannah and checked his watch. "We're probably looking at another hour before Roland gets here."

"Oh, my word. What's wrong with me?" Dixie jumped straight up from where she was sitting. "You kids haven't eaten, have you?"

"Don't worry about us, Dixie. I'll make us a peanut butter sandwich." Hannah stood.

"No, no, no . . . I'll put something together for you." She tied her apron around her waist. "Jake, do you like chicken salad?"

"Yes, ma'am," he said. "Unless you try to hide some of those exotic fruits and vegetables—like pineapple and kiwi—inside." He laughed. "My mother used to try that. We learned to spot a kiwi from a mile away."

Dixie chuckled. "I won't do that, honey. My chicken salad is pretty standard." She smiled. "Although I have to put a Dixie twist to everything. I think you'll like it."

"I'm sure I will," he said.

"Hannah, would you mind helping me cut vegetables?"

"Of course not." Hannah said, following Dixie into the kitchen.

Jake leaned his head back and let out a deep breath. It had been a long day. First his conversation with Poe Allan. Then his meeting with the case investigation team, followed by a mad dash to Hendersonville to make sure that Hannah was OK. He suspected that, given the chance, he would sleep well tonight.

He was all but dozing on Dixie's sofa when she announced that supper was ready. Hannah and he ate at the bar, while Dixie catered to their every need. Chicken salad sandwiches with fresh garden pickles and homemade potato chips.

"This is delicious, Dixie. You don't have another room you can rent, do you?"

Hannah laughed.

Never one to be left without a comeback, Dixie thought for a minute and said, "Well, I suppose I could put you in the basement."

"Don't do it." Hannah pretended to whisper in Jake's ear but spoke so Dixie could hear her. "It's dark and dank down there."

"I have a woodworking shop in my basement." Jake crunched on a potato chip. "And it's not much different."

"You do woodworking?" Dixie asked.

"Yes, ma'am. It's a hobby. My grandfather used to flip houses before that was even a thing, and I picked up the woodworking trade to help him on weekends."

"How cool." Hannah dabbed her mouth with her napkin. "What have you made?"

"I made the fireplace mantels in my house."

"You have more than one?" Hannah asked before taking a bite of her sandwich. "By the way, Dixie, you outdid yourself on this chicken salad."

"Thanks, honey. But I suspect you're just extra hungry."

"I have three." Jake took a drink of iced tea. "One in my living room, kitchen, and master bedroom."

"Where's your house, Jake? If you don't mind my asking."

"I don't mind at all." He looked at Hannah. "Hannah saw it today."

"It's in Germantown," Hannah said. "One of those beautiful early 1900s cottages that everybody would like to buy, but no one wants to sell."

"Was it in your family?" Dixie grabbed a potato chip from the serving dish and popped it into her mouth.

"Yes, ma'am. Rylie and I bought it from my grandparents after we were engaged. My grandfather bought it as an investment many years ago and gradually upgraded all of the basics—electric, heating, plumbing." He smiled at Hannah. "Everything but the basement."

She laughed.

"It's actually not that bad," he said. "It's dry and clean. Those things are necessary if you're doing woodworking."

Ophelia, who had been sitting at Jake's feet hoping for

a handout, jumped up and ran to the front door just as Roland walked inside.

"Roland!" Dixie rushed to greet him. "I'm so glad you're back."

"Me, too." He rubbed the back of his neck.

Jake got up from his seat and walked across the room. "How did it go?"

Roland reached to shake Jake's hand.

"You work with some nice people, son. They were very gracious to me." Roland greeted Hannah, who had joined the others in the entry. "Very professional." Roland straightened his back. "Can't say I'd like to go through that again, though. It was a humbling experience."

"Roland, let me get you a glass of tea."

"That sounds good, Dix."

"Are you hungry? The kids were just eating. I can make you a sandwich."

"Oh, no. Not at all." Roland shook his head. "I'll have a seat on the sofa and relax a bit. Maybe Jake and I can talk after they finish their supper."

Ten minutes later, Jake and Roland walked to the backyard. Ophelia followed them.

"How did it go?" Jake asked.

"Well, I wouldn't call it an interrogation." Roland chuckled. "At least not after they were able to verify my alibi. I'm sure glad I ran into my old high school buddy that morning. Actually, I ran into my son too. I forgot to mention that." Roland picked up the ball at his feet and threw it across the yard for Ophelia. "My friend Alan was able to verify the time down to the minute. I'm sure glad it turned out the way it did."

"Me too, sir." Jake took a seat on a bench on one side of the brick patio and the dog ran up to him with the ball. Jake picked it up and studied it, then tossed it again. Ophelia took off running. "Did they explain to you why we had to clear you before we could cross you off the list of suspects?"

"Yes, they did. And they explained why I was on that list." He scratched his head. "Law enforcement is a lot more complicated than it used to be. I did some part-time security work in my younger days, but that was a time when about all you had was your gut. We didn't have the fancy technology you have nowadays."

"We still use our guts," Jake said. "In fact, that's often what keeps us alive."

"I can understand that, son."

"So they explained everything to you?"

"They did. They gave me the simple version."

"What's their working theory on how you crossed paths with Hannah's attacker?"

"Based on what I told them today, I'd say they have a few ideas." Roland picked up a stick and threw it for the dog to chase. Then he took a seat in an Adirondack chair. "I made several stops that morning, including dropping my car off at the dealership for service. They gave me a loaner car, which I understand added another layer to the investigative onion. And I stopped at two grocery stores on my way back to the dealership."

"That leaves a lot of possibilities."

"Yes." He laughed nervously. "I could have done myself a big favor if I had stayed home that morning."

"In theory, I suppose," Jake said. "But then again, you might have helped us find the most important lead we have right now." Jake glanced to the back door to be sure that neither of the women was nearby. "To be honest, we haven't had a lot of success with leads so far. Everything is coming up empty. Whoever assaulted Hannah did a good job of covering his tracks." Jake hesitated and then continued. "I hope we find him soon. I don't have a good feeling about this case. And, to be honest, I'm concerned that there's a group of people behind the killer who are even more evil than he is."

"What are you thinking?" Roland asked.

"That we're dealing with a human trafficking ring. And those people are ruthless."

"That's scary for Hannah's sake." Roland frowned.

"Yes. I don't know if she just happened into it that day, or if she had been targeted. Either way, she's on their radar now, and that's

why we need to do everything we can to protect her at all times."
Jake stood. "We have a lot of work cut out for us."

CHAPTER 20

As soon as Jake and Roland walked back into the house, Jake asked Dixie and Hannah to join them in the living room. Dixie wiped her hands on a towel and untied her apron. "Hannah, I'll finish these dishes later. Let's go sit with them."

The four filed into the living room, taking seats across the room from each other, their body language speaking volumes that had yet to be said aloud. Jake and Roland chose the gray side chairs. Dixie and Hannah took seats on the sofa. Ophelia jumped up between them and rested her head on Hannah's knee. Perhaps the dog was the only one truly comfortable.

"Hannah." Jake broke the silence. "I need to ask you not to go to your showcase on Saturday night."

Hannah's face flushed. "I thought we had already talked about this."

"We did." He chose his words carefully. "But things have changed since then."

"What has changed? I don't understand."

"I don't have a good feeling about it."

"That's it? I'm not a three-year-old." She crossed her arms. "You can tell me what's going on." She looked around the room, as if to see if anyone else was enlightened.

"I don't want to put your life in danger," he said.

"Jake." Hannah sat up straight and looked at him. "I really did think we had this settled. I'm not afraid. I want to live my life, not cower inside the house hiding from something that may never happen." She took a long breath, let it out, and continued. "Besides, I want to help you catch this guy, and I can't do that sitting around here."

"Hannah, I'm not so sure . . ." Dixie interjected.

Hannah's shoulders tensed. Despite her earlier declaration about not being afraid, her body language told Jake otherwise. And, perhaps, it was more from what she didn't know than what she did. She deserved to have all the facts.

He shifted in his chair. "When I returned that call earlier this evening, it was to my boss. He had just talked to a colleague at Homeland Security. They're concerned that we could be investigating one of Middle Tennessee's largest trafficking rings. They may even have national ties."

Dixie gasped. This had already been a difficult day for her. Now he was, unfortunately, making it worse.

"We don't want to put your life in danger—in any more danger than it already is—by trying to flush out the bad guys and using you as bait." He glanced to Dixie, who was clutching her hands. "You need to think about Dixie too."

"But what you're trying to tell me is that they're going to find me, either way. Is that right?"

"If my gut is right, they're most likely going to try," he said.

Hannah looked to Dixie, and then to Roland, as she rubbed her hand across the top of Ophelia's back. "If my being in this house is what's putting Dixie in danger, I'll find some other place to live."

"Hannah! Where would you stay?" Dixie reached out to her. "I promised your mother that I would take good care of you, and that means you need to stay here with me."

Dixie looked to Roland and then to Jake. "I'll ask Roland to bring over one of his guns. I'm not afraid to protect myself."

"Dixie—" Roland almost came off his chair.

"Ms. Carmichael—Dixie!—please." Jake interjected. "That isn't necessary. There will be law enforcement officers watching your house day and night."

"People!" Hannah said. "Why are we arguing? Unfortunately, I've brought all of you into this, but . . ." She looked around the room. "We need to work together."

"I agree," Dixie said. "So you need to stay here."

Jake chuckled under his breath. *One for Dixie.*

"Jake," Hannah said, "I appreciate your telling me everything.

Or at least everything you can. I realize there are some things that are privileged." She shifted her gaze to Ophelia. "And I trust you, even when you can't tell me everything."

She looked up at him, and her blue eyes compelled him to want to take care of her. Or to draw her into a hug. Instead, Dixie moved closer to Hannah on the sofa and wrapped her arm around her. "We'll get through this," she said. "With Jake's expertise and God's help."

"Amen," Roland said. "So . . . I don't know about the rest of you, but this has been a hard day."

"Who wants coffee?" Dixie asked, jumping up.

"That sounds good," everyone said in unison, sparking group laughter. Perhaps nervous laughter, but laughter nonetheless.

While Dixie was preparing the drinks, Jake moved to the sofa with Hannah. "OK. If you really want to do the showcase, I'll work with you on it."

"Really?" Her face lit up.

"I will increase the security detail, both here and at the showcase site while you're there." He continued, "We've finally been able to get the paperwork we needed for a release, and I have a team of forensic experts going through Ginny Williams's computer right now. I've also asked forensics to do another sweep at Shannon Bridges's house, because we now have access to an ESD K-9." He paused to explain. "An electronic storage detection dog that can sniff out hidden hard drives or similar computer storage devices. If we can find computer files, or even one set of fingerprints, we may be able to solve this quickly."

"Thank you." Hannah nodded appreciatively.

"I promise you we won't stop until we find this guy."

Markham turned right off Hillsboro Road onto Hobbs Road, then made a left onto Van Mir Drive. His red Jaguar sports coupe hugged the pavement as he navigated the many twists and turns of the street, finally taking a left into the paved driveway of his two-story home in Nashville.

For several years he had lived about a mile west of Green Hills Mall in one of the most prestigious communities in Nashville. His home was convenient to most of his favorite stores and restaurants on the west side of the city. Whole Foods, Trader Joe's, Great Harvest Bread Company, Green Hills Grille, and his neighborhood Kroger, where he routinely bought cat food, were close by. Yet, despite its convenience to retailers in the area, his two-acre property had been carved out of a cozy hillside with lots of trees. It was surrounded by a six-foot-high cedar-and-stone fence, which provided additional aesthetics and privacy.

He had bought the place at a time when Nashville was one of the hottest real estate markets in the country. But a single man living on a civil engineer's salary in Nashville could do quite well. Especially when he had a side job. He had been anxious at first about getting into the second business. But, at the time, it had looked like an offer he couldn't refuse. Unfortunately, it didn't take long for his partner in crime to leverage him in a way that made it difficult to buy himself out of debt.

Until now. Now he had the upper hand.

He had no intention of being hauled off to jail. The truth was, he hadn't meant to kill that girl. It had been an accident. A careless use of force that had created a lot of trash talk within his business community.

It was deadly to call attention to yourself in his line of work. It was a multi-billion-dollar industry, and no one wanted to lose their share. One slipup and you were out. You could spend more than a decade of your life in jail. Or never be heard from again.

He pressed a button on his key fob. His gates opened. He drove around to the side of the house and pressed a second button, and the first of three garage doors opened. Markham drove the Jaguar into his oversized garage, which also housed an old Ford F-150 XLT work truck. He closed the garage door and stepped out of his car. After he opened his back door, he waited for an onslaught of cat feet.

He was home, and he could relax for now. But he had plans. Soon.

CHAPTER 21

Friday, September 3

Hannah rushed around all day. There was something about knowing that she would be performing, or at least rehearsing, tonight that energized her.

She made phone calls to producers about songs she wanted to pitch to their artists. She worked on an idea for a new song. And she exchanged last-minute texts with the manager of tonight's venue, as well as with other songwriters who would be rehearsing this afternoon.

Soon, Dixie's grandfather clock struck three, and it was time for her to take a shower and get ready for Jake to pick her up at four thirty. She wondered what his day had been like. *What does a TBI agent do all day?* She knew he had meetings and phone calls. And, of course, he was sometimes "out in the field," as he called it, chasing bad guys. But there had to be more. She would ask him sometime, and he would laugh at the question. He had a great laugh.

Why was she thinking about him again? She was enjoying his company too much. She didn't have time for a relationship. Not a serious one anyway. And Jake was a serious kind of guy. His heart was tender. That was evident in hearing him talk about Rylie. How many men would spend hours in the garden to keep a woman's memory alive?

Rylie had been a blessed woman. It had to be difficult to leave a man who loved her so much. Every woman—herself included—could only hope for that someday.

Hannah picked up her brush and ran it through her hair. Someday. Right now, she had too much ambition. Too much of a career ahead of her. Jake would be long gone from her life by the time she was ready to settle down. In the meantime, she would enjoy the time she spent with him. He was a storybook prince of sorts, and she hoped he would one day find his storybook princess.

Jake stepped out of the shower and glanced at the clock on his bathroom wall. He had an hour to get ready and get to Hannah's house. Where had time gone today?

He grabbed the comb from his vanity and ran it through his hair. What was that? A gray hair? It couldn't be. He had gotten up early every morning for nearly two years to practice martial arts. He worked out with his weights at home. And he ran three or four miles at least four or five days a week.

Apparently, you didn't outrun genetics. He could thank his mother for that. She'd had gray streaks in her hair since she was thirty, and he was now thirty-one.

Where had the last ten years gone?

Walking into the closet between his bathroom and master bedroom, he filed through rows of polo shirts, pulled one out, and then picked out a pair of his best blue jeans. He decided to wear a sports jacket too, at the risk of being considered overdressed in Hannah's music business world. He didn't want to embarrass her.

They had both agreed last night that she would introduce him as a friend, as she had at the riding academy, so they didn't need to explain why she had security with her. The fewer people who knew about her potential stalker right now, the better.

Jake finished dressing, picked up his truck keys, and headed out the door. He was pulling into Dixie's driveway at 4:29, with a minute to spare. It was Dixie who answered the door.

"Hey, honey. Don't you look nice! Come on in." She stepped aside so he could enter. "Would you like a glass of tea or fresh lemonade?"

"No, thanks, I'm good, Dixie."

"Have a seat. She'll be down in a minute." Dixie walked to the bottom of the staircase. "Hannah! Your handsome date is here."

Jake laughed. Even Dixie was getting into the act.

She stepped back into the living room and had a seat. "You two stay safe tonight." She raised her wrist to look at her watch. "I'll be anxious for you to get home."

"I'm not sure how long we'll be out," Jake said. "Is Roland not coming over tonight?"

"No. Tonight is his bowling night." She laughed. "He bowls once a month. Not enough to get good at it, but they have fun."

"Why aren't you with him?"

"I go with him once in a while, but honestly I have enough to do around here to keep me busy." She gestured toward the kitchen. "I'll be making a peach pie later. Roland may come over after bowling to eat a piece with me."

"Just so you know, there will be security outside the house. Don't let it startle you if you see someone out the window." Jake nodded toward the front yard. "Do you have my cell number handy in case you need it?"

"I do. Don't worry about me, honey. I've got Ophelia, and Roland brought me a .38 this afternoon."

Jake sat back in his seat. "Now, Dixie, you be careful with that thing. That's why I have security here." He shook his head. "I don't want you hurting yourself or someone else."

"Jake, I grew up shooting. My daddy had me practicing with targets when I was ten." She grinned, revealing the dimples in her cheeks. "I might not be able to do it now, but I've hit my share of bulls-eyes in my life. I want to get my carry permit as soon as I have time."

"I'm all for the Second Amendment, ma'am," Jake said. "But I want you to stay safe."

"Hey! Sorry, I'm a few minutes late . . ." Hannah strolled into the room. "Wow! You look nice. But why did you dress up?"

Jake got up from his seat. "I didn't want to embarrass you," he teased.

She looked at him and then down at herself. "I think I'm the one who will embarrass you."

"I like the way you look," Jake said. And he meant it. She was wearing a white blouse, faded jeans, and red boots.

"You kids both look great." Dixie jumped up. "Go have fun." She hesitated. "And be careful."

"We'll be fine, Dixie. Don't you worry about us. It's just a rehearsal, so we'll probably be back about seven o'clock."

CHAPTER 22

Jake picked up Hannah's guitar case and opened the door for her. "See you later, Dixie," he said. "Make sure you lock this door behind us."

Hannah walked to the edge of the porch and waited for him. It was warm outside, but the breeze made it a comfortable afternoon. Jake joined her, took her arm, and escorted her down the front steps. He opened the passenger side door of his truck and helped her inside.

"This is a serious truck," she said.

"Yeah. Sorry if my need for off-roading is showing." He chuckled. "Are you comfortable?"

"I'm good!"

He closed her door, opened the rear passenger door and stowed her guitar case, then walked around to the driver side. "Have you ever been off-roading?" he asked, starting the engine.

"One time. It's intense."

"Can be." He laughed. "I do it to burn off adrenaline from too many days in the field."

"I'm sure that's intense too."

"Can be." He smiled, shifted the stick into reverse, and backed onto the street. "Where are we headed?"

"City Winery," she said. "They graciously give us a place for the fundraiser every year. Have you ever been there?"

"A time or two. Not in a while."

"Ever since COVID, they've held some of their shows in their outside garden area. It's a fun venue to play. And the staff is great."

"That's on Lafayette, right?" He took a right on Caruthers Avenue.

"Yes. Almost hidden from the street."

"I've probably missed that turn every time I tried to get there."

Hannah laughed. "You and everybody else."

She leaned back into her seat. "So, what made you want to be a TBI agent?"

He took a right on Twelfth Avenue South and glanced her way. "It's pretty simple, really. I've always loved cops and robbers. That kind of thing. When I was about ten or eleven, I started watching all of the CSI shows and got hooked."

"That's hilarious."

He laughed. "I know. Be careful what you let your kids watch on TV."

"Are you glad you made that decision?" she asked.

He looked at her. "I haven't regretted a day of it." He took a right onto Division Street. "Even though I quickly learned that television was a lot different than the real world."

"How's that?"

His expression sobered. "For a starter, the bad guys are a whole lot worse in the real world. And when the good guys are killed, it's for keeps." He hesitated. "That's why I've tried to convince you to be careful, Hannah. When you mess up in the real world, it's a lot more unforgiving."

She nodded. "I understand." She turned to him. "I really do. It's just that I'm—I'm stubborn, I guess."

"Yes, you are." He smiled. "So how about you? What made you want to be a songwriter?"

She laughed. "I wish I could say it was a TV show, but it was something even more stupid than that. I used to sing to my dolls. I made up songs, pretending I was a star." She covered her face with her hands. "My mother has videos of me. It's humiliating now to think about it."

He chuckled. "What happened after that?"

"I guess I never grew out of it. I would sing in church. And in high school talent shows. I even tried out for a part in a high school musical."

"Did you get it?" He stopped at a red light and looked at her.

"Yes! And I'm sure I was a real ham." She sighed.

"I'm sure you were great in it."

"I don't know about that, but it was a turning point for me." Hannah thought back over those years. "I realized that was what I wanted to do with my life." She turned to him. "And I realized it was really about the songs. I love performing too, but I really love the songs. I started studying the music industry and how all the pieces fit together. Everything . . . everybody from the producers to the roadies to the radio folks has a part to play." She stared at the Nashville skyline through the window of the truck. "But it always starts with the song."

Jake made a left onto Eighth Avenue South, executed the round-about, and took a right at Lafayette. The entrance to the City Winery entrance was just past the sprawling parking lot of the Union Mission, off the main road and halfway hidden by another building closer to the street.

Despite its name, the Winery was a lot more than a place to buy wine. As a performance venue, it hosted a number of events each year—from gospel brunches to rock-and-roll legends to classic pop artists. Hannah had told Jake that her event, like many songwriter nights in town, would be low-key. The event poster, which was displayed on a tripod stand near the main entrance of the building, described tomorrow night's event as a "relaxing night of music under the stars."

Jake pulled to a stop a few yards beyond the main entrance and hopped out of his truck. He hurried around to the passenger side, opened Hannah's door, and helped her out. Then he opened the back passenger door of his Tacoma and grabbed her guitar case.

"Do you want me to carry your guitar to the stage?"

Hannah reached for the case. "No, I'm fine."

"Be right back," he said.

He turned his truck around in the small holding area in front of the building and drove back down the hill to the first available spot in the large lot that was designated for Winery guests to park.

Before leaving his truck, he grabbed his badge and tucked his gun inside his belt. Then he started hiking up the hill.

It was a gradual climb, probably a quarter of a mile, although not challenging for someone who had been a runner since high school. At the top of the hill, Jake turned left and walked over to the girl at the valet desk under the canopy.

"Which way to tonight's rehearsal?" he asked.

"Straight back on your right, sir." She pointed to the side of the building. "It's under the big white tent."

Jake smiled and thanked her.

The canvas doors of the oversized tent were pulled back. Jake could see rows of small tables that had been positioned at least six feet apart. A wide center aisle between them led directly to a stage, which had been set up against the back wall. Lights and simple decorations had been hung around the outdoor room. Plants had been used to add additional color.

The far wall of the tent was, of course, canvas. The masonry wall of the winery building was on the right. Even this early in the day, servers were already hurrying in and out of a door near its center. They carried tablecloths, candles, and other amenities in preparation for the show that would be playing tonight. Hannah had told him earlier that her rehearsal had to be over by six for-ty-five so doors could be opened for guests to arrive at seven.

Jake saw Hannah standing near the front of the stage talking to a group of people. Even from the distance, it was evident that she was the person in charge. He smiled. From all appearances, she was a woman without fear. So far, he hadn't seen her back down from anything. Not to a would-be kidnapper. Not to promoting a show a week after her recent trauma. And, apparently, she didn't think twice about standing on stage in front of hundreds of people. Just yesterday, he had watched her connect with the elderly residents at the assisted living home in Hendersonville.

When Hannah saw him, she motioned him forward. He pre-ferred to stand in the back and monitor everyone and everything in the room. But, if he wanted to remain anonymous, he had to play the role of the doting boyfriend. He walked up to Hannah and placed his arm lightly around her waist. She looked up at him and smiled.

"Jake, I'd like for you to meet everyone. Everybody, this is Jake Matheson." From there, she went on to introduce everyone—Francie, Bella, and Billy. All were songwriters performing on tomorrow night's show. "We will also have Troy Jones, but he's not going to be able to make it to rehearsal tonight."

Jake chatted briefly with the two women and then struck up a conversation with Billy, who said he had been out of town for a week and had only returned yesterday. Jake made a mental note to ask Hannah how well she knew the guy—and all the others here tonight. Until he learned the identify of Hannah's attacker, anyone and everyone was a suspect.

After the rehearsal started, Jake took a seat at the back of the room so he could keep an eye on both entrances as well as Hannah, which was sometimes difficult because she was all over the room, running from one thing and one person to another. Between performers, she would run on stage, conference with the person going off or coming on, and talk about the banter she had planned between performances. She carried a pad with her to make notes about each person so she could share biographical and other information about each one with the audience tomorrow night.

Jake wondered what motivated her, especially right now, when she could have been focusing on the man who had tried to steal her life last week. Was it the human instinct of survival that kept her going? Or was it the idea of helping others? He knew how much the riding academy—and the kids it helped—meant to her.

More than either of those things, Jake guessed she was really just fulfilling her natural calling. The thing that had been born deep inside of her, motivating her to write songs and to share them with others.

CHAPTER 23

Saturday, September 4

Jake's alarm went off at seven thirty the next morning. By eight, he was on his way to his martial arts session. On his way home, he would stop at The Turnip Truck in the Gulch to pick up fresh produce for the week and a grilled panini from the deli for his lunch. He spent most Saturday afternoons, sometimes working into the evening, on a project in his woodworking shop in the basement. But tonight he would be working.

He glanced at the time on the dashboard of his Tacoma. He had four hours to spare before picking Hannah up at her place. She had told him last night that she needed to be there no later than six for a seven-thirty show. Doors would open at seven, and each of the performers would be doing a final sound check between six and seven.

Jake switched on his radio and was surfing through the channels when his phone rang. It was Poe. Jake muted the radio.

"Payday," Jake answered.

"Hey, man. I've got something."

"Great, buddy. What is it?"

"There's something going on. I haven't heard specifics, but there's a rumble about exacting vengeance because of the recent law enforcement heat. I'm not sure what it means, but it seemed like it was important."

"Thanks for the heads up." Jake ran through a few scenarios in his head. "When can you get me more information?"

"I'll work on it," Poe said, sounding out of breath. "You might want to watch your— Hold on."

Jake could hear Poe talking to someone nearby. In a few

130

seconds he returned.

"That's all I have."

"Are you still asking around about the name of the guy who killed the girl?"

"For sure . . ." Poe's voice faded. "Hey, I need to run. I'll be back in touch soon."

Jake punched end on the call. Poe's concern wasn't all bad news. It meant they were getting close enough to cause a stir. And that meant they were getting close to their killer.

He dialed Tolman.

Markham pushed his chair back from his desk, stood, and stretched. It was only four in the afternoon, but his back hurt and his head didn't feel a lot better. He checked his watch for the third time in an hour. The day was passing slowly, as a day will do when awaiting good news.

He had tried to stay productive, but he had spent a lot of time just staring at his computer screen since sitting down at his desk at nine o'clock this morning. Working from home, as he had done for almost two years now, suited him much better than working at the office. He could focus better here. And, besides, he didn't care that much for his coworkers. People, in general, could get on his nerves.

Especially when his work was tedious, like it had been today. When he was drafting plans for transportation infrastructure, millimeters mattered. He had to stay on focus. If his drawings were off by even a little bit, a train could derail—and that could bring on a domino effect of disastrous portions.

Markham returned to his chair and continued to work. He had earned two degrees from the University of Tennessee, one in civil engineering and one in computer engineering. They were similar, yet very different disciplines. He had graduated near the top of his class in both. And that meant he'd had no problem finding a job back in Nashville. It had made sense to him to return to his hometown. He knew his way around the area. Nashville had a vital nightlife. And, most importantly, Markham liked the idea of living closer to his father, who was the only person in his life who had ever cared about him.

Civil engineering had a been a solid first career move. Designing railroad infrastructure paid good money, and it had taken only a few years for Markham to upgrade his lifestyle with the move to Green Hills. As people in the South liked to say, although disparagingly, he had been living above his raising for a while now. He liked it that way.

He hadn't been looking for a second income; he hadn't needed it. It had found him at a coffee shop one day by way of a chance meeting. Markham had been able to utilize his other degree in this second business, but he had also had to use his brawn, which was considerable. Standing six foot two and weighing two hundred pounds, his physical presence could be intimidating. It had kept him out of a lot of fights through the years. The truth was, he was a peace lover, not a fighter. He did his fighting on the inside, and often found himself battling between two distinct personalities.

When he used his computer degree in his second job, he was essentially an enforcer. A dog catcher, to put it in vulgar vernacular. Except the renegades he hunted were human. He had no use for anyone who shirked their duties, and it had never bothered him to bring them to justice. Street justice, maybe. But justice nonetheless.

Everything had gone smoothly for well over a year. The work had been easy, and the money was good. Then, last week, he had grabbed the wrong girl, and the domino effect had set in. Soon after that, another girl was dead. And now everything was in jeopardy.

He looked at his watch. It was finally five o'clock. Good news should be a few hours away. And that would be the first step in putting everything else in motion.

He closed down his computer, got up from his desk, and walked downstairs. Crossing the foyer, he went into his kitchen, where he was greeted by a dozen empty cat food cans littering his countertops. He retrieved the trash can from the corner of the room and slid the debris into it. Once he was rid of his houseguest, he would hire a pest control company to exterminate the roaches that had invaded his kitchen.

Returning the wastebasket to its place, he opened the refrigerator and selected two individual containers of lasagna. He carried them to the countertop, peeled back the plastic wrap on the containers, and discarded it. After he put both containers in the microwave, he turned it on and set the timer.

While the lasagna was cooking, he retrieved a bag of salad from the bottom drawer of the refrigerator, divided its contents into two bowls, poured salad dressing over the top, and added the croutons. He pulled a serving tray from beneath the sink, wiped it with a wet paper towel, dried it with another, and set the tray on the counter.

Soon, Markham was carrying two meals upstairs. One for his guest and one for him.

When he reached the media room, he knocked before opening the door. Shannon sat in one of the two chairs in the room watching television, an amenity he had added for her in the last two days. He set the food on the table and pulled up the second chair.

"I thought we would eat together tonight," he said.

"Why?" She threw him a disdainful look.

He ignored her venom. He was used to it by now. "You need to eat it while it's hot." He unfolded a napkin and placed it in his lap, then took a bite of lasagna. "You should try it. It's good."

"I don't want to eat." She refocused on the television.

"I thought you might want some good news."

"The Yankees won the series." Her sarcasm had become boring.

"Well, there's always that," he said. "But this is good news for you."

She swiveled in his direction.

He leaned back in his chair, enjoying her attention. "I'm expecting to make a great deal of progress tonight in getting back the girl."

She shrieked with laughter. "You're obsessed with that woman. I thought you had good news for me."

133

"It is good news for you," he said. "As soon as I have her in my possession, you can go home."

CHAPTER 24

Hannah was sitting in the living room with Dixie and Roland when Jake arrived a few minutes early. "Wow. You look nice—again!" she said, when she opened the door. He was dressed more casually tonight than he had for rehearsal. He was wearing a white shirt, tucked into somewhat faded jeans, and—

And then she realized there was someone with him.

Hannah blushed and Jake smiled. Then he changed the subject. "Hannah, this is Special Agent Beau Gardner. You've probably never seen him, but he has been watching Dixie's house. Can we step inside for a few minutes?"

She wanted to run somewhere to hide. Instead, she said, "Of course, I'm sorry." She opened the door for the two men.

"Dixie, Roland . . . Jake is here, and he has someone for you to meet."

"Ms. Carmichael," Jake said, "I'd like you to meet Special Agent Beau Gardner. Agent Gardner is working with me on Hannah's case. In fact, he has been watching your house for almost a week now."

"Thank you so much." Dixie stood and walked toward them. Roland followed.

"Beau, this is Dixie Carmichael and Roland Davis."

"Nice to meet you, Beau," Dixie said. "Just call me Dixie. Everyone does." Roland nodded and reached to shake Beau's hand.

"It's nice to meet you both." Beau smiled and then turned to Hannah. "It's nice to meet you too."

"Likewise," Hannah said quietly, hoping he hadn't heard her comment to Jake. "Thanks for your help."

"It's my job," he said. Then he added a smile.

"Would you two gentlemen like to have a seat? Something to

drink?" Dixie asked.

"Thank you, but no. We need to be going. I just wanted you to meet Beau in case you see him around here." He turned to Hannah. "Are you ready?"

She nodded.

He spoke to Dixie again. "Beau is going with us tonight to help with security, but there will be another agent watching your house."

"Thank you." Dixie smiled. "You know I appreciate you all."

"We sure do! Take good care of our girl," Roland added.

Hannah picked up her guitar case, and Jake took it from her hand.

"Cinderella, let's get you to the ball," he said, and then before turning toward the door, he added. "And, by the way, you look nice too."

"Thank you." Hannah ducked her head and walked straight past both agents and out the door, her cheeks burning.

"Beau, we'll see you over there," Jake told the other agent as soon as they had closed the door behind them. "Hannah is riding with me."

"Have a good show, Hannah," Beau told her. "We've got this."

She nodded, said "Thank you," and Jake escorted her to his truck. He had told her that he would be attending as a "civilian" again tonight because he didn't want to attract attention to himself or create questions for Hannah.

After they were both inside the Tacoma, Hannah grimaced. "I wish you had told me you were going to have someone with you. He probably thinks I'm a ditz or something."

He laughed. "Don't worry about it. Everybody likes to be complimented."

"Thank you for your help tonight," she said, wanting to change the subject. "I can tell that you've pulled out all of the stops to protect me."

"We're doing our best," he said. "There will be a couple of other of guys there too."

"Wow . . . I appreciate it. But I think you will find that there will be no trouble at all."

"I hope you're right, Hannah. But I would rather be safe than sorry."

They rode in silence the rest of the way until Jake pulled into the City Winery parking lot. "You're quiet tonight. Are you thinking about the show?"

"Sorry. Yes. Just rehearsing some of my lines. Introductions of the other performers, charity information, that kind of thing."

"I predict you'll do just fine with no trouble at all," he said.

She looked at him and smiled. "Thanks."

He stopped the truck in front of the building. "Want me to get out and help you with your guitar?"

"No, I'm good. But thanks."

"OK. I'll be right back after I park the truck." He nodded straight ahead. "I see Beau standing beside the entrance to the tent. Let him know if you need anything while I'm not here."

Hannah got out of the truck and was walking toward the tent when she was joined by Troy Jones.

"Hey, girl." Troy put his arm around her shoulders and pulled her to him. "What did I miss last night?"

"We had a good rehearsal," she said, glancing in his direction. "But you're a pro. I have no doubt you'll do fine without it."

Her words had been an understatement. At this point, Troy was the most successful artist on the show tonight. He wrote both Christian and secular songs, but he'd had chart success on contemporary Christian radio. And he had toured on some of the major Christian music tours.

"How long do I have for my set?" he asked, stepping back so Hannah could enter the tent first. As she did, she noticed that Beau was watching them, or, more specifically, watching Troy.

"Everybody has twenty minutes. Then we'll do a group finale and check presentation at the end."

He nodded. "And if there's an encore?"

"How about you leading us in 'People Get Ready'?"

"I'm happy to do that."

"We have about thirty minutes. Would you like to run through that right now?"

"That would be great." Troy took Hannah's arm and helped her onstage. She walked directly to the microphone and clapped her hands.

"Are all of our performers here?" She looked around the room and saw Francie and Bella and Billy running toward the stage.

She stepped to the microphone and tapped it with her fingers. It was hot. A few minutes later they were running through "People Get Ready" with Troy, and then did a quick verse and chorus of "Don't You Forget About Me," which was their planned finale.

She looked at her watch. "If anyone wants to do a mic check, we have fifteen minutes until the doors open. Forty-five minutes until showtime."

Cars were filing into the parking lot when Jake reached the bottom of the hill. Most of the first and second rows of the lot, as well as some of the third row, were already filled. He maneuvered his Tacoma into a spot on the fourth row, secured his badge and pistol, and got out of the truck. After locking the doors, he started the long walk up the hill. In this humidity, he would be wet with sweat when he got to the top.

As he walked, his conversation with Poe earlier today started replaying in his head. What did "exacting vengeance" really mean? Should he have put more security on Hannah tonight? Taken literally, exact could mean an eye for an eye. If that was the case, then one dead woman could only be avenged by the death of another.

Jake increased his pace. He would be glad when this night was over. He had told Hannah over and over that advertising her whereabouts when someone was trying to harm her was a bad idea. From the looks of the number of cars filing into the parking lot, plenty of people knew about the show tonight. He just hoped they weren't the wrong people. Maybe Hannah had been right, and this would turn out to be an ordinary evening.

Beau Gardner stood at the entrance to the tent. Jake nodded as he walked by, sidestepping the early arrivals hoping for a good seat. Soon many others would join them. Jake stepped inside the tent and looked around. None of the performers was visible at this point. And only a few servers were milling around. He walked up to one of the young women, told her he was with Hannah, and asked about reserved seating. She led him to a table marked "Cassidy."

"Would you like to see the menu, sir?" Jake's stomach rumbled, but he told her that he only wanted a soft drink. He would eat a peanut butter and jelly sandwich when he got home.

"I'll be right back with it, sir."

Jake was scanning the stage and backstage area about ten minutes later when Hannah appeared from behind him. She took a seat in the chair next to him. She had a big smile on her face.

"How's it going?" He knew the answer before he asked the question.

"Good!" She was almost jumping up and down in her seat. "Sound check went great. I can't wait for you to see how it has all come together."

"I don't know what you're drinking," he said with a laugh. "But I want some of it."

She looked at his glass on the table. "Actually, I haven't had anything to drink, and I'm parched. Is that diet or regular?"

"Regular," he said. "Want a taste?"

"If you don't mind." She picked up the glass and took a long drink. Then she took another and jumped up. "I'd better get back there."

"Go get 'em, kid."

"Thanks!"

"Sir, may I get you another drink?" his server asked a few minutes later.

Jake laughed to himself. "Yes, please. I hardly remember tasting the first one."

He had found himself laughing more in the past week than at any time in the last two years.

CHAPTER 25

The show was almost over when Jake stepped out of the tent. A breeze that had been absent earlier helped stir the hot air. He nodded to Beau Gardner, silently passing the torch to his associate for Hannah's security, while he went to get the truck.

Beau responded with a smile and a nod and walked into the tent.

The only people who were milling about outside were venue staff preparing for the crowd's final exit in about fifteen minutes. So far no one had left their seats to go home early. Hannah deserved the credit for that. She had put together a show that had captivated them.

He pondered that thought. Things had really come together from last night to tonight. Rehearsal had been loose and relaxed. He'd had no idea how it would transform into such an exciting show. He chuckled to himself. Apparently, he didn't know anything about the music business. Last night they had spoken in some kind of code.

"I'll vamp here."

"You take the lead on this verse."

"Big finish in the key of G."

Hannah was a seasoned professional. A talent who deserved to break through. If such a thing was possible, it seemed evident that she had been born to stand on stage.

Jake took a right at the north side of the Winery and started walking down the hill. From this vantage point, the Nashville skyline dominated the horizon with the Music City Center in the foreground and the iconic "Batman Building" rising above. The Cumberland River stretched beyond.

The narrow lane of asphalt before him that led to the parking lot below was almost completely bathed in semidarkness. Only the distant streetlamps and the stars above helped to light his path. Jake stumbled on a pothole in the uneven pavement, almost falling face forward.

He chastised himself for taking his eyes off where he was going. The massive parking lot was almost filled was cars now. There were only a few empty spaces, and the muted colors of the night made it difficult to pick out his truck in the midst of them.

The air was hot and thick. The breeze had temporarily gone. Rain was supposed to be coming in overnight. He reminded himself to turn off the timer on his sprinkler system as soon as he got home to save water. For the most part, it had been a long, dry summer. Deep in thought about what he would do tomorrow, he was surprised when two men stepped out from between parked cars, one man from each side. Jake's gut told him they weren't here to see the show. As a precaution, he reached for his gun and then remembered that he had stowed it in his boot, along with his badge. Too bold of a gesture.

Offense always had the advantage, and he shouted to the men, who were no more than twenty yards away. "Can I help you?"

It was more of a demand than a question.

"Yeah. You can mind your own business," the taller man, standing on the right, replied.

"Hey, I don't want any trouble, guys, and I don't think you do either. I would suggest you turn around and walk away."

The first man, who looked to be the spokesman for the two, laughed and then spat on the ground.

"I'm an officer of the law," Jake said. "You don't want that kind of trouble."

"Ooh. I'm scared," the man on the left mocked.

When Jake swiveled slightly to gauge the proximity of the second man, number one stepped closer.

"We're here to give you a message," the first man said, poking a finger into Jake's face.

"I wouldn't try that," Jake warned.

The man pitched his body forward and took a punch.

Jake blocked his opponent with his right forearm, deflecting and throwing him off-balance. In a matter of seconds, number one recovered and took another swing. This time Jake pivoted and landed a kick squarely mid-torso, knocking him down.

Jake turned and prepared to defend himself against number two.

The second man lunged forward, aiming for a one-two punch. Jake grabbed his hands, wrung them unmercifully, and threw the man backwards into a nearby car.

Before Jake could turn around, number one reached around him from behind, enveloping Jake's neck in his arms. Jake grabbed the man's forearms, braced himself, and then squatted, pulling the man forward, up and over Jake's right shoulder. His attacker landed on his back on the hard pavement and cried out in pain.

At this point, number two returned. Jake prepared himself, holding his hands in front of his upper torso, keeping his elbows close to his side. He bobbed and weaved, avoiding every punch the second man tried to land. Then, with an uppercut, Jake connected a fist to the underside of his opponent's chin, sending him stumbling backwards onto the ground.

Jake turned to counter a rushing attack from number one, who, although he was a taller, spindly guy, appeared to be quicker on his feet. Jake sent a knee into the man's groin, and then slammed a fist into his jaw. But number two grabbed Jake's ankles and pulled, dragging him onto the ground.

Jake covered his head and prayed, just before number one landed a kick to his ribs. Jake writhed in pain.

"Now you're the one who has been warned," number one said before kicking Jake in the head.

"Who sent you?" Jake asked, barely above a groan.

"Let's just say it's someone who doesn't like the way you're sniffing around. We've taken care of your snitch too, by the way."

Jake heard the sound of a knife being pulled from its sheath. Then a woman screamed.

"Stop that!" a man shouted.

Jake heard footsteps running toward him . . . and then footsteps running away.

Then he lost consciousness.

◦⟋⟍◦

"What happened?" Hannah screamed and started running for the parking lot.

"Hannah!! Stop!" Beau chased after her, finally catching her at the top of the narrow lane leading to Jake Matheson below.

She stared at him and started to pull away. Then she heard a siren shrieking up Lafayette Street. An ambulance, with its flashing red and yellow lights heading toward them, weaved in and out of the jagged line of traffic with cars that had stopped all along the road to let the emergency vehicle pass.

The Nashville Fire Department ambulance turned into the parking lot, and Hannah's focus shifted to the swarm of blue lights gathered below. There were four Metro police cruisers forming a circle around a cordoned-off area. A small crowd had started to gather, and Hannah saw police officers milling around with high-beam flashlights flashing. Once the ambulance sirens had been disengaged, she heard shouting being directed at the crowd, asking them to move out of the way so the ambulance could pass. Finally, the orange-and-white ambulance pulled to a stop near the center of the circle, and several people rushed out. They pulled a gurney from the back of the vehicle and rolled it toward . . .

Jake Matheson.

"I don't understand, why . . ." And then she realized she did understand.

She understood everything completely.

This was all her fault.

Hannah could feel her entire body start to tremble. She had the urge to run. Down the hill. Past all the people. To the center of the circle. To tell Jake she was sorry.

Beau put his arm around her shoulders, pulling her closer to his side.

"You can't do anything to help him right now, Hannah. We have to keep you safe. That's what Jake would want. That's why

143

we're here, remember?"

That's when the tears came. She couldn't stop them. The fear she had refused to give in to a few days . . . a few hours ago, now shook her.

When she could finally speak again, she turned to Beau.

"Who attacked him?"

"We don't know that yet," he said. "But we'll find out. Witnesses who saw the end of his altercation have said they saw Jake fighting with two men. I'm sure he gave them a run for their money, but they eventually got the best of him. They kicked him in the ribs—and in the head—multiple times."

Hannah knew she was going to be sick. "Why would somebody do something like that?" She looked at the agent, Jake's friend, standing beside her. And then to the ground. "It's my fault. He was trying to keep me safe, and he was hurt. If I hadn't insisted on doing the show, he would be OK right now."

"Don't blame yourself," Beau said. "We make a lot of enemies in our business. It's just part of the risk we take when we sign up for this job."

Hannah shook her head, pulling away. She had selfishly denied that doing this show was dangerous. She had been willing to take the risk for herself. But it hadn't been she who was attacked. And, if Jake was badly hurt . . . or worse?

It would be on her.

"Let me take you home." Beau gently pulled Hannah in the direction they had come. "We can't do anything for Jake right now. The medics are doing that."

Hannah nodded.

She had let Jake down. Why would he want to see her anyway? She turned and walked toward the black SUV, which was parked near the tent. Another man, dressed in khakis and a sports coat, was waiting for them at the vehicle.

"Hannah, this is Agent Andrew Robb. Do you want to wait here, or do you want to go with me to get your guitar?"

"I'll go with you so I can say goodbye to everyone." She wiped the smudged mascara off her face.

Beau nodded, and the two of them walked silently to the back of the tent and into the backstage area. The production crew was already breaking down stage gear, and Hannah's guitar case was lying open with the guitar inside. When she walked around the corner of the stage, she noticed a small circle of people gathered around someone. It was Troy Jones leading a group of singers, musicians, and stagehands in quiet prayer.

". . . And we ask this in Jesus' name. Amen," Troy said, before the circle of people started to disperse.

At that moment, Troy looked up and saw Hannah. He hurried over to her and put his arm around her. "We just heard," he said. "If there's anything I can do, let me know."

Hannah nodded. Her friends thought she was dating Jake, although they would have been praying for him no matter who he was. It was nice to have praying friends. Spiritual warriors, as Dixie always called them.

"Thank you," she said, wiping a tear from her eye. "I'll keep you updated."

Troy acknowledged Beau and walked away.

"Do you need to speak to anyone else?" Beau asked her. He had closed her guitar case and was carrying it.

She shook her head. "I'm not really up to it. I'll send them a note after I get home . . . or tomorrow." When she looked at Beau, she saw exhaustion in his eyes. "May I go home now?"

"Of course." He led her back to the front of the tent and helped her climb inside the SUV. He stowed her guitar in the backseat, and then walked around the vehicle to the driver's side, where Agent Robb was standing.

The two men spoke briefly, and then Beau climbed inside the SUV. He looked at her. "The ambulance just left."

"When will we know more?" she asked.

"It will take a while for the doctors to evaluate him. I think we might know something by midnight or a little later." He shifted the car into reverse.

"After I drop you off," he added, "I'm going to the hospital. As soon as I know more, I will call you."

"Do you need my number?"

"Jake gave it to me."

"Of course he did. He's good at what he does."

"One of the best," Beau said.

They drove back to Dixie's house in silence. Beau escorted her to the front door and handed her the guitar case. "Do you need anything else?"

She shook her head. "Just call me."

He nodded and left.

Dixie was waiting inside the house when Hannah entered. "How did it go?" The older woman peeked around the corner, as if looking for someone else. "Where's Jake?"

That was all it took. Hannah rushed to Dixie's side and fell into her arms sobbing.

"Honey." After a few minutes, Dixie gently pulled her away. "What happened?"

Hannah wiped her face with the back of her hand. "He was attacked by two men in the parking lot. He's on the way to the hospital." She broke down again. "It's all my fault!"

Dixie wrapped her arm around Hannah's shoulders and led her to the sofa. "Come over here and start from the beginning."

Hannah knew that Dixie was trying to distract her, but she was thankful for the attempt. Dixie made hot tea, and they curled up on opposite ends of the sofa. Hannah was almost to the end of her story when her cell phone rang.

Beau Gardner's name came up on her caller ID.

"How's he doing?" she asked.

"They're doing a CT scan right now to determine brain injury." Beau's voice sounded thin. "Most likely he has several broken ribs, and they're concerned about damage to his lungs."

Hannah's breath caught in her throat.

"Until he wakes up, we won't know how bad it is. Or if there's any cognitive damage."

Please, God.

"I'll call you in the morning when I know more."

CHAPTER 26

Sunday, September 5

Hannah awoke the next morning to a message from Beau Gardner. Jake was showing signs of improvement. Beau said he would call her later with more results. "Special Agent Robb is outside your house," Beau said. "If you need anything, check with him."

After replaying the message twice, Hannah jogged down the stairs. The older woman was sitting at her kitchen bar working on her laptop, with a half-empty cup of coffee sitting in front of her. "Hannah! Have you heard any news on Jake this morning?"

Hannah took a seat next to Dixie. "He's a little bit better." Hannah managed a smile.

"How did you sleep last night, honey? You look tired."

"Not great." She shrugged. "May I have a cup of your coffee?"

"Of course." Dixie jumped up. "Have you eaten anything this morning?"

"I'm not really hungry." Hannah took a seat at the bar, and Dixie set a cup of hot coffee in front of her.

"You need to eat something. I was just about to mix up a batch of sweet potato pancakes." She was already pulling bowls and ingredients from her cabinets. "Would you like to go to church with me after breakfast?"

"Maybe," Hannah said, watching Dixie measure flour and spices and dump them into a blue mixing bowl.

"It might be just what you need to get your mind off last night."

"Nothing is going to do that," Hannah said before taking a drink of her coffee.

"Honey, God's got this." The older woman opened the

refrigerator and took out buttermilk, eggs, butter, and a plastic container. She held up the container. "Pureed sweet potato from my garden."

Hannah did her best to smile. "I live with Martha Stewart."

Dixie sliced off a chunk of butter, threw it into a cast iron skillet, and lit the flame beneath the pan. "Roland made plans to have lunch with his son after church, so he isn't picking me up today. He's meeting me there." Dixie turned to her. "I'd love to have your company."

"Sure. Why not . . ." Hannah said as Dixie measured buttermilk, poured it into a second mixing bowl, and then added eggs, vanilla, and her sweet potato puree. Hannah took another sip of coffee as Dixie mixed the contents of the first bowl and then added the ingredients from the blue bowl. A few minutes later, she ladled batter into the hot skillet and turned down the heat. The smell of butter and batter wafted through the air.

Ten minutes later, they were eating pancakes topped with butter, maple syrup, and toasted pecans, and an hour later they were on their way to church when Hannah's phone rang with a call from Beau. "Agent Robb just told me that you and Dixie are going to church this morning."

"Yes." Hannah looked in the rearview mirror. "He's right behind us."

"You two stay safe," Beau cautioned.

"Yes, sir."

He chuckled. "I called to give you more good news."

"What is it?"

"Jake may be released from the hospital tomorrow. He's completely awake now, and he's already giving us orders." He laughed. "He called me this morning."

"Oh . . . that's wonderful!" Hannah turned to Dixie in the driver's seat and gave her a thumbs up. Dixie smiled and pumped her fist.

"He'll be on bedrest for a few days after he gets home. And, if you know Jake, you know that's not going to be easy for him to do. We may have to tie him to a chair." Beau sighed. "The main thing is that he's on the mend."

"Thanks for calling me!" Hannah said.

"I'll call you if anything changes, or if something else comes up," Beau said. "You and Dixie stay out of trouble. If anything happens to you, Jake will be after all of us."

"We'll be good, I promise." Hannah laughed. She pressed the end button on her phone and slipped it into her pocket.

"Jake's going home tomorrow."

"Oh, honey." Dixie reached across the console to take Hannah's hand. "God is so good."

"Beau said he will be on bedrest at home for a few days after he goes home, but he's better!"

"We have a lot to be thankful for," Dixie said, as she pulled her car into the church parking lot and eased into an empty spot.

Markham waited for the traffic light to change at the corner of Woodmont Boulevard and Hillsboro Pike. Traffic was always heavier than usual on Sunday mornings with cars trying to navigate the busy intersection as they made their way to one of two large churches on opposite sides of the road. Woodmont Christian Church and Woodmont Baptist Church had commandeered this corner for as long as Markham could remember.

With or without the traffic, he had never liked Sundays anyway. Not since his mother had dressed him up and taken his sister and him to church. He had been six or seven years old, wearing a suit and tie and was expected to act like a little man. His sister was usually dressed in something more casual.

He had never been his mother's favorite child, but he had been the one she held accountable. She had free rein in the house after his father left for the army. And, although she never harmed him physically, she had left an indelible wound on him emotionally.

If anyone knew about it, they certainly didn't try to intervene. Including the church people, who praised his mother openly for her well-disciplined son. Markham's father had been the only one who had ever interceded on his behalf.

He and his sister had spent eight long years alone in the house with the woman who was in name only his mother, while his father was serving overseas. After his father returned from the military, things started changing for the better. His parents eventually separated, and Markham never had to see his mother again. Even if she had wanted to see him, he wouldn't have let that happen.

He heard it said once that "What we don't receive in childhood, we spend the rest of life trying to find." That wasn't true for him. He had no aspirations for the perfect family. Not even the perfect wife. At the moment, there were only a few women in his life. All of them were business associates. Women tried to use their wiles to take advantage of a man, and he had no use for that. Apparently, a lot of men did. It was what drove the success of his business. He had spent a lot of his time in the last week trying to keep that business running. And that meant working directly with his manager on the street. Candy did a good job, but she was no less manipulative than the others. She had lavished him with compliments, telling him that he did a much better job than his partner, and even begged him to take over the business full time.

Markham knew she was trying to get on his good side so she could eventually take advantage of him. And what she didn't know was that he had no interest in taking over the business. He wanted out. And he would be negotiating his exit soon.

Hannah always loved to watch Dixie and Roland in church together. They would usually hold hands throughout the service. It had always struck Hannah as an act of worship. Just as when they held hands around the dinner table when praying before a meal. She thought back to the meal they had shared with Jake. Even though he no longer attended formal worship, he had seemed completely at ease with their informal prayer around the table.

Jake had occupied her mind a lot lately. She made an attempt to refocus her attention on the pastor's message about the trials of life.

"Many of you may think that you are out of God's will when you have trouble in your life," he said. "But that's often not the case. Many times it is when we are most in God's will that we find ourselves in the midst of trials." He looked around the room of more than a thousand congregants. "It is usually when we're exactly in God's will, doing exactly what we're supposed to be doing that we're attacked by the Deceiver."

Hannah thought about her best friend, Casey. And Jake's fiancée, Rylie.

"So what do we do to defend ourselves against those attacks?" the pastor asked. "Well, the first thing we do is pray. Jesus provided an example for us when He went to the Garden of Gethsemane to pray before His greatest trial in this life, crucifixion. And just as Jesus did, we need to pray over our trials. By all means, we should ask for deliverance. But we should also pray for strength, in case deliverance doesn't come."

Just like with Casey and Rylie.

"By the way, the Bible tells us that it's OK to question God, to ask Him why He is allowing us, or others, to go through something. We may find that His answer is a part of our solution." He lowered his voice. "But we should also be prepared to not receive an answer, or at least the answer we had hoped for."

His eyes swept the congregation once again, and he outstretched his arms. "We should also draw closer to each other. The Bible tells us in Hebrews 10:24-25 to seek fellowship with other believers, and to edify and help one another. When we share our trials with others, we diminish them.

"And finally"—he closed his Bible—"we should trust. We need to turn our trials over to God and remember that He is in control. When we think about trials, we almost always think about Job. He was a man who trusted God through his trials. And he not only trusted, he also praised God through them all. In Job 2:10, we are told that Job asked, 'Shall we accept good from God, and not trouble?'"

The pastor stepped back from the podium. "In summary, what do we do when we are going through troubles? We pray. We ask for God's help and for discernment. We share our burdens with others. And, most importantly, we trust God. For those of you who may not have noticed that spells PAST. Put your troubles behind you by *praying, asking, sharing,* and *trusting.*" He held up a finger for each point.

Hannah pulled a pen from the tray attached to the pew in front of her and scribbled a few notes onto her printed program. She wanted to share them with Jake when the time was right.

A few minutes later, the pastor asked them to stand. He closed the service with an altar call and a benediction, then Hannah followed Dixie and Roland down the center aisle, through the front lobby, and into the bright midday sunshine.

"I will see you later," Roland said to Dixie, as he walked them to their car. "After my lunch with R. J."

He turned to Hannah. "Have you ever met my son?"

"I haven't," she said. "But I'm sure he's a wonderful man if he has you for a dad."

"Thank you, honey." Roland smiled. "I'll introduce you to him sometime. I don't get to see him very often. He has his own life. His own friends." Roland walked to the driver's side of Dixie's car, opened the door, and gave Dixie a kiss on the cheek before she slid into the car. "Y'all be careful this afternoon."

Dixie threw Hannah a sideways look. "We're going straight home and wait for an update on Jake."

CHAPTER 27

Monday, September 6

Hannah pulled back her bedroom curtains hoping for sunshine, but clouds hung low in the sky as far as she could see. She retraced her steps across the room and headed straight to her kitchen. After inserting a pod into her coffee pot, she pressed the button. While her morning cup of caffeine was brewing, she grabbed a fruit bar from the basket she kept on top of the counter.

A few minutes later, she sat in the window seat that overlooked Dixie's backyard and scrolled through the newsfeed on her phone. Her mind was miles away when the phone rang. She saw Beau Gardner's name on the screen. Hannah's throat tightened.

"Good morning," he said. "I'm calling to let you know that Jake is on his way home."

Hannah gave a sigh of relief. "That's great news!"

"I'm on my way to your house right now. I'll be keeping an eye on things today. Robb has a day off."

"Thanks. I'll be here under house arrest."

He chuckled. "Is it that bad?"

"Not really. It's just that I have a lot to do, and I can't get it done here."

"Well, I have more news to make you happy."

"Yes, please!" Hannah said, jumping up from the window seat.

"We took one of our ESD—electronic storage device—dogs to Shannon Bridges's place this morning, and he found a stash of thumb drives hidden in the wall. Our digital forensics team is going through them right now."

"What do you expect to find?" Hannah asked. "She's a college professor, not a terrorist."

"I'll let Jake explain that to you when you see him," Beau said. "He asked me to bring you over to his place this afternoon."

"He did?" Hannah's heart pounded, and she wondered if she was more excited about the prospects of seeing him or concerned about what he might tell her. "What time are we leaving?"

"Is one o'clock OK with you?"

"I'll be ready," she said. Maybe the clouds were lifting after all.

Hannah looked at the clock on the wall. She had time to fill before one and thinking about seeing Jake had given her an idea. She hurried across the room to her storage closet and dug deep, pulling out the Korg D888 multitrack digital recorder she had retired after investing in The Gold Mine studio with her friends. The Korg would work well for what she had in mind, which was to put down a simple piano and vocal track for her new CD. This would be the final song.

Until now, she couldn't decide what to record. But looking forward to seeing Jake had reminded her of "Unchained Melody," the song she had sung for Harriet at the senior center in Hendersonville a few days ago. It had gone over so well there, and then again at the City Winery on Saturday night, she had decided to add it to her show for a while. A piano-vocal version of the old classic would fit perfectly with the nine songs she already had recorded for the CD.

Hannah carried the recorder to her work desk, dusted it off, and hooked it up to her AT2035 microphone and Yamaha keyboard. She rehearsed her arrangement a couple of times, and then hit record for the piano track and rough vocals.

Once she was happy with the piano track, it was time to add her final vocals, one lead and a harmony. After she finished recording and mixing the track, she uploaded it to a CD duplication company based in Nashville. If their turnaround was as quick as usual, she would have new CDs delivered to her front door by the end of the week.

After she carried her equipment back to the storage closet, she went downstairs to tell Dixie about her invitation to visit with Jake.

"I have an idea," Dixie said. "Why don't we bake a batch of cookies for you to take to him?"

"Dixie," Hannah said, "I just realized something. You use your cooking as a way to express your love for other people."

Dixie tilted her head. "I'd never thought of it that way, honey. But I think you're right."

"Just so you know," Hannah teased, "I feel loved. I've gained ten pounds since I moved in with you."

Dixie laughed. "And you needed to. You were too skinny."

"My point exactly," Hannah said. "And I'm sure Jake will love the cookies. What can I do to help?"

Dixie glanced at her watch. "We have two hours. Let's do something simple. Maybe chocolate chip peanut butter?"

"Sounds great."

Dixie hurried around the kitchen bar and started rifling through a file cabinet next to her desk. "Here it is!" She pulled a piece of paper from the file and handed it to Hannah. "Would you please get everything we need from the pantry?"

While Hannah was gathering ingredients, Dixie preheated the oven and retrieved the necessary bowls and utensils. As soon as they had everything on the countertop and organized, Hannah started measuring dry ingredients.

Dixie creamed butter and sugar together in a bowl, and then added what Hannah had prepared. Once the dough was made, Dixie started washing dishes, and Hannah spooned dollops of cookie dough onto parchment-lined baking sheets and put them in the oven to bake.

In less than an hour, the house smelled like warm sugar and butter, and the last batch of cookies was in the oven.

"Go on upstairs and get ready," Dixie said. "I'll watch this batch."

"Thanks!" Hannah said and then ran upstairs to take a shower, put on fresh clothes, and apply makeup, something she hadn't done much lately. She made it back downstairs with five minutes to spare.

Dixie was waiting for her at the bottom of the stairs. She held a plastic-wrapped platter of cookies in one hand and a sandwich bag full of cookies in the other. At one o'clock sharp, Special Agent Beau Gardner rang the doorbell. As soon as he stepped inside, he zeroed in on the platter of cookies Hannah was now holding. He looked over her shoulder toward the kitchen. "It smells great in here."

"Thank you, Agent Gardner." Dixie handed him the small bag of cookies.

His brown eyes danced. "Are these what I think they are?"

"Peanut butter chocolate chip," Hannah said.

"Oh, thank you! My mother used to make these."

"I hope you enjoy them," Dixie said, and then winked at Hannah as she walked out the door behind Beau.

It took less than fifteen minutes to get to Jake's house. As soon as they pulled to a stop, Beau hurried around to the passenger side door of the black SUV. Hannah checked her lipstick in the visor mirror and grabbed the cookie platter before he opened the door.

"Have you been here before?" he asked.

She nodded. "Jake brought me by one day so he could change clothes. He went running with me because I was whining so badly about it."

Beau laughed. "He's a genuinely nice guy." He paused, perhaps to question if he should say what he was about to say next. "And, in case you were wondering, he's exactly like he appears."

Hannah felt heat rise to her cheeks. Was Beau insinuating she had a crush on Jake? Or vice versa? Of course, she might have had a few passing thoughts . . . but their relationship had always been professional. She planned to keep it that way. No way did she want to become—or have Jake become—the brunt of his office jokes.

She straightened her t-shirt, and they walked up the sidewalk to Jake's front door. It opened before they stepped onto his porch.

"Hey, buddy!" Beau said. "You're looking good."

Hannah wasn't prepared for what she saw next. Jake's face was bruised and battered. And his arm was in a sling. She wanted to run away. Or run to him. But, most of all, she wanted to cry.

I did this to him.

Jake croaked out a laugh. "Come on in," he said. He held the door open.

Hannah stepped inside with Beau Gardner behind her.

"Can I get you something to drink?" Jake asked.

"I'll have a water," Hannah said before she remembered that she was carrying the cookies. She held the platter out to him.

"These are from Dixie . . . and me. We made them this morning."

Jake's smile widened. "That's amazing. And they look soft enough that I can chew them too." He gestured to his jaw. "I may lose a little weight until this heals. It hurts to eat right now."

"I'm so sorry, Jake." The words finally made it from Hannah's heart to her mouth.

His expression softened. "It's not your fault," he said. He reached toward her but had second thoughts and pulled back. "You didn't do anything," he said. "And, besides, you should see the other two guys."

Beau chuckled. "I told her you could hold your own," he said, taking a seat on the sofa. "I'll take a water too, while you're in the kitchen."

Jake set the platter of cookies on a coffee table that looked like an antique trunk that that had been fitted with a piece of thick glass on top. "You got it. I'll be right back." He looked to Hannah. "Have a seat and make yourself at home."

She nodded, but she didn't take a seat. Instead, she walked around the small living room, taking everything in. Every piece of art hanging on his walls was original. And, although she wasn't familiar with some of the artists, she recognized many as local artists who had just started to make a name for themselves. Most of the furniture in the room was antique, except for the seating, a contemporary, cream-colored sofa that dominated the center of the room, and two red leather chairs near the front windows. There was a wide-screen television hanging on the wall.

The floors in the house were beautifully finished wood, probably oak, and a large rug in blue, gold, and deep red added a punch of color. Even though the decor had a woman's touch, it had a certain masculinity about it. In fact, it fit Jake perfectly. Rylie had left him with a physical reminder of her love.

A tear fled from Hannah's eye. She wiped it away. If Jake and Beau saw her on the verge of crying again, they would begin to doubt her emotional stability. She walked to the red leather chair in the corner of the room and took a seat just as Jake returned. He gave her a bottle of water and took a seat on the sofa, handing one of the two remaining bottles to Beau.

"Hannah," he said, "I asked Beau to bring you here today because we have new information." He cracked open his bottle of water and took a drink. "But, before I tell you about it, I want to ask you a few questions."

Had he invited her here to interrogate her?

"OK."

He set his bottle on the coffee table and exhaled a shaky breath. "Do you remember meeting—or ever seeing—Shannon Bridges before the day of your attack?"

"What?" The question caught her completely off guard. She shook her head. "No. I don't remember ever seeing her before that morning. May I ask why you're asking?"

Jake glanced from Hannah to Beau and then back again. "Because," he said, "we've found a hidden stash of Shannon's thumb drives. She's operating a human trafficking ring in Middle Tennessee."

CHAPTER 28

Jake studied Hannah's reaction.

She stared at him in disbelief. "What?"

"It's pretty crazy, isn't it?" Beau picked up a cookie. "A college professor who was running a sex trafficking ring."

"And to make it worse," Jake added, "she likely met—and groomed—most of her victims through her work. It's convenient, if you think about it."

"Are you saying Ginny was one of her girls?" Hannah's expression clouded.

"That appears to be the case. At this point, we have no real explanation of how it connects back to you except that you were an unintentional victim." He hesitated. "Unless, of course, you were targeted."

"By Shannon?" Hannah laughed. "That's ridiculous. I had never met the woman, not before that morning."

"I think it's more likely that your attack was a case of mistaken identity." Beau took a bite of his cookie. "Trafficking doesn't usually happen by chance. A victim is almost always manipulated over time, not grabbed off the street, and you and Ginny looked a lot alike."

"So, the man who attacked me was working for Shannon?" Hannah directed her question to Jake. "And he thought he was grabbing Ginny?"

"Most likely," Jake said. "Your attacker was probably trying to bring Ginny back into the fold. She may have been wanting to leave the business."

"And she was killed because of it." Hannah's voice was weak. She looked down at her hands. "So Shannon's story that morning was completely made up?"

"At least some of it," Jake said. "Our working theory is that Shannon invited Ginny to meet with her that morning and then asked her to return the books to her office. That way, Shannon would know exactly where Ginny would be so the goon could pick her up."

Hannah frowned. "That's just evil."

"If you'll remember, Shannon said she was running late that morning. What she probably meant was that her conversation with Ginny ran late, throwing off the timing, if only by a few seconds, and—"

"Then the attacker saw me and thought I was Ginny!"

"Yes," Jake said. "The goon saw you, and you fit the general description, so he grabbed you, setting everything in motion."

"When you put up a fight and bested the guy," Beau said, "that threw the timing off even more. Jake arrived, found you in the parking lot, and called the police."

Jake grimaced. "I'll always regret not getting there five minutes sooner."

"You had no way of knowing," Hannah said.

"And neither did Shannon," Beau added. "She thought everything had gone as planned until she gave up on Jake and started to leave."

"That's when she walked right into a parking lot full of cops, with Jake among them. That's when she had to manipulate her story a little bit," Beau said.

"Just like she no doubt manipulated her victims," Hannah said.

"I'm guessing she's a pathological liar," Jake agreed. "She may even be a sociopath."

Hannah remained quiet for a few seconds, processing everything she had just heard. "So, now that you know that Shannon is involved, what do you do next?"

"First of all, we'll tighten security around you," Jake said. "While I'm sidelined for a few days, Beau will be heading up that effort."

Hannah glanced to her lap, where her hands were folded, and then to Beau. "Thank you, Agent Gardner." She turned to Jake. "I can't tell you enough how sorry I am that you're detained because of me."

Jake started to object, but she raised her hand to him, palm out. "Please, let me finish." He fought back a smile. She was a fighter. He loved that about her.

She took in a deep breath and sat straight up in her chair. "I want you to know I'm not afraid. I'm scared, of course. But I'm more scared of doing nothing than I am of Shannon—and whoever she has working for her."

Jake let her continue.

"How many girls, like Ginny, will be hurt or killed before she is stopped?" Hannah thought for a moment. "I can't look at myself in the mirror in the morning if I don't do what I can to help. After all, I'm already involved."

"Are you finished now?" he asked.

"Please let me help, Jake." She was begging now. "That's all I'm asking. Don't hide me away in a bubble. I'm willing to take a few risks to get that woman off the street."

Jake looked from her to Beau, who was shaking his head.

"We'll keep that in mind," Jake said. "But I want you to understand, I'm calling the shots. I'm not going to let you take any chances that might get you hurt."

Markham took his time preparing lunch. He wanted it to be extra nice. He had heard that the best deals were made over meals, and he wanted to make a deal with his guest. Not that she had any leverage right now. She wasn't going anywhere until he was ready to pull the trigger.

He carried the tray of food up the stairs and into her private quarters. "Sorry lunch is a little late," he said. "I made something special." He set the tray on the table. "Teriyaki shrimp with rice."

"That smells awful," she said. "I'm not hungry."

Markham took a seat and unfolded his napkin. "I'm eating with you today because I want to catch you up on some business."

His last comment must have piqued her interest because she turned to look at him. "Go on." Her words were spoken like an order rather than a request. The woman had no manners. At least he had been taught manners when he was growing up.

She said nothing while he picked up his fork and took a bite. He wanted to take several bites because it tasted good. But he put his fork down and dabbed his mouth with his napkin. "The cops have been asking a lot of questions," he said.

"What do they know?"

He could hear concern in her voice. "Don't worry about anything. I'm taking care of it." Markham took a drink of his water. "But I have a proposition for you."

Her interest was piqued again.

"I need you to give me your word that, if I can get everything taken care of so you and I both come out of this clean, you will let me out." He leaned back in his chair. "No strings attached."

When she didn't answer, he shook his head and picked up his fork again. "I mean it, Shannon. I didn't intentionally kill that girl. Her death was an accident."

"You're a bumbling fool!" she screamed. "If you had been more careful, we wouldn't be dealing with the cops right now." She stood and paced around the small room, taking a seat at the foot of her bed. "I can't promise you anything."

"That's fine," he said. He was prepared to play hardball. "But if you can't give me your word, I'm warning you now . . . your death *won't* be an accident."

"Is that a threat?" She jumped up and ran to him.

Markham stood. He dwarfed her five-foot-two diminutive frame. He could put his hands around her neck and choke the life out of her now. And maybe he should. She was nothing but evil. Even he knew that.

Shannon seemed to enjoy everyone else's misery and that had never been his intent. It still wasn't. She had tricked him into doing her dirty work. If he had known more in the beginning, he would have walked away from her that first day in the coffee shop.

She had been charming then. Sweet and cute. Even funny. And

he'd had very little attention from the girls in his lifetime. He had fallen under her spell temporarily. Until the clock struck midnight, figuratively speaking, and she had become the ugly stepsister.

He looked down at her. "Not if you make a deal."

"I'll tell you what," she said, seeming to acquiesce. "I will—"

She raised her knee and delivered a hard punch into Markham's groin.

"Oh—!" He bent at the waist, trying to catch his breath, paralyzed.

She stomped his foot with the heel of her shoe.

Markham fell to the floor.

Shannon ran around behind him and encircled his neck with her arm. She pulled him back just enough to temporarily cut off his airflow. He was starting to lose consciousness.

"This is how it's done, jerk." She let him collapse onto the floor, and then the room went dark.

CHAPTER 29

Tuesday, September 7

Jake turned his truck toward the Bureau headquarters. Sick day or not, he needed to file paperwork. Besides, what else did he have to do that was more important? Whether he felt up to it or not, he could sit in his office chair as easily as he could sit in his chair at home.

Rylie had often told him that he always put his work first. He hated the thought of that now. He was consoled only by knowing that she had accepted him as he was. She had been independent enough, strong enough, and she had loved him, despite his misplaced priorities. What he wouldn't give to have the chance to hold her in his arms one more time and tell her that she had always been the most important thing—the most important person—in his world.

She had brought perfect balance to his life. Not many women could handle his intense competitiveness. Or his fast-forward ambition. But she respected him for those things. She was never in competition with him, but she loved to compete alongside him. If there had been a t-shirt saying as much, she would have worn it.

He smiled at the thought of that and all the things they used to do together. Rylie had always been ready to try new things. When he bought his first four-wheeler, she had been the first to hop on for a ride. Later on, she had encouraged him to buy his truck, and they had gone off-roading together every weekend, usually on Sunday afternoons.

After church. After family time. They had taken off together for something they could do exclusively on their own. It had always been an adventure. They would go exploring, either in the truck or on foot, off-roading, taking the backroads, hiking a trail, caving or canoeing.

Don't let the memories get you down, Jake, Rylie's father had said to him a few days after the memorial service. Build on them instead, he had said. You can't dwell on the past and participate in the present. Or the future. The future is not ours anyway. God only gives us today.

Benjamin Richmond was a pastor, and encouraging people was his nature. It was also one reason Jake hadn't returned to church. The Richmond family church held too many memories. Jake had stayed away for their sake, as well as his. No one in Rylie's family would want to stare at the empty seat on the pew where she would have been sitting next to him.

On a typical day, it took less than fifteen minutes for him to get to his office from his house in Germantown. His usual route was North Sixth to northbound Ellington Parkway. The Ben Allen Road/Hart Lane exit was the second exit off Ellington Parkway. Once on Ben Allen Road, he would take the first right onto R. S. Gass Boulevard, and the entrance to his office building was only a few hundred yards up the road. When he turned right into the Bureau entrance this afternoon, everything appeared to be normal. He drove past the empty guard station and headed around back to his usual parking spot.

He was locking his truck when his phone rang. It was Hannah.

"Hi! How are you feeling today?" She was perky.

"Better, although not a hundred percent."

"Great!"

"So were those peanut butter cookies. I ate two for breakfast with coffee."

"That's why I'm calling. Dixie wants to know if you would like to come for supper."

"I—I don't think . . ."

"I told her you might not feel like leaving the house yet."

"It's not that. I just got to my office."

"Jake! I thought you had doctor's orders!"

"You're not going to tell him, are you?"

She laughed. "No. But I will tell Dixie that you had no legitimate excuse for turning down supper."

He chuckled. "Please don't make me laugh. It hurts."

"Sorry."

"Of course you are." He could imagine the mischief he would see in her eyes if she were standing in front of him.

"So, you can actually turn down Dixie's fried chicken . . . and peach pie?"

"You're making this impossible."

She broke into song. "To dream . . ."

"OK, you can stop now. I told you not to make me laugh."

He could hear her stifle a laugh. "Is my singing that bad?"

"Hannah . . ."

"Yes."

"What time do you want me there?"

"Is seven o'clock OK?"

"See you then."

She hung up. And he wondered why he had ever thought it was a bad day.

When Markham woke up, Shannon was sitting in the chair next to him with a gun pointed at his head. "Did you enjoy your nap?" she asked.

Markham slowly pulled himself into a sitting position, leaning against the wall next to him. "I barely remember what hit me."

"If you give me any more trouble, I'll be happy to remind you."

That's when it all came back to him. Shannon had crippled him and then overpowered him. Maybe he was a fool, just like she had said. "How long was I out?"

"Long enough for me to find this." She flaunted the gun in her right hand. "Nice piece. It was in your bedroom side table."

"Let me have that." Markham reached for the .45 caliber. "That was the pistol my dad carried in the army."

"I'll take good care of it," Shannon said. "And you need to stop being so pushy. I'm the one calling the shots now."

Markham rubbed the back of his head. "Did you hit me with it?"

"That might have happened," she said. "And it might happen again."

"All right. All right. Enough," Markham said, closing his eyes. "I don't have any fight left in me right now."

"Good," she said. "We need to talk." She relaxed her grip on the pistol. "I need you to tell me what happened two weeks ago that got all of this started. Who's the girl you're so hot to find? And why do you need to find her so badly?"

"The girl I grabbed in The Pancake Pantry parking lot. I thought she was Ginny—"

"That was a rookie mistake."

"I'm concerned she may have seen my face," Markham said. "I recognized her after she broke free."

"Hannah somebody . . ."

"I know who she is. She's a singer," Markham said. "Although I don't think she saw enough of me to know me unless she sees me again."

"Well, that's not likely to happen. Not unless you're some kind of weird star stalker."

"It might."

"And that's because . . . ?"

"She lives with my father's girlfriend. I saw her one day when I dropped him off at his girlfriend's house."

"You know where she lives?"

"Yes."

"So why not go grab her from her back yard?"

"That's not possible." Markham shook his head, a reminder that it hurt. "The cops are watching her house. My father told me."

CHAPTER 30

Jake had decided there was nothing better than Dixie's fried chicken, unless it was eating Dixie's fried chicken *and* hearing Hannah tell Dixie stories.

"Dixie started a ministry for single adults during the 2020 pandemic," Hannah said, smiling at the older woman.

"Is that how you met Roland?" Jake asked.

"Oh, no," Dixie said. "I met Roland online before that."

Jake almost choked on his potatoes. "You and Roland met online?"

"Oh, yes. That's why I started my ministry."

"You need to tell Jake the whole story. He needs a good laugh," Hannah teased.

Jake held his hand on his ribs and gave her the evil eye.

"Well, maybe just tell him the serious version. Without all the funny stuff." She ducked behind her napkin in jest.

"Hannah . . ." Jake cautioned her. "You're going to regret this someday. I will get even." He laughed and then cried out in pain.

"Jake, are you OK?" Dixie asked.

"I'm OK, Dixie. It's just that it hurts to laugh. If Hannah makes one more funny remark, I may throw a chicken leg at her."

"Pea fight!" Hannah said, picking up a green pea from her plate.

Dixie held her hand out. "There will be no food fights at my table, young lady."

Hannah apologized and then winked at Jake.

He looked directly at Dixie, trying to avoid any peripheral view of Hannah. She was probably making faces at him. "Dixie, I would love to hear your story."

Dixie leaned back in her chair with her hands on the table. "Roland, forgive me. You've heard this story one too many times already."

"No worries, dear," he said. "I'll clear the table and slice the peach pie in preparation for dessert." He turned to Hannah. "You might want to come with me so you can stay out of trouble."

Hannah laughed and started picking up plates. "Who wants coffee?" she asked.

"I'll have a cup," Jake said.

"Cream, right?"

"Yes, please."

Jake turned back to Dixie. "I'm ready now. But first, tell me what dating app you used to find Roland."

Dixie dabbed her mouth with a napkin. "You know . . . I'm not sure I remember. I was on several at one time or another." She playfully slapped Jake on the hand. "And that's why I wanted to start my ministry . . ."

He sat back in his chair. "So, you started an online dating ministry with your friends at church?"

"Yes. Sort of." Mischief flashed in the older woman's eyes. "That sounds really crazy, doesn't it?"

"Maybe a little." He did his best not to laugh out loud.

"It's OK, honey. You can laugh. The ladies at my church did."

Jake shook his head and smiled.

"I remember thinking, you know, this may not be a good idea." She patted his hand again. "But you know what? It was!"

Hannah walked into the dining room with coffee. She set one mug in front of Dixie and gave the other one to Jake. "I'll be right back with the cream," she said.

"So how did that work?" Jake asked. "How do you start an online dating ministry?"

"Actually, the first question would be *why* do you start an online dating ministry?" Dixie said. "I know you're not going to believe this, but it was obvious to me from the beginning. I chatted with so many widowers online, and it just hit me. There was such a need." She took a sip of the coffee. "You have to understand, the concept is only applicable to older women like myself. Women who are either widowed, divorced, or have never been married, and are hoping to meet someone in their age group."

She sipped her coffee again, while Hannah set a small pitcher of cream in front of Jake and then took a seat. "Those were the same kind of men we met. Mostly widowed . . . and unhappy. Many weren't sure what to do next. They had just lost the love of their lives, and probably the mother of their children, and they were all of a sudden alone in this world."

The thought of that pinged Jake in the gut. He grabbed his rib. Dixie stopped.

"I'm OK," he said. "Just rib pain."

She looked at him closely.

"No, really. I'm OK, Dixie. Go on."

"Long story short, I began praying for them. Every one of them I talked to online or met for coffee. It started to feel like a calling."

"Why not? God called Moses into the wilderness." Hannah laughed.

Dixie raised an eyebrow.

"Sorry," Hannah said. "Kind of . . ." She took a quick sip of water.

"Do you see that?" Dixie laughed and pointed at Hannah. "That's exactly what I got from the women I invited to our first meeting."

"I can't say I'm surprised." Jake hid his smile behind his coffee cup.

"I know . . ." Dixie agreed. "But eventually the ones who laughed the most started to understand my vision." She leaned back as Roland placed a plate of peach pie on the table in front of her. "And do you know what else happened?"

Jake shook his head and reached for the plate Roland was holding out for him. "What happened?" he asked and then took a drink of his coffee.

"Several of them found husbands."

Jake almost spat out his drink.

"I told you it was funny," Hannah said.

"Dixie, you're too much." Jake took a bite of his pie. "And so is your cooking."

Roland shook his head. "Can you see now why I fell in love with this woman?"

"I knew she was special the first time I met her," Jake said. "How long did it take you?"

Dixie crossed her arms over her chest and looked at Roland. "This should be good."

"We met almost three years ago, if that's what you're asking," Roland said.

"That's not what he's asking," Dixie prodded. "When did you know I was a keeper?" She winked at Jake.

"Well . . . let me think about that for a minute." Roland sat back in his chair and Jake's phone rang.

"Hang on . . ." Jake waved a finger in the air and stood, walking quickly to the foyer.

Hannah watched his demeanor change. It had to be a call from his office. She held her breath.

"Yes . . . OK . . . That's not good . . ." Jake said, walking across the living room. He was pacing now.

Hannah exchanged glances with Dixie and Roland, and in a few minutes, Jake walked back into the room. He sat down and laid his phone on the table next to his plate.

"That wasn't good news," he said. "Metro just confirmed another death related to the case. This one was a suicide."

CHAPTER 31

"Jake," Roland said, while Hannah was in the kitchen, "why don't you and Hannah go outside and enjoy the evening. It's beautiful out there. I'll help Dixie in the kitchen."

"Well, thank you, Roland." Dixie jumped up and started grabbing plates.

A few minutes later, Hannah and Jake stepped out onto the back patio. Ophelia was following closely at Hannah's heels.

"That dog follows you wherever you go," Jake said.

"Sometimes." Hannah took a seat on Dixie's glider. "I try not to encourage her too much. She's Dixie's dog."

Jake picked up a ball that had been left on the patio, and Ophelia redirected her attention.

"Oh . . . so I've figured out how to win you over," Jake said. He threw the ball as hard as he could, and it landed in Dixie's garden.

"Oops," he said, taking a seat next to Hannah.

"You're going to win over the dog and bring down the ire of Dixie," she said. "My money would be on sticking with Dixie."

Jake cringed. "I'm sure you're right about that."

Hannah nodded and looked down at her hands. She hadn't said much since he had broken the news about another death related to her case.

"So, what do you think? Was Roland trying to give us a chance to relax or was he wanting time alone with Dixie?" Jake tried to lighten the mood.

"What was her name?" Hannah asked.

"I don't know yet. The office didn't give me a lot of details. I'll find out tomorrow."

"When is this going to stop, Jake?" She turned to him, a tear in her eye.

He wanted to reach out to her, but he checked himself.

"Hannah," he said. "These kinds of things happen in my line of work. That doesn't make it any easier." He repositioned himself on the glider. "But, as awful as this is going to sound, bad things are still going to happen after we bring Shannon to justice. She's one of thousands of bad people out there. And we can only stop one of them at a time."

Ophelia was back with the ball in her mouth, begging Jake to throw it again. He wanted to laugh, but thought better of it, considering Hannah's mood, but the dog didn't just wag her stub of a tail. She wagged her entire bottom.

"You'd better do what she wants," Hannah said. "She won't stop until you do."

Jake removed his hand from Hannah's and reached for the ball in Ophelia's mouth. She gave it to him without a fight. He stood and threw the ball up and out, careful not to put as much muscle behind it this time.

"You did good." Hannah was smiling again. "She'll have you trained in no time."

"I can handle that," Jake said as he retook his seat beside her.

The Hannah he loved was back.

Wait . . . *Loved?*

Where had that come from?

The dog returned.

"Do you want to walk around?" Hannah asked, jumping up. "She'll keep doing this if we just sit here."

"Sure." Jake stood and grabbed the ball from Ophelia. He threw it into the side yard.

"I'll give you the grand tour of Dixie's garden," Hannah said, walking in the direction of the dog and the ball.

Forecasters had predicted a gray day, and they had gotten that mostly right. Only a sliver of the moon was visible, and the stars had taken center stage in the sky.

"I've never been able to find the constellations," she said. "Are you good at that?"

He looked up.

"Do you mean the Big and Little Dipper and those kinds of things?"

She nodded.

"That's Camelopardalis." He pointed to the north. "It's supposed to look like a giraffe. What do you think?"

"I'm not seeing it."

"It's harder to see than some of the stars and was only discovered in the early 1600s. The first astronomer to include it on a star map a few years after its discovery likened it to a camel, instead of a giraffe. Thus the first part of its name, which also sets up a biblical reference to the Book of Genesis when Rebekah rode a camel into Canaan to marry Isaac."

Hannah turned to him. "That's fascinating. How do you know all of that?"

"Trivia games," he deadpanned, then grinned. "No. Not really. I've always been fascinated by astronomy. Look . . ." He took her arm and turned her slightly to the left. "That's the Ursa Major constellation. It's known as the Great Bear. The Big Dipper is in there. It's one of only a few star groups in the Bible. It's mentioned in Job. 'He is the Maker of the Bear and Orion, the Pleiades and the constellations of the south.'"

"You're blowing me away," Hannah said. "Tell me something else about you I didn't know."

"That's a tough question. Why don't you go first?"

Hannah laughed. "I suppose it is a tough question." She thought for a few seconds. "How about this . . . my favorite color is yellow, and I've always dreamed of living in a yellow farmhouse . . . with a red roof!"

"And a barn?"

"How did you know that?"

"That's easy," Jake said. "You love horses."

"OK, your turn. Where have you always dreamed of living?"

"I'm pretty much there," he said. "There's just something about

Nashville. I like living in the city. There's a lot of energy here. Tourists, locals. Diners, five-star restaurants. High rises, cottage homes. It's a good balance. We're a little bit country and . . ."

"And a little bit rock and roll." Hannah laughed.

"Yes. That's a good way to put it."

"Don't you remember the song?"

"There's a song?" He appeared to be genuinely surprised.

"It's from the seventies. It was recorded by Donnie and Marie Osmond."

"I know who they are. She does those commercials . . ." His expression grew serious. "You're not going to sing it, are you?"

Hannah laughed. "Not unless you want me to. But I do know it."

Jake shook his head. "You're a virtual jukebox when it comes to old music."

"I've always loved it."

"You're a little bit country and a little bit rock and roll too."

"I'll take that as a compliment," Hannah said. "You may be a city boy, but you have a country boy heart."

Jake laughed. "What exactly does that mean?"

"You love off-roading. And gardening . . . and I think you know more about horses than you were letting on the other day."

"You might be on to something," he said, taking her hand and turning her toward the house.

"Can I ask you something?"

"Sure."

"What attracted you to Shannon when you started talking to her online?"

He stopped walking. "Wow . . . that's an interesting question."

She could feel the heat rise to her cheeks. Had she really asked that?

"If you would rather not—"

"No! I'm good with it. It's just interesting because it's not necessarily something a person thinks about consciously." He sat down on the bench across from the glider they had occupied earlier. Hannah took a seat beside him, and he put his arm around her—not on her but resting on the back of the bench. "You're going to think I was naive. Me, of all people, naive about online dating. I mean, I'm an agent of the TBI and investigating online crimes and scams are part of what we do."

Hannah didn't say anything but watched instead as he thought about his answer.

"But her photos gave me the impression that she was sweet, even shy."

"And maybe she is . . . at least, shy."

Jake chuckled. "You're being too kind. I knew I was wrong the minute she sat down at the table to give me her deposition. There was something off about her." He thought for a minute. "Have you ever heard the word *charlatan*?"

"Sure." Hannah nodded.

"That's the best word I can think of to describe her. Especially in retrospect."

"Can I ask something else?"

"Absolutely." He grinned.

She leaned back and looked at him. "You find me amusing, don't you?"

"Refreshing is more the word."

"Hmm." She thought about that for a few seconds. "I'll take that as a compliment. My question is why did you look for someone online? I've had friends who did that—some very successfully, although I've never done it. I'm curious why someone, especially in your line of work, would do that."

"Do you think it's a bad thing?"

"Oh, no. Don't let me give you that impression. I guess I'm just not comfortable with it."

"You're right to be cautious. I thought I was too savvy to be misled, and I wasn't. It's easy to see now how people can be victimized."

Neither of them spoke for a few moments.

"Unfortunately, there are a lot of them who are." He looked at his watch. "Do you realize it's almost ten o'clock? What are you doing tomorrow?"

Jake stood and walked her to the back door, where Ophelia was already waiting for them.

She laughed. "I'll be here under house arrest. Remember?"

"Why don't you let me pick you up, and we can go for a walk at Radnor Lake? I'm not sure I'm up to running yet, but I would love to stretch my legs."

"You can always count on me for that! What time tomorrow?"

"Does one o'clock work for you?"

"Sounds good."

CHAPTER 32

Wednesday, September 8

"So is your father helping you?" Shannon asked.

"Not intentionally," Markham said. "But he's feeding me information that's helpful."

"You need to talk to him regularly."

Markham didn't respond. Shannon was the bossiest woman he had ever met. Well, except for his mother.

It didn't take a psychoanalyst to explain why he disliked women so much. He had run into a lot of difficult ones in his lifetime. Shannon was no doubt the worst of the lot. He should have killed her when he had the chance. Then again, maybe it wasn't too late. Now that he had done it once, even if unintentionally, it wouldn't be that hard to do it again. His father had talked about that very thing once when recalling his time spent in the Persian Gulf and Iraq in the late '80s and early '90s.

Markham jumped back to the moment, realizing that Shannon was still talking.

"You haven't been paying attention, have you?"

"Sorry," he said, although he wasn't. "I was thinking about something my father told me once."

"I should just shoot you now and put you out of your misery." She pointed the gun, *his* gun, at him. "If you listen to me, I will get you—both of us—out of this mess that you got us into in the first place."

She shook her head in disgust. "We're not going to let them take us down. Do you understand?"

At least they agreed on one thing.

Hannah was ready before Jake picked her up Wednesday afternoon. She had slept late that morning, and lunch had been a breakfast bar and two cups of coffee. Last night had been one of those unusual times when she'd had problems sleeping, although she had still felt somewhat rested when she woke up at 11:00 a.m.

"Music business hours," Dixie always teased when Hannah slept late.

But Hannah knew it wasn't the music business that had kept her awake for half the night. It might have been because she ate too much of Dixie's good cooking at supper. Or it might have been Jake's tales about the stars that had disturbed her. Whatever it was, she had awakened in the middle of the night with a feeling of foreboding.

Still . . . she wasn't afraid. In fact, she was eager to embrace what was coming. God had this, whatever it was. All she had to do was hang on for the ride.

Now, in the light of day, sitting in the swing on Dixie's front porch, while waiting for Jake, she thought about how God had never failed her. He had always been there at the right time, whenever she needed Him most. Even in the little things. And even when her faith was barely hanging on.

Those were the times when she had realized that faith didn't have to be bold. It could be childlike and meek. It was that kind of faith that was at the heart of the stories that Jake had told about the stars and the constellations.

After he left last night, she had gone upstairs and looked up the biblical references he mentioned. Rebekah had gone into Canaan riding a camel because she believed that God was calling her to marry Isaac. And, because of that faith, she had become the mother of two nations. Nations that would change the landscape of the earth forever. One of those nations would bring about the prophesied Messiah.

It didn't get much better than that.

But it had been Jake's reference to the Book of Job that had really pulled her in. Sitting on her upstairs window seat, looking out at the stars, she had read ten chapters, from twenty-eight to thirty-eight, and they were fascinating. She wondered why she hadn't read the Book of Job more often.

Sitting on the porch, she scrolled through the Bible app on her phone and found the words she had underscored in Job 39:19-25.

> Are you the one who gave the horse his prowess
>> and adorned him with a shimmering mane?
> Did you create him to prance proudly
>> and strike terror with his royal snorts?
> He paws the ground fiercely, eager and spirited,
>> then charges into the fray.
> He laughs at danger, fearless,
>> doesn't shy away from the sword.
> The banging and clanging
>> of quiver and lance don't faze him.
> He quivers with excitement, and at the trumpet blast
>> races off at a gallop.
> At the sound of the trumpet he neighs mightily,
>> smelling the excitement of battle from a long way off,
>> catching the rolling thunder of the war cries.

Another version translated the word *danger* to *fear*. She loved that.

Hannah darkened the screen and tucked her phone into the pocket of her shorts. Bad dreams and foreboding aside, if God could make the horse laugh at fear, He had surely created her to do the same.

Jake's pulse quickened when he saw Hannah waiting for him on the porch. He had stayed awake much of last night replaying their evening together. Had he really held her hand? And then gone on and on about the stars? If that hadn't been enough, he had asked her to go walking with him today.

Thankfully, she had accepted.

He glanced in the rearview mirror. He had enough bags under his eyes to carry home the groceries. Sleep would have been nice. But he couldn't stop thinking about her. There was something about her that made him feel comfortable. He could talk to her about anything.

She was easy to look at too, with her big blue eyes and long, blonde hair. *Remember why you're here, Jake. This is not a date.*

He looked at his tired face in the mirror again. It was the best he could do. He pulled the truck to a stop in front of Dixie's house and rolled down the window. "Are you ready?"

"I am!" She jogged down the front porch steps. Apparently, she had slept better than he had.

He hurried out of the truck and met her at the passenger side door so he could open it for her. He gave her a boost up into the cab. "I apologize again for this truck. It's not the easiest vehicle to get in and out of."

"Don't apologize. I like your truck," she said.

He walked to the driver's side and climbed inside.

"How was your night?" she asked.

"I didn't sleep very well. How about you?"

"Me either! What's up with that?"

"Well, at least we're two for two. We should be a lot of fun today."

She laughed. "We'll watch out for each other. I'll try not to let you fall in the lake."

"You would probably push me in," he teased.

"I would not! Although now that I know how you think, I'm keeping my eye on you."

"I would never do that. Not unless it was a matter of life or death."

"Whose? Yours or mine?"

He chuckled. "Yours, of course. I took an oath to serve and protect."

Hannah leaned back in her seat. "And you're doing a good job,

Agent Matheson. I feel completely safe with you."

About fifteen minutes later, they looked for a place to park in the Radnor Lake west lot. Even though the park was still one of the best-kept secrets in Nashville, it had grown in popularity over the last few years. Relatively few Nashvillians visited the park despite its proximity to the heart of the city. Still, the parking lots were rarely empty.

All fourteen hundred acres of the park grounds were inside the Metropolitan Nashville city limits, less than a half hour from downtown Nashville. And although visiting hours were limited to daylight hours, a hiker could spend most of a day there, exploring one or all of the nine trails.

Jake pulled into a vacant parking place near the main administration building. "We got lucky," he said.

Hannah glanced at her smartwatch. "The Radnor Lake lunch crowd must have just left."

He stepped out of the truck and walked around the front to open Hannah's door. "Do you have everything you need to take with you?"

She patted her pocket. "Just my phone."

"Do you want to stop by the restroom first?"

She gave him a crooked smile. "How far are you planning to walk me?"

"Around every trail and up every hill."

"I can do that," she said.

"I'm sure you could, but since neither of us slept that well last night, how about we go a little bit easier on ourselves? Maybe a round or two on the Lake Trail? I'm not feeling up to Ganier Ridge Trail quite yet."

"Sounds good." She hopped out of the truck.

Jake closed the passenger side door and locked the truck, and they set out at a moderate pace. There was a steep incline up Otter Creek Road, which led to the main trail encircling the eighty-five-acre lake. Once the terrain leveled off, they hung a right and increased their pace.

Radnor Lake State Park was a natural area, which meant

that no trees or brush were cut unless they endangered park visitors or personnel or obstructed the right-of-way for visitors or groundskeepers. It was also a wildlife refuge and visitors could see everything from rabbits and squirrels to wild turkey and deer. There were almost always wildflowers in bloom. And in summer months, turtles sunned on logs floating in the lake or on the bank.

Because the area was never poached by hunters, and hikers weren't allowed to leave the trails, the wildlife had no reason to feel threatened. Jake had once watched a flock of seventy-five to a hundred turkeys parade across the Lake Trail, all in single file. The big birds had taken their time, in complete disregard of their human visitors, who waited patiently as they passed.

"My guess is that this place gets quiet, and a little creepy, at night," Hannah said, looking around. "Can you imagine?"

"I've heard they sometimes have astronomy night hikes out here."

"That would be fun!" She turned to him. "I enjoyed last night."

"Me too." He took her hand, and they kept walking.

CHAPTER 33

"Would you like to get something to eat?" Jake asked. "Maybe on Twelve South or in the Gulch?"

Hannah looked down at her attire. "Maybe something casual. I'm not exactly dressed to go out."

"Do you like Monell's? We could pick up to-go and take it to my place." He glanced at his watch. "They're still open."

"That works!"

Hannah called the restaurant and placed their orders on the way, and within the hour they were carrying food and drinks into Jake's little cottage. "Make yourself comfortable," he said. "Would you like to eat in the kitchen or on the sunporch?"

"The sunporch sounds great!" She hesitated. "Do you mind if I use your restroom first?"

"Straight down the hall." He set the bag of food on the coffee table and took the drinks from her hands.

A few minutes later Hannah joined him in the kitchen.

"I'm hungry, how about you?" he asked.

"Starving. I had a breakfast bar for lunch and that's it today."

"You must have gotten up late." He led her into the sunporch, where he had the table set and ready.

She took a seat in a brown wicker chair that faced a wall of windows overlooking his garden. "It's beautiful out there."

"I have a lot more to do." He opened his to-go box. "I have everything I need in my woodworking shop downstairs to build a gazebo in the backyard. I was hoping to finish it this year, but my ribs may not be up to the heavy lifting for a while."

"I'm so sorry, Jake."

"Stop that!" he chastised her. "Remember, that was not your fault." He took a bite of his food. "If you want to place blame, you're in this mess because of me."

She set her glass on the table and stared at him. "Why would you even think that?"

"If I hadn't asked Shannon to lunch, Ginny probably wouldn't have been in the parking lot that day, and you would have never been assaulted."

"I'm not sure how you figure that," she said. "Shannon's meeting with Ginny had nothing to do with your lunch."

"Can we agree to not blame anybody except the bad guys?"

"Deal," she said, taking a bite of her baked chicken. "This is good. Thank you for dinner. And the walk. I've enjoyed it. It almost felt like a normal day."

"You'll get there," he said. "We're learning more about the case every day."

"I hope so." She reminded herself that it had been less than two weeks since her attack.

After they'd finished eating, Hannah asked to take a walk in the garden. "It's beautiful out here. You're doing a great job with it," she told him.

"It's not nearly as put together as Dixie's, but I'm getting there a little at a time. Rylie left me with a good foundation."

Hannah's heart climbed into her throat. Would he ever be ready to move on again? She hated to admit it, even to herself, but that now mattered to her.

"That's because she loved you," she said. "She wanted you to have this place, and the other special things she left you, to build on." Hannah fought back threatening tears. "You were blessed to have her."

Jake took her hand. "Do you want to go inside for a little while?"

Jake, you have to get a handle on this. Why did he continue to talk about Rylie? That wasn't fair to Hannah or anyone else. Most of all, it wasn't fair to him.

He held the door to the sunroom open for her.

Hannah glanced at her watch. "I should probably be getting home soon."

"I'll have you home by seven," he countered. "How would that be?"

She stepped inside ahead of him.

"I still have some of Dixie's cookies left. Would you like one warmed?"

She studied his face, and he knew she was weighing her decision. "You've talked me into it," she said. "But only one."

"You got it!" He gestured toward the living room sofa. "Make yourself comfortable. I'll be right there."

He put three of Dixie's chocolate chip cookies on a plate, set the plate in the microwave, and dialed in ten seconds. While they were heating up, he stuck his head around the door. "Anything to drink?"

"No, I'm good."

"OK," he said. Within thirty seconds he was setting the plate of cookies on his coffee table. He offered Hannah a napkin and joined her on the sofa.

She picked up a cookie, broke a piece off, and wrapped the biggest piece in her napkin, which she put on the table in front of her. "They're good warmed up," she said.

"Microwave. My favorite method of cooking."

She laughed, took another bite, and made a funny face. He wasn't sure if she knew how beautiful she was. She had a way about her that made you feel good about yourself. He could—

"Where did you go?" She broke into his thoughts.

"Oh . . . sorry. What did you say?"

She smiled. "I asked if you can boil water too."

"I think I did one time, but it was sheer luck." He gestured behind him. "That's why you see so many Monell's boxes in my trash can."

"You need to live with Dixie," Hannah said. "I'm the luckiest person on earth to have that gig."

Jake smiled and drifted off again. He hated to ruin the mood, but he had promised to keep her updated about their latest findings. He took a bite of the cookie in his hand and set it on a napkin on the table. "I want to fill you in on Shannon's case."

Hannah's expression darkened. She reached for a nearby pillow, pulling it close to her.

"I know more now about the woman whose body was found yesterday."

Hannah nodded.

"Her name is Lillian Haynes. Her alias was Candy Hayes, and she was found inside her home. Her autopsy is still pending, but she mostly likely died of an intentional overdose."

Hannah readjusted her position on the sofa, and Jake took a breath. "She left a suicide note, and in it she mentioned Shannon Bridges."

"In what context?" Hannah hugged the pillow closer to her chest.

"She said something to the effect that she wanted out. She said suicide seemed to be the only way."

Hannah closed her eyes. "I can't even imagine . . ."

"She ended the note with 'If you know Shannon Bridges, you'll understand why I had to do this.' The investigating officer at Metro didn't connect it to our case until a few days later."

Hannah's hands knotted into fists, and her cheeks flushed with anger. "How much evil can that one woman cause? I don't understand. Does she have no conscience?"

"It gets even worse," Jake said. "It was Lillian's six-year-old daughter who found her."

Tears welled up in Hannah's eyes. Jake leaned closer and offered her a fresh napkin.

"You're a blessed woman, Hannah," he said. "If you hadn't managed to break free of your attacker, I'm not sure how bad it could have been."

She nodded, remaining silent. Jake suspected that she couldn't speak, judging from the tears welling up in her eyes. He reached to wipe a tear from her cheek.

She smiled. A weepy, questioning smile.

Vulnerability. It was the first time he had seen it in her eyes. The child deep down inside. Hannah had always presented herself as a strong, almost confident, woman. And he had no doubt she was most of the time, but a scared little girl was also in there.

Jake wanted to pull her to him, surround her with his arms. He wanted to give her his heart. Or maybe he had already done that. He had shared more with her in the short time he had known her than he had shared with anyone since Rylie died.

Jake, you have to move on.

He reached out to her, and she came willingly, settling into his embrace. She laid her head on his shoulder, and his arms encircled her, as she gently swayed back and forth. Jake breathed in deeply. The sweet scent of her perfume, anchoring him to the here and now. She filled an emptiness his arms had longed to fill for almost two years. At this moment in her life, Hannah needed him. But he needed her too. That thought ambushed him. He was also vulnerable. Vulnerable to the possibility of losing her, just like he had lost Rylie.

Jake pulled her closer still. He could hold her in his arms forever. But, before he could do that, he had to keep her safe. He had to let her go. Until his work was finished. He had to focus on the most important thing. Finding Shannon—and Hannah's unknown attacker—and bringing them to justice.

He kissed her softly on the top of the head and gently pushed her away. She turned her chin upward and smiled. Her tears were gone, although the vulnerability remained. Jake brushed a wisp of hair from her forehead and held her face in his hands, for a second too long. He moved toward her, barely touching his lips to hers.

When he pulled back, she smiled. He kissed her again, and she was willing. He pulled her back into his arms again and held her for a while longer.

CHAPTER 34

"Oooo!" Shannon jumped back. "What are those awful bugs doing in here?" She had just turned on the light in Markham's kitchen to heat up something to eat.

"That's the least of our problems," Markham spat back at her. "Candy is dead, and she mentioned you in her suicide note."

"She was always weak." Shannon tossed her head and opened his refrigerator door.

"Shannon, are you so stupid you don't understand? She named you in the note." He shook his head. "It's a good thing you're at my place. The police have to be crawling all over your house right now."

"They're idiots too," she said, closing the refrigerator door and opening the freezer. She rifled through boxes of frozen entrees, finally pulling out a tilapia dinner.

Markham laughed. A bitter laugh. "You have no idea how much trouble we're in, do you?"

She turned and stared at him. Her dark eyes wide and menacing.

"You're weak too." She ripped the frozen meal out of its cardboard carton, and then ripped the plastic off the top of the container. "And stupid. We're going to be proactive. I will get all of this handled." She opened the microwave door, set the container inside, and shut the door. She dialed in the time, punched the start button, and then looked back at him. "That's why I'm in charge."

Markham slammed his fist on the countertop, almost breaking his hand. "You have no idea, do you? Candy killed herself because of you. She told me over and over again how much she hated you. How hard you were to work with. How completely unmerciful you are. She begged me to take over the business—"

He looked up at the ceiling and back to Shannon. "I just wish

I had. I was doing just fine on my own. Now that Candy is gone, we have nothing. None of the girls will know what to do. Did you ever stop to think about that? Candy was our main manager. Now we have nothing. My guess is that one, if not all, of the girls will be down at the police station—or will catch the first bus out of town—in the morning, if not sooner, spilling their guts about you. And me."

He huffed. "You've done it now, Shannon. This is the end. I really should have killed you while I had the chance, because you're bringing both of us down." He turned to walk away.

"Where are you going?"

Markham turned and saw the gun pointed at him. "You've forgotten who's in charge." She laughed. "But it's your lucky day. I would shoot you if I didn't need your help." She tossed her head again. "Get a grip, Markham. Don't you understand?" She walked around the room, looking around, deep in thought, as if trying to find the answer. "I will figure this out." She pointed the gun at him again. "If you will just listen to me, everything will be OK."

The timer on the microwave went off.

"The first thing I need you to do is to find out from your father how we can get to Hannah Cassidy. And if he doesn't know, we'll work it out ourselves. We will grab her and start again in another place. She will pay for all of the trouble she has caused. Or I will start over on my own." She smiled. "If you want out, help me with this one last thing, and I will let you out."

That was all he wanted. To be free. He took a seat at the bar. "Are you leveling with me?"

"Yes." She smiled and nodded. "For real. You do this one more thing, and we're square. No strings attached."

"OK," he said. "I'm in."

She turned her back to him and started searching through his cabinets. "Good," she said. "We'll get started on a plan tomorrow. In the meantime, where are your plates?"

The woman was crazy, and the sooner he had her out of his life the better. If she was willing to let him walk away, he was willing to do whatever it took.

It was almost seven thirty when Jake escorted Hannah to Dixie's front door. "I'll see you tomorrow," he said.

She nodded.

He left without a kiss. Had the moment they'd shared earlier meant anything to him? Or had it been one of those mistakes they would regret later?

Maybe Jake was already regretting it.

After walking in the door, she was happy to see that Dixie and Roland were preoccupied with television.

"Did you eat?" Dixie asked over her shoulder.

"Yes, ma'am."

"Did you have a nice time?"

"I did. It was a beautiful day to walk at Radnor, and we had Monell's for supper," she said, conveniently leaving out the fact that they had eaten at Jake's place. She stifled a yawn.

Hearing Hannah's voice must have awakened Ophelia because the dog came running up to her. "Has the dog been outside lately?" Hannah asked.

"I don't think she has, dear."

Roland started to get up. "I'll take her out."

"No! No worries. You're watching something. I'm happy to do it. Come on, girl."

Hannah hurried across the living room, through the kitchen, and down the back hallway. As soon as she opened the back door, the terrier rushed outside.

Hannah followed her, taking a few steps onto the flagstone patio. The sun had already set for the evening, but the night air was warm and reassuring. Everything would be all right. She prayed, asking God to help her believe it.

Jake and his team at the Bureau would find Shannon—and Hannah's attacker—soon and put a stop to the madness that was going on around them. They had to be found—and stopped—before they hurt someone else.

Please, God. *Please.*

Hannah thought about the six-year-old girl who would be going to bed tonight without a mother. Forever. And because of what? Greed?

It was evil. Pure evil.

Suddenly, a memory returned to her. It was only a flash, but it was there. She remembered something about the man who had grabbed her. It was his face. Or was it? She could almost see him. She closed her eyes and tried to let the memory come. Had she been keeping it inside for fear she couldn't live with it?

And then she screamed.

CHAPTER 35

Markham was fixing supper for himself and thirteen cats when Shannon rushed into the kitchen. "We have to leave immediately!" she screamed. "Put food out for the cats and pack a bag."

"What?" He already had a half-dozen cats gathered around his feet.

"Do it! Now!"

"Why?"

"I'll tell you when we're in the car. Do you know where we can go and stay for a week or so?"

Markham thought for a minute. "My family has a house near the lake in Hendersonville. It's an old ranch-style place. A log house built on five or six acres. It's not remote, but the neighbors aren't close. And I have the key. Dad asked me to check on it once in a while when I'm in Hendersonville for work. We can stay there for as long as we want. The electricity is on. The water is on—"

"That works for now! We leave in fifteen minutes!"

"Why can't we take the cats?" he asked. But Shannon was already on her way up the stairs to pack the few things he had brought from her house.

Jake heard Hannah scream and pivoted. He ran beside the house, opened the gate, and rushed into the back yard. Roland and Dixie got there just as he did. "What is it?" he asked.

The look on Hannah's face was pure terror. She ran to him and fell into his arms.

Dixie and Roland stared, saying nothing.

"What is it, Hannah? What did you see?"?

He pulled away and drew his gun from its holster. "Who is here?" He looked frantically around the yard.

"Not here," she said. "He's not here, but I remember what he looks like. I remember the face of my attacker."

Dixie rushed to Hannah's side. "Honey." She grabbed her into an embrace. "Please tell us."

Hannah turned to look at Roland. "It's your son. It was your son who tried to kidnap me. It was your son who killed Ginny."

Jake looked at Roland, who was staring at Hannah in disbelief. "What's she talking about?" Jake asked.

Roland shook his head. "I have no idea. But that's impossible . . ."

"No, I'm sorry. I'm really sorry." Hannah had tears running down her face. "But it's him. I know it's him."

Dixie looked from Jake to Roland and then back to Jake. "What do we need to do?"

"Let's go inside," Jake said, reholstering his gun. He opened his arms wide, herding the others into the house. The dog followed, and Jake shut the door.

"I'll fix coffee," Dixie said.

"Good idea." Jake turned to Roland and Hannah. "Let's go into the living room and sit down." Roland nodded, and they followed Hannah into the room. He motioned Roland to the side chair closest to the front door. "Hannah, sit with me on the sofa."

She took a seat, drawing one of Dixie's bright yellow pillows into her lap. "Roland," she said. "I'm sorry."

Roland nodded, rubbed his hand on the back of his neck, and shifted his eyes to the floor.

"Hannah," Jake said. "You need to tell us why you think it's Roland's son . . ." He stopped and addressed Roland. "What's your son's name?"

"I call him R. J. His mother used to call him Markham. That's his middle name. He was named after me. His full name is Roland Markham Davis Jr." The older man broke down, and Dixie rushed across the room to put her hands on his shoulders.

"It's OK, Roland. We'll get through this."

He nodded.

Jake turned to Hannah. "Hannah, have you ever met R. J.?"

She shook her head.

Jake looked to Roland again. The older man, who had composed himself again, wiped his eyes.

Jake turned to Hannah again. "If you haven't seen him, how do you know it's him?"

Hannah looked at Jake with tears in her eyes. "I've seen his picture." She turned to Roland and Dixie. "You showed me several photos of him a few weeks ago. Do you remember? It was you, Dixie, and your son. You had gone to dinner somewhere."

Roland nodded. "Amerigo's. We took R. J. to supper one night about a month ago to celebrate his birthday."

Jake put his hand on Hannah's arm. "Hannah, this is important. Are you sure?"

"Yes."

"Can you tell me why you're so sure about this?"

"Because I remember his face now. And . . ." She looked from Jake to Dixie and then to Roland. "And in one of the photos, you can see the back of his arm. He has the same tattoo."

"A computer chip," Roland said. "He has a tattoo of a large square with wavy marks running through it."

"Yes," Hannah said. "That's it."

"OK." Jake got up and started pacing around the room.

"Roland, I'm going to need your son's address . . . and his phone number. I'm under obligation to follow up on this."

"You don't believe me?" Hannah stared up at Jake.

"Yes . . . I do," he said. "I believe that you believe every word you're saying." He paced to the front of the sofa. "It's just that an accusation is only that until we prove that someone is guilty."

"OK." Hannah looked down at her hands. "But I'm sure."

Dixie walked over to the sofa and sat down next to Hannah. "It's OK, honey. We're not questioning you. And I think I can speak for Roland in saying that he's not upset with you."

Dixie looked back at Roland, and he nodded.

"Roland, can you and I talk outside?" Jake asked.

"Of course." Roland stood and started walking toward the back door.

"Hannah," Jake said, putting his hand on her shoulder again. "We'll get to the bottom of this. I promise. You and Dixie need to stay in here for a few minutes while I talk to Roland."

She nodded.

Jake turned and followed Roland out the back door. The older man walked to the far side of the patio, stared at the cloudless sky, and then turned around. "I'll tell you whatever you need. I don't think my son is capable of doing what Hannah is accusing him of doing, but I know you have to follow up."

Jake took a seat on the glider. "Let's sit here for a few minutes. Can you tell me a little bit about R. J.?"

Roland took a seat on the bench. There was a moment of awkward silence between them, and then Roland spoke.

"R. J. had a rough childhood. His mother was his sole caregiver while I was in the military for eight years. When I would come home on leave, I never noticed that there was a problem. But—" He looked at Jake. "When I came home for good, I realized there was one."

Jake nodded.

"Lorraine hadn't physically abused R. J., but she had done a number on him emotionally. He was a bright kid—still is. And I'm sure he was a handful for a single mom." Roland shook his head. "You know, I blame myself a lot for what happened. I should have been here, instead of off defending the world. Sometimes you lose your own family when you're trying to save everybody else."

"I'm sure you did the best you could do."

Roland nodded and continued. "Anyway, Markham was fourteen or fifteen when I came home to stay. I took a teacher's job, and I started reinvesting my life in my family. Especially my son because I could see that there was a problem. Like I said, he was smart as a whip. He excelled in school. He never had a problem with his grades. But he was emotionally handicapped. Lorraine had bootstrapped him to a regimen that put the Army restrictions to shame. I mean, his clothing, his language, his actions. Everything he did was controlled by her. At least as much as she could."

"Go on," Jake said.

"R. J. didn't rebel by drinking and partying." Roland looked up at Jake. "He never was one to drink or even chase the girls. But he would sass his mother. I'm not saying she didn't deserve it, but she *was* his mother, and she was owed his respect. She kept on him . . . Day and night. She would nitpick. Bully. Anything for control.

"That eventually led to Lorraine and my arguing." Roland studied something on the ground as he talked. "And one night, she left."

"Did you divorce?" Jake asked.

Roland looked up. "We never did. But we also never got back together." He stopped for a minute, as if reliving that moment in the past. "And she never asked to see the kids again. She didn't even take me to court. She just moved across town. I knew where she lived, and I would reach out to her from time to time, but she never responded. Not positively anyway. She would acknowledge my call, even talk for a few minutes and ask how we were doing. But it was like she didn't want anything to do with us."

"That had to be hard on your kids."

"It was hard for his sister. But not for R. J. He would have refused to see her if she had reached out. And if I even alluded to the fact that I wanted her to come back home, he would lash out and tell me that he would leave before he would see her again."

Roland had to compose himself. "You know, R. J. isn't much of an emotionally connected man. But he would hug me. Still does today. He trusts me. And, as much as he resented that I left him alone with his mother for all those years, he loves me for defending him and knows that I have his best interest at heart."

"I'm sorry," Jake said. "All of this—all of your past—has to be hard."

"It was." Roland shook his head. "But after Lorraine passed away, I could tell that R. J. relaxed a bit. It was like the biggest threat in his life had gone, and he could actually live without fear of being confronted by it again."

"Where does R. J. live?"

Roland's face brightened with obvious pride for his son. "He lives in Green Hills. He has a big house over there. Much too big for a single man. But he has a great job. I think I've told you before, he's a civil engineer. Works for the railroad designing infrastructure."

Jake nodded. "Do you get to see him very often?"

"Oh, yes. I just saw him Sunday. We went out to lunch."

"Has he been acting any different lately? Maybe in the last two or three weeks? Or even in the past year?"

Roland thought about the question for a minute and then shook his head. "Not really. I may have noticed something, but it's hard to put my finger on it. He may be just a little more withdrawn. Even depressed."

"Does your son take medication?"

"He does. Right after he left for college—he graduated with two degrees from UT—he was diagnosed with DID. Dissociative Identity Disorder."

Jake stood. "Roland, I know Hannah's accusation sounds like a far-fetched notion, considering she has never met your son. But I need to follow up. Let's go inside." He laid his hand on the older man's shoulder. "I need R. J.'s contact information so I can get my team on it immediately. I also need a current photo."

CHAPTER 36

While Roland wrote Markham's address and phone information on a scratch pad Dixie kept in her office, Jake took Hannah into the dining room for a quick conversation. After she took a seat, he pulled his chair closer to hers.

"How are you feeling?"

"I'm OK. It's somewhat of a relief to have finally figured it out. My subconscious has been working on it for more than a week."

"Are you afraid to stay with Dixie? Would you like for me to ask Roland to stay away for a few days, until we have this thing figured out?"

Hannah shook her head. "I don't know how I feel. It's not like it's Roland's fault. The thing that puzzles me is that I've never met his son. I'm not sure why . . ." Her voice drifted off into a whisper, and she looked away.

"Hannah." Jake brought her attention back to him. "I think you may be in more shock now than you were right after the attack. What do you think?"

"Maybe." She was looking right at him, but her eyes seemed to be focused on something in the distance. "It is worse now, you know? Being able to see his face." She offered him a weak smile. "It's somewhat terrifying."

Jake reached for her hand and cupped it in his. Her fingers were cool, despite the lingering heat outside. "I'm sure it is."

She leaned toward him.

"Roland knows that I'll be sending a team of men to his son's house, and he's OK with it."

Hannah's free hand flew to her mouth. "I hate this!" She looked away again. "What if I'm wrong?"

"Do you think you are?"

"No." She shook her head. "I'm sure it's him."

"Can I ask you again why you're sure since you've never met him? Is it just the tattoo that has convinced you?"

"Not really," she said. "I see a lot of faces in crowds and at industry events, and I've made it a practice over the years to never forget someone. I've heard it said that Garth Brooks remembers everyone he meets, and I want to be like that. It pays in my line of work. People love to be remembered. We all do! The problem comes when they know you through your music, but you may not have met each other. They may know who you are, but they forget that you don't know them. Does that make any sense?" She had a frustrated look on her face.

"Of course it does. I can't tell you how many times I've run into someone on the street, the local weather girl, for example. I don't know her, and she certainly has no idea who I am, but I might speak because I recognize her."

"Exactly." Hannah's face lit up. "I have the same thing happen to me, but on a different level. I'm not a household name, but a lot of people know my face because of the shows I perform locally."

Jake nodded.

"I've had a lot of people speak to me when we meet on the sidewalk. And then, almost immediately, I'll see fear in their eyes because they're not sure *how* they know me. I can literally see them panic because they're not sure what to say next." She laughed. "I always try to say something appropriate. Even if it's just, 'How are you?'" She shrugged. "There are other times when people know who I am, but they forget that we've never met. Or maybe we have met, but only in passing. Even so, I want to call them by name."

She stopped talking and took a long breath.

"You're exhausted," he said. "It has been a full day."

"Yes. All of that to say, I've seen several photos of Roland's son, and I guess I just memorized his face because I thought I would probably meet him one day. I wanted to know who he was out of respect for Roland."

"Unfortunately, you did meet him, but not under the best of circumstances." Jake lowered his voice. "Hannah, your theory is credible. Probably more than Roland wants to believe."

"I understand why he wouldn't want to believe his son did it," she said. "I don't want to believe that either."

"None of us do, but your story is more compelling than you may know. It fits perfectly with the DNA findings from last week," he said. "Do you remember the mix-up last week about Roland's DNA being on the steering wheel of the attacker's car?"

"Of course. But this isn't about Roland. It's about his son."

"You're right," he said. "However, your indictment of Roland's son is further substantiated by the DNA evidence we have on file."

"I'm accusing Roland's son, not Roland."

"That's right. But the first and most important rule of DNA profiling is that a child inherits about half of his or her DNA from each parent, which means that Roland's son and Roland have many of the same DNA markers."

"I get it." Hannah's face lit up.

"But it's not just that," Jake explained. "Roland said he sees his son as often as he can. If he saw him on the morning of your attack, it's quite possible that they shook hands or touched the same object, setting up the DNA transfer I suspected in the first place."

Hannah bit her lip. "So you believe me?"

Jake took her hand. "I believed you even before I put all of those facts together."

Within twenty minutes, Markham was making a left turn out of his driveway. At Shannon's insistence, he would be taking back-roads all the way to Hendersonville to avoid as many cameras—and police cars—as possible. The route he had chosen would take them west then south through White's Creek.

Markham glanced in his rearview mirror. Shannon was following him, driving his old Ford truck. She had insisted they take two vehicles to the lake house. The woman had a plan for every-thing, and he was right back where he had started, taking orders from her again. At least this time he had made a deal with her that he could walk away, no strings attached, after they took care of the business at hand.

Markham had already made up his mind. If for any reason Shannon went back on her word, he would kill her. Or he would die trying. He wasn't going to spend the rest of his life being pushed around by her.

Taking the backroads would add an extra forty minutes or more to their trip, which would also suit Shannon's purposes. She wanted them to arrive at the lake house well after dark.

Once there, they would be stuck inside four walls for a few days, until all their plans were in order. The lake house wasn't big enough—actually, no house was big enough—to hold the two of them comfortably, but Markham had his computers with him and a lot of work to do. Fortunately, there was an active Wi-Fi connection at the house because he used it occasionally as a getaway from his nine-to-five.

Granddad Davis had passed away a few months before Markham graduated from college. His grandmother had moved into a senior living facility shortly after that. So, when Markham moved back to the area, he became the main caretaker for the property in exchange for living there rent free. Although the deed to the lake house was still held by his father—and, as it stood now, Markham and his sister, Rebecca, would one day own it jointly— Markham had the option to purchase it until that time at fair market.

While he was living there, he had made a lot of structural upgrades to the house and barn. But he had made few cosmetic changes. Shannon would no doubt find the decor offensive, but that was her problem. She was the one who had insisted on their quick escape from Nashville. Something he still didn't understand. The woman was probably more paranoid than he had ever suspected. If there was such a thing as paranoid narcissism, Shannon was the shining example.

The truth was, she needed his help to thrive, if not survive. She owed him much more than she would ever admit. Without his help, it would have been almost impossible to keep "her girls" in check. Not to mention that, without him, she would probably be in jail right now.

Markham dialed back his ego, something he actually knew how to do. *Pride came before the fall.* He may have hated every minute he had spent in church—a little boy dressed up in a grown man's suit—but he had learned the Bible backward and forward. And it had served a good purpose in his life. *Every way of a man is right in his own eyes. But the Lord weighs the heart.*

Markham had never been able to justify his business dealings with Shannon. And, if he could do it all over again, he would have walked away from her at that first meeting. But she had drawn him in, in a way that only Shannon could. The woman was a master at manipulation. And he had been burned.

Unfortunately, he now found himself running from the law because of it.

CHAPTER 37

As Shannon had planned, it was dark when Markham pulled his Jaguar into the long, gravel driveway leading to the lake house. The narrow lane wrapped around a row of fir trees that had grown up in an old fencerow, making the house completely invisible from the road. Beyond the trees was an open area where the house had been built almost forty years ago.

One window inside the house was lit, thanks to the automatic timer system he had set up to ward off would-be burglars and over-zealous teenagers. Markham pulled a remote from his center console and pressed two buttons, one that activated the garage door opener and one that lit up every room in the '80s-style ranch house.

Shannon pulled up behind him in the Ford X-150 LXT and stopped. She was not happy to learn that the house had a one-car garage, so they would have to leave the truck parked in the driveway. But Markham assured her that the neighbors weren't close enough to see it, and that his family never darkened the door to the place. His sister lived on the other side of town, and his father had left the care of the place up to him.

Shannon carried her small bag of toiletries and the few pieces of clothing she had with her into the garage, and Markham closed the big door behind them. He unlocked and held the back door to the house open so Shannon could make her way inside. She wrinkled her nose the moment she stepped into the kitchen.

"It's a little musty in here," Markham said. "It's been vacant for a long time, but it will be fine after we open the windows and let in some fresh air."

He led Shannon down the hall, stopping at the first door on the right. "This is the best of the two guest bedrooms," he said. "Make yourself comfortable."

She gave him a sideways look that had contempt written all over it and walked into the room without saying a word.

"The Jack and Jill bathroom is to your left," he said.

She slammed the door.

Markham shook his head and cursed under his breath as he continued down the hall to the master suite, which was on the left. His bedroom wasn't much bigger than either of the guest rooms, but it had its own bathroom. And he already had clothes in the closet for the occasions he wanted to stay here.

Markham threw his bag on the bed and looked around. With a little more work, this house with its quiet surroundings could have suited him fine. He wasn't sure now why he had bothered to relocate to Green Hills. He had started back to the garage for his computer gear when he heard Shannon scream. He met her half-way down the hall.

"Come here, quick," she said and rushed into the bedroom. "Look!"

Markham stared at the small black arachnid resting on her windowsill. "It's a spider, Shannon. Have you never seen one of those?"

"Kill it! Kill it! I hate those things!"

He opened the window and the screen, pulled a business card out of his pocket, and scraped the spider out into the yard.

"Why did you do that?"

"Because he has as much right to live as you do."

"I hate those things!" She wrapped her arms around herself and swiveled back and forth.

Markham tried not to laugh, but he couldn't help himself. "You probably scared it to death with that scream."

"I hope so." She took two steps back.

He sighed. "It's a good thing you won't be living here long because spiders are just a way of life in a lake house."

"Ewwww."

"I'll show you the lake tomorrow. It's only about a hundred yards behind us."

"I'm in no hurry. Thanks." She straightened and hurried into the hallway. "Do you have any bottled water here?"

"Sure. It's in the fridge in the kitchen."

Markham followed her out of the room and down the hall. "Help yourself," he said. "I have food in the freezer in the garage, as well."

She opened the refrigerator door and snagged a bottle of water. "I didn't think anyone lived here."

"They don't. But I keep food in the house because I use it for a getaway once in a while."

"Oh." She twisted the cap off the water bottle. "We'd better be safe here like you said we would be. I have too much to think about to have to worry about the cops coming down on us."

Markham shook his head. "I can't guarantee anything except that I'm going to pick up Hannah Cassidy on Friday."

CHAPTER 38

Thursday, September 9

The wheels were already turning in his head when Jake woke up early Thursday morning. After talking to Hannah last night, he had called Frank Tolman and shared everything he knew, which included Hannah's visual revelation about her attacker and details from his conversation with Roland Davis. All of that was damning enough. But when paired with DNA results from the crime scene, it seemed obvious that the younger Davis was their man.

Tolman had ordered Jake to go straight home and get some rest, reminding him that he was still on sick leave. "I will take care of everything that needs to be done tonight, but I need you rested and back at work on Friday," he'd said.

Jake had been grateful for the respite. He had overdone it today. If things were heating up, as it looked like they were, he needed to be at his best for the days ahead. His first job today was to follow up with a call to Tolman.

"What's the word?" Jake asked after his boss answered.

"After we hung up last night, I expedited a search warrant and a swat team to the Davis home. We have it staked out now. No one has come or gone since last night."

"Do you know if he's home?"

"That we don't. If there's no movement in or out of the house in the next few hours, we will move in on him."

Jake told his boss about his DNA transfer theory and how it made sense in light of Hannah's accusation.

"It looks like a solid case," Tolman said. "What's interesting is that Davis's background check is stellar. And the man's a genius. He has two degrees in engineering."

"Yes, but he's on medication for Dissociative Identity Disorder," Jake said. "His father told me that he had a tough childhood."

"There you go," Tolman said. "We're dealing with two people fighting to gain control of one body."

"I think we may be dealing with more than that," Jake said, almost to himself. "R. J. has three people pulling at him right now . . . the good and the bad sides of his personal identity. And Shannon Bridges."

And she was trouble. Big trouble.

Hannah spent the morning sitting on a barstool in Dixie's kitchen commiserating over coffee. Neither had slept much the night before because of Hannah's accusation of Roland's son. It had upended everyone's world.

At eleven o'clock, Dixie suggested making lunch. "We can't just sit around here drinking coffee all day." She opened the refrigerator door and stared inside. "It's almost lunchtime."

"I'm not hungry." Food was Dixie's fix for everything.

"You have to eat," the older woman insisted. "And I'm not going to cook it for you. I'm going to teach you how to make something. What would you like to learn today?"

Hannah suspected this was Dixie's way of taking her mind off everything else. "You could show me anything, and it would be helpful." Hannah drummed her fingers on the black granite bar in front of her.

"Tuna salad? Chicken salad?" Dixie stepped away from the refrigerator. "It's too hot for soup. How about quiche?"

"I love quiche," Hannah said. "But I'm not sure that's the best choice if you want me to make a good impression on a future husband."

"You're right." Dixie laughed. "I know what we'll do! I'll be right back." She turned and hurried down her back hall, taking a right into the storage and laundry room.

A few minutes later, she reemerged holding a roast of some kind.

"Look what I had in my fridge. A brisket."

"You don't really expect me to learn how to do that, do you?"

"It's simple." Dixie glanced at the clock. "And we have just enough time to make it for lunch. It's only eleven. We will be eating by twelve thirty."

"No way. I may not know much, but I know enough to know that you don't cook that kind of thing quickly," Hannah said.

"Easy." The older woman wasn't going to be deterred. She hurried back to her storage room and within a few seconds returned with an instant pressure cooker.

"No way! I'll blow the roof off your house." Hannah hid her face in her hands.

Dixie chuckled. "Well, if you do, you'll be living in the open air. What are you waiting for, girl? Get over here and let me teach you how to cook."

Hannah stood and walked around the bar. "It's your roast—and your house," she said. "But I wouldn't trust me if I were you."

"Here." Dixie handed her the brisket. "Unwrap this thing, while I look for the rest of our ingredients."

A few minutes later, Hannah was wearing an apron and a pair of disposable kitchen gloves, watching Dixie mix spices in a bowl.

Dixie gave her a bottle of olive oil. "I want you to rub some of this on the brisket."

Hannah poured a small amount of the oil into one hand and started rubbing. "Like this?"

"Try to give it an even coating all over." Dixie watched as she worked. "Perfect! Now, here are your spices."

"What's in here?" Hannah sniffed the tangy, musty-smelling herbs.

"Today I used salt, pepper, thyme, and equal parts garlic powder, ground mustard, and smoked paprika, but I sometimes change that. It depends on the mood I'm in. You can come up with your own special formula, based on what you like."

"That might be dangerous." Hannah laughed.

"OK," Dixie said. "Pour a little bit of the spice mixture into your hand."

Hannah did what she was told.

"Now, pat the mixture gently onto the surface of the roast. Do that until you've used all of the spice mixture and every part of the brisket is coated."

Hannah worked for a few minutes, doing her best to put an even coating on the meat.

"Good job!" Dixie said. "Take off your gloves and throw them away, while I pour a tablespoon of olive oil into my pot, which I've already set to sauté."

Hannah took off her gloves and watched.

"Once the pot is heated up, you're going to add the roast. Careful. Don't burn yourself. We're going to sear, which means brown, each side of the beef."

Hannah followed Dixie's instructions, turning the roast every three or four minutes until each side of the meat was a golden-brown color.

"What's next?" she asked. "This is fun."

Dixie handed her a clean bowl. "Take the roast out of the pan and set it in this bowl."

Hannah did what Dixie asked.

"Now, you're going to pour the liquid out of the pan and deglaze the pan."

"That sounds like something I can't do."

"Here, watch me." Dixie grabbed two potholders from the counter and poured hot liquid from the cooker into a glass measuring cup. "See how I'm scraping the bottom of the pan?"

Hannah nodded.

"You're going to return the roast to the pan, with the juice, and secure the lid. Then set the timer."

Hannah did everything she was asked and stepped back. "My work here is done."

"Not yet." Dixie laughed. "We need to make the barbecue sauce."

"Couldn't we just use store-bought?" Hannah asked.

"We could. But you wouldn't learn anything that way . . . Besides, this is a scratch kitchen."

"You're a good teacher," Hannah said.

Dixie grinned. "I can't wait to teach you how to make biscuits. But right now . . . let's go to the pantry and find everything we need to make the sauce."

About twenty minutes later, after Hannah had mixed up the sauce, the two women washed their dirty bowls and utensils.

"It's much easier if you clean everything as you go," Dixie told her. "When you're hosting a party, or even just cooking for your family, you will be able to relax more after the meal. And your guests won't have to stare at a messy kitchen."

"Never let 'em see you sweat," Hannah said.

They were putting away the last of the clean dishes when the doorbell rang. Dixie stepped to the window and peeked through the curtain.

"It's Jake."

She walked to the door and opened it.

"Your timing is really good. Have you eaten?" Dixie asked. "Hannah and I are making lunch."

"It smells great," Jake said. "What is it?"

"Just a little barbecue beef brisket we threw together." She winked at Hannah.

Hannah laughed.

"Please tell me you haven't eaten," Dixie cajoled.

"I haven't. But I don't want to intrude."

"Jake, you're family," she insisted. "You are never intruding."

"OK, if you insist. I just stopped by to check on both of you."

"We appreciate that, don't we?" Dixie turned to Hannah.

Hannah nodded and took off her apron. "Is there any news?"

"Nothing so far. We have R. J.'s house surrounded—and have had since last night." He looked at his watch. "In about an hour, a SWAT team will be going to the door and, if no one answers, will force their way inside."

Dixie and Hannah looked at each other.

"Say a little prayer," Jake said. "This could be interesting."

CHAPTER 39

It was almost one o'clock in the afternoon, and Markham was working at his computer at the kitchen table when Shannon walked into the room looking for breakfast.

"You're up early." He looked at his watch.

"What are you doing?"

"I'm working," he said. "Something you haven't done in a while. You've been AWOL from your teaching job for almost two weeks now. I wonder if they've missed you yet?"

"Very funny. What do you have to eat around here?"

"I told you last night, there's food in the fridge and there's more food in the freezer in the garage. Do you expect me to cook it for you too?"

She glared at him. "I'll be happy to have you out of my life. You're such a negative person."

Markham burst into laughter. "Well, if that's not the pot calling the kettle black."

She harrumphed, opened the refrigerator door, and took out a bottle of canned soda.

"I never drink this stuff, but my stomach is killing me."

"What's the matter? Are you worried about something?" Markham taunted again. He closed the cover of his computer. "Everything will work out. Did you not listen to anything I told you yesterday? We will have Hannah Cassidy in our hands by the end the week."

Shannon pulled up a chair. "What's your plan?"

"First, you tell me why we had to leave my house in such a hurry to get here."

"That's an easy one," she said. "I knew it wouldn't be long after Candy died before everyone on the street would know that the cops were looking for me. I also knew that after our girls found out, they would scatter like flies. It's only logical that one of them would go to the cops—or the other way around. When that happened, I knew your name would come up eventually."

Markham nodded. "That was a good call."

"Thank you," she said, but there was sarcasm in her voice. "So, what's your plan for picking up Hannah Cassidy?"

Markham leaned back in his chair. "She volunteers at a horse-riding academy in Franklin every Tuesday and Friday. She helps groom the horses and works with the special needs kids, who ride at the facility. She's especially close to one six-year-old boy named Brandon. If I can get to Brandon, I can get to her."

"How do you know all of this?"

"My father talks about her all the time. Hannah does this. Hannah does that. You'd think she could do no wrong. He talks about the little boy too. He's the grandson of my father's girlfriend."

"You really are close to this family." Shannon studied him. "Are you sure you're on our side?"

Markham gave her a hard look. Did she *ever* listen to him?

"I'm tired of repeating myself, Shannon," he said. "I've told you over and over that I'm *too* close to them, and that's what scares me about Hannah. With our connection, I knew that I would eventually run into her. And when that happens, she will figure out who I am." He opened his computer. "If it weren't for that connection, I would take my chances with her, because she didn't get a good enough look at me that day."

"Level with me, Markham." Shannon leaned closer to him. "You're feeling sorry for her, aren't you? I can see it in your eyes."

"She's a good person. And all of this is my fault. But what does that have to do with it?"

"I knew it!" Shannon stood from her chair and began pacing. "You were never right for this job. You're too emotional. Too soft. That's why Candy—and all of the girls—wanted to work with you and send me packing." She huffed. "They would have run over you in a righteous minute. They would have had you working for them before it was over."

"So what if they like me better?" Markham challenged. "I've always treated them fairly, but I also made them toe the line. Anybody who works for me knows they'd better do their job or pay the consequences. The girls have always known that I wouldn't tolerate laziness or obstinance. But . . . they also knew that I wouldn't hurt them."

"Looks like Ginny found out otherwise."

"That was an accident, and you know it. I wouldn't have hurt her if she hadn't tried to get away from me. Even at that, it was a mistake. I was emotional. I had just messed up by grabbing Hannah, and—"

"What did I just say, you idiot? I just said that you're too emotional." Shannon pitched her empty soda can into the trash. "And even you know it."

"I—"

"Shut up!" she screamed. She took a seat in the chair she had vacated a few minutes before. "You don't have what it takes to finish this job."

Markham remained silent. His father had always told him, "Never argue with a fool, or you'll look like one."

"The truth is you like having women tell you what to do. Without us—without me—you wouldn't know how to deal with anything except"—she pointed to his computer—"that mind-numbing, geeky world you retreat to every day. You're good at that, but you're not good at real life."

Markham wanted to argue, but he knew she was right. He had been controlled by a woman since the day he was born. Maybe some things never changed, after all.

His mother had bullied him, molded him, taunted him. Just like Shannon did now. That was the reason he had retreated into his own world as a child. A world that he could control, even build, without interference or help—from anyone else. It was, ultimately, that world that had earned him self-respect, as well as the respect of others. He was one of the best in his field.

"You're book-smart," she said. "But you're not street-smart. Not enough to figure yourself out of this mess."

He slumped in his chair. She was right again. He had succeeded in business, but he had failed in life. "What am I going to do?"

"You're going to listen to me. You're going to do exactly what I tell you to do. And we're going to get through this."

He nodded.

"Tomorrow, you're going to pick up Hannah Cassidy. And you're going to bring her to me. After that . . . you're free. You can go on with your safe little life, playing with trains like the five-year-old boy you always were, and always will be."

"What will you do with Hannah?" he asked. "She's too old for most pimps."

"You really are soft, aren't you?" She tsked. "I'm not going to kill her if that's what you're worried about. I've already found a buyer for her. Top dollar from a man who knows who she is." She laughed. "I may have found her biggest fan."

Markham grimaced.

"Your little mess up is working out rather well," Shannon smiled. "Hannah will finance my new start . . . in Dallas, or Carson City, or wherever I decide to land." She glared at him. "And I certainly won't tell you where that is."

Markham shrugged his shoulders. "And I really don't care to know."

"Now," she said. "Please fix me something to eat. I'm starving."

CHAPTER 40

Hannah prepared a basket of rolls, while Dixie depressurized the cooker. If only if it could be as easy to "depressurize" herself. They were all on pins and needles, waiting on word about R. J.

Jake was sitting on the sofa, playing with Ophelia, when the doorbell rang. "Are either of you expecting anyone?" he asked.

Hannah and Dixie both shook their heads.

"I'll get it," Dixie said, wiping her hands on a kitchen towel.

"No! Let me." Jake stood. "I don't want to take any chances."

Hannah watched him take his gun from his boot and tuck it into his belt. He hurried to the front window and peeked outside. Hannah saw his shoulders relax. "It's Audrey and Brandon," he said.

After their guests had stepped inside, Jake closed and locked the door behind them.

"You're here!" Brandon said. "I brought you something." The six-year-old held up his left hand and waved a paper in the air.

"What is it?" Jake bent slightly to see what the boy was holding.

"It's a get-well card," Audrey said. "He made it for you as soon as he heard you had been hurt. He insisted on bringing it here today in case you were here."

"Well, thank you!" Jake said, taking the paper from Brandon. "That's a good-looking card, buddy. Did you draw that?"

Brandon nodded.

Hannah and Dixie walked closer so they could see the paper. Brandon had drawn a photo of a stickman lying in bed with a bandage around his head. At the top he had written *To Mr. Jake*, and at the bottom he had written *From Brandon*.

Hannah's heart melted. Even Brandon had fallen in love with Jake Matheson.

"We were just about to sit down to lunch. Have the two of you eaten?"

Audrey blushed. "We haven't, Mom. We were planning to stop at McDonald's after we left you."

"Happy Meal!" Brandon said, jumping up and down.

"Why don't you eat with us instead?" Hannah suggested. "There's plenty, isn't there, Dixie?"

"Goodness, yes," the older woman said. "We're having brisket sandwiches and potato salad."

"It smells delicious." Audrey bent down to her son. "Are you OK with eating lunch here, Brandon?"

"Sure!" the boy said. "Can I sit with you, Jake?"

"Of course, buddy."

"Go wash your hands—" Before Audrey had time to finish her sentence, the boy took off for Dixie's bedroom.

"He thinks he's at home here." She shrugged and laughed.

"He is, honey." Dixie put her arm around her daughter's shoulder. "Why don't you and Jake go ahead and have a seat at the table. Hannah and I will finish up."

It was just past one when Dixie and Hannah took a seat at the table. Dixie had sliced homegrown tomatoes and set out homemade pickles, which she served along with potato salad she had made earlier.

"This looks and smells great, Mom." Audrey turned to Jake. "Now you know what it was like growing up at my house. I had friends regularly dropping by around mealtimes."

Jake laughed. "Can't say that I blame them."

"No one loved it any more than me," Dixie said. "Because of it, I was able to stay more involved in my daughter's life. And that's the way I wanted it. Your dad did too."

Audrey smiled and bit her lip. "I miss Daddy."

"I do too, honey," Dixie said.

Hannah looked around the table. Every person here had experienced loss. But they were all doing their best to move on with their lives. *How had they all found each other?*

It had to be a God thing. And, as always, He was working

everything to the best.

Hannah couldn't think of another group of people she would rather be with at this moment, and she reached to take Jake's hand as Dixie bowed her head to say grace.

At the end of her prayer, Dixie looked around the table and said, "Everybody eat! We're glad to have you with us, aren't we, Hannah?"

"Mr. Jake, will you go with Hannah and me to the riding place tomorrow?" Brandon asked.

Jake looked to Hannah for help, but she smiled and said nothing.

"I don't know, buddy. I didn't even know you were going to St. Francis tomorrow."

The six-year-old took a bite of his sandwich, chewed, and then gave Jake a puzzled look. "But Hannah and I go there every Friday."

"Oh. OK. I guess I should have known." Jake cleared his throat and gave Hannah a sideways glance. "I'm not really sure if Hannah needs to be there tomorrow. Maybe we should wait until—"

"Of course you're going, aren't you, Hannah?"

"Brandon, wipe your mouth with your napkin, please," Audrey said. "Maybe we should let Miss Hannah make up her own mind."

Brandon swiped his mouth. "But you're going, right?" He was beginning to get upset.

"Of course I'm going," Hannah said before turning to Jake. "Can we do that?"

"I don't really think it's smart."

"Please, Mr. Jake. You can go with us too."

Jake looked from the six-year-old to Hannah and then back to Brandon. "OK, buddy," he relented. "Miss Hannah will go. And I will go with her."

He turned to look at Hannah, who was trying to cover a laugh with her hand.

"But we have to be careful," he said. "Can we do that, Brandon?"

"Sure!" The boy took another bite of his sandwich. His focus had moved on.

"Thank you," Hannah mouthed.

"I hope it's a good idea." Jake frowned.

"It will be fine. We—"

Jake's phone rang, and Hannah and Dixie froze.

Jake stood. "Excuse me a minute. I need to take this call." He hurried toward the back hallway. "Matheson."

"We've just raided the house," Frank Tolman said.

"And?" Jake opened the backdoor and stepped outside.

"And there was no one inside."

Jake's heart dropped. Had R. J. been tipped off? Surely Roland hadn't told him. Jake would have a hard time believing that, even if Frank Tolman might not. R. J. was Roland's son. It would take a big man not to want to save his own child. But Jake knew that Roland understood.

This was life or death. *For Hannah.*

He refocused on the conversation. "What's next?"

"I'm not sure." There was strain in Tolman's voice. "We're going through the house now, lifting fingerprints, looking for clues as to where he may have gone. He left a dozen or more cats in the house, so he must be planning to return."

"I'll be right over—"

"You stay where you are. I don't want HR coming down on me because you're at a crime scene when you're not released to work yet. Where are you now?"

"Hannah Cassidy's house."

Tolman chuckled. "Well, keep it social. You're not back on duty until tomorrow."

"Yes, sir." Jake was chomping at the bit to get back into the middle of everything.

"Just relax, Matheson. We'll stay on this." He waited for a beat and then said, "We need to talk to Roland Davis again. Can you call him and arrange the meeting?"

"I'll give him a call as soon as I hang up with you," Jake said. "Then I'll pick him up and drive him to the Bureau."

"That will work," Tolman agreed. "In the meantime, let's arrange additional security for Hannah Cassidy. R. J. Davis has been pushed into a corner, and he might do something drastic. We've seen what happened when he acted out of fear the first time." He hesitated. "Ginny Williams paid that price."

The thought kicked Jake in the gut. "I'll call Beau and have him assign extra men."

"See you at the office," Tolman said.

Jake hit the end button and found Roland's number on his phone. Roland picked up after the first ring.

"I've been waiting for your call." The older man sounded tired. And scared. Jake could only imagine what he was going through.

"Are you at home?"

"Yes."

"Stay there. I'm on my way. We need you to answer a few more questions."

"Is—is my son OK?"

"We don't know for sure, Roland." Jake said. "He has disappeared."

CHAPTER 41

"What are they doing?" Markham shouted as he watched the video of a dozen men, who were dressed in special-ops clothing and converging upon his Green Hills home. Two of the men carried a long pole that looked like a battering ram. They heaved it into his front door, while the other men shielded their faces from the glass shards and splintered wood flying everywhere.

"No!" Markham screamed.

"What's going on?" Shannon rushed into the kitchen through the dining room door.

"I'm watching video from my home security system. The police broke into my house."

"I told you so . . ."

She seemed almost happy to hear about it because it proved her theory to be right.

Markham cursed at her under his breath.

"I want to see it." Shannon hurried around the table to stand behind him.

Markham switched from the exterior cameras to the interior cameras and saw a swarm of men carrying automatic weapons running through his front door and dispersing in every direction. Two or three of the men ran up the stairs. Two took off for the back of the house. Another pair turned right into his dining room.

He switched to his back hall camera and saw the garage entrance door open and more men milling about.

"My kitties!" His cats were being terrorized. "I told you we should have brought the cats."

Shannon growled at him. "Calm down. The cats will be fine." She patted him on the shoulder. "Switch to your office feed."

Markham cued up the camera in his office. Two men were

inside. One was rifling through his desk, while the other was checking his credenza and bookshelves. The second man walked over to his printer and pulled out a piece of paper. He studied it and then ran out of the room.

"Bingo!" Shannon said. "They found the bait!"

At Shannon's insistence, before they left, Markham had printed several maps that included directions to Toledo, Ohio, Shannon's hometown. He had also printed information for a few hotels in the area, all in different parts of town.

"Toledo is the last place I'd go," Shannon said. "But they don't know that. And it will take them a few days to realize we're not there."

"I hope you're right." Markham chewed his thumbnail and switched back to his living room camera.

The men were now walking about in a leisurely manner. Satisfied that Markham wasn't home, they switched into offensive mode. One man was dusting for fingerprints. Another was systematically going through his trash can.

"It won't take long for them to figure out that you're with me," he said.

"So what? They probably knew that before they broke into your house."

Markham shrugged. She didn't have a clue as to how hard this was for him. She wasn't concerned about the damage to his house. Or that the kitties were being terrorized. His home was being violated, and she didn't care.

His rights were being violated too. Why did the police have the right to do this to him? There had to be compelling evidence. Had Hannah Cassidy identified him? His heart stepped up a beat.

If Hannah had identified him as Ginny's killer, they wouldn't stop until they found him. If they weren't talking to his father by now, they would be soon. Would he think to tell them about this house?

Markham swallowed. He no longer felt safe here.

"I think we should leave," he said.

"Why?" She walked around the table, apparently bored by the action on the screen.

"They must know more than we thought."

She took a seat in the chair across the table. "They're not stupid. We just have to stay ahead of them."

"But what are we going to do?" He closed his computer.

"I know what I'm going to do. I don't know about you. I'll be leaving town as soon as you get your hands on Hannah Cassidy."

Markham shook his head. "We need to talk about that. I'm not sure it matters now."

"Of course it matters. Have you lost your mind?"

He didn't respond.

"Hannah Cassidy is the difference between jail time and freedom for you, Markham. She was the only eyewitness to Ginny's murder. If she's out of the picture, you get off with a slap on the wrist."

"Are you going to hurt her?"

Shannon cursed. "I told you what I was going to do. And why do you care? You told me two days ago that you were going to kill her when you found her. Now, you're worried about every hair on her head?"

"I couldn't really hurt her. I didn't mean to kill Ginny."

"Listen to me." Shannon pointed her finger at him. "We wouldn't be in this mess if it weren't for you. But you killed Ginny, accident or no accident. I knew the morning that this thing came down that we were in trouble."

She was right. Again. Maybe he should listen to her.

"Listen to me," Shannon repeated. "I'm going to get you out of this. Just get me Hannah Cassidy. She's the only person in this world who can send you to jail for life. Or get you the death penalty. Your freedom depends on whether or not you can deliver Hannah Cassidy to me tomorrow."

He nodded.

She leaned forward. "After you do that, it's in my hands."

She hated Hannah Cassidy. He could see it in her eyes. Hannah had been the beginning of trouble for her. Most likely, Shannon was jealous of her too . . . jealous of her looks. Jealous of Hannah's successful career.

Markham shrugged. It wasn't going to end well for Hannah Cassidy. He was sure of that. But there was nothing he could do about it. Not if he wanted to save his own life.

CHAPTER 42

Roland was standing at his open front door, waiting for Jake when he arrived.

"Are you ready?"

The older man nodded, stepped off the porch of his three-story townhome, and closed the door.

"Where are we going?"

"To the Bureau. My boss wants to talk to you."

"I've already told you everything I know," Roland said. "But I understand. I'm not upset with you, Jake. You're just doing your job. It's my son who has caused this problem."

Jake clapped the older man on the shoulder. "You'll get through this, Roland."

Roland swiped moisture from his eyes. "I feel like I've let him down. If only . . ."

"Go easy on yourself, man. You did your best." Jake opened the door to his SUV. "And you'll walk along beside him to help him get through this."

Roland got inside the SUV and closed the door. Jake walked to the other side of the vehicle, climbed inside, and started the car.

"I hope he's OK. I hope he's OK . . ."

They rode in silence for the rest of the trip, and within twenty minutes, they were walking through the door of the Arzo Carson TBI State Office Building. The TBI's motto, "That Guilt Shall Not Escape, Nor Innocence Suffer," was displayed on the front.

Jake escorted Roland into one of the small conference rooms. Frank Tolman and a small group of men were already there. "Come on in, Matheson," Tolman said. "Mr. Davis, please have a seat."

Roland didn't speak but took a seat next to Jake.

"Agent Matheson may have already told you, but we did a

search of your son's house this afternoon. He appeared to have left in a hurry. Dirty dishes were in the sink. He had left bowls of food for his cats. And both of his vehicles were missing from his garage. Our records indicate that he owns two vehicles, a 2020 red Jaguar F-Type sports car and a 2010 Ford F-150 XLT pickup. Does that sound right to you?"

"Yes, sir."

"When was the last time you saw your son?"

Roland thought for a few seconds before responding. "It would have been Sunday. I took him to lunch on Sunday."

"Is that also the last time you spoke to him?"

"It was."

"And what was his frame of mind that day? Did he appear to be aggravated? Maybe worried about something? You know your son better than anybody. Were you concerned when you left him that day, or did everything appear to be normal?"

"No, sir. I didn't notice anything especially unusual." He glanced to Jake, and then back to Tolman. "My son is not the strongest man emotionally, but he manages. And as far as I know, he is taking his medication."

"What kind of medication?"

"It's some kind of antidepressant to stabilize his mood swings." Roland's face paled. "You don't think he has done something to hurt himself, do you?"

"We don't have any reason to believe that, Mr. Davis. In fact, we're quite confident he has someone with him, because both vehicles are gone. Do you have any idea who he might have taken with him? Does he have a girlfriend? A close male friend?"

Roland shook his head. "R. J. keeps his personal life to himself, and I don't try to interfere. I was young once too, Agent Tolman, and after I left home, I didn't want my parents too involved in my day-to-day life."

"Do you have any idea why he might want to go to Ohio?"

"Ohio? No . . . not at all. I've never heard him mention it. Why?"

Tolman held up a piece of paper. "We found this in his

computer printer. It's a map, actually, one of several, to Toledo. We also found information on hotels in that area. Does your family have any ties to Toledo?"

"No, sir. None at all."

Tolman turned to Jake. "According to Shannon Bridges's background check, she was born and raised in Toledo, Ohio. Everything we're finding right now indicates that she is with him. We'll know more as soon as forensics gets back to us about the fingerprints that were found in the house."

"What are you thinking?" Jake asked. "That she initially left her home to take refuge at Roland's son's house?"

"Interestingly, no." Tolman said. "We found a secret room in Markham's house, and it appears that he may have been holding her there without her consent."

Roland Davis bowed his head and started to silently weep.

Jake put his hand on the older man's shoulder.

"It may not be exactly as it seems, Mr. Davis," Frank Tolman said. "We also have reason to believe that your son is in business with Ms. Bridges." He glanced at his other associates in the room. "The business of human trafficking.

"Mr. Davis, I have one more question for you. Did you call your son to alert him to the fact that Hannah Cassidy had identified him as her attacker?"

Roland didn't respond. Instead, he dug his phone out of his pocket and slid it across the table to Frank Tolman.

"I'm an honorable man, sir. I served my government faithfully for eight years, while denying my family the time I should have spent with them. In all honesty, did I consider calling my son? Of course, I did. He is my son." Roland took a deep breath and exhaled slowly. "But that wouldn't have been doing him, Hannah Cassidy, or you any favors."

Tolman studied him.

"Please," Roland said. "Take a look at my phone and see for yourself."

After everyone left, Hannah helped Dixie clean the kitchen and put the dirty dishes in the dishwasher.

"I hope Jake will get back to us soon," Dixie said. "I'm worried about Roland."

"Me too," Hannah agreed. "None of this is his fault."

Dixie smiled and wiped moisture from her eye. "Hannah, you're an amazing young woman. You're wiser and stronger than your years."

"I think I just grew up quickly," Hannah said. "I had to do that or regress after Casey died."

"Death has a way of making us introspective. And it can be a cruel teacher. But we have a God Who is much bigger than our situation—whatever it may be. We also have His word that everything works to the good for those who love Him."

"That has always been one of my favorite verses," Hannah said. "It is, at once, one of the most comforting—and most difficult—concepts in the Bible to understand."

Dixie nodded. "I want to read you something."

She walked from the kitchen to her living room and took a book from the bookshelf. "I've always loved *The Message* translation of the Bible. It frames the Word in a way that's easier for those of us in the modern world to understand. This passage from Romans 8 really gets to the heart of it. 'Meanwhile, the moment we get tired in the waiting, God's Spirit is right alongside helping us along. If we don't know how or what to pray, it doesn't matter. He does our praying in and for us, making prayer out of our wordless sighs, our aching groans. He knows us far better than we know ourselves, knows our pregnant condition, and keeps us present before God. That's why we can be so sure that every detail in our lives of love for God is worked into something good.'"

CHAPTER 43

Hannah paced the floor of her small apartment. It had been a long Thursday afternoon. She hadn't heard from Jake since he left them after lunch.

Finally, around seven o'clock she went outside, with the dog trailing behind her. The sun was setting as she walked toward the garden. There was a slight chill in the air. A fall chill that signaled the eventual coming of winter, although she was sure there would be many more hot days before winter came.

Autumn sunsets in Nashville were always beautiful. Perhaps it was God's way of sending extravagant beauty before the barrenness of winter. Maybe they were a sign of His promises that winter would eventually pass, and warmth would return again in the spring. Or maybe it was His way of leveling out everything, because it had been an especially hard day. No . . . make that an awful day.

If that was the case, and if this beautiful sunset insinuated promises, then why did her skin prick with fear?

Despite the devotional time she and Dixie had had earlier, her fear persisted. She turned toward the house and saw Dixie looking out through the glass of her back door.

Did she feel it too?

Hannah glanced at her watch. It was two minutes past seven and the sky to the west was transitioning from ethereal hues of blue, orange, and pink to black.

Her phone rang, and it was Jake. "I've been worried," she blurted out.

"It's been a busy afternoon, but we're finally on our way home."

"We?"

"I have Roland in the truck with me. Are you and Dixie OK if we stop by your house on our way home?"

"Or course."

"We're going to get something to eat first, but we'll be there by seven thirty. Maybe a few minutes after."

Hannah turned to make her way back to the house. Her path was dark now, and Dixie's security lights were flickering on. She called the dog and opened the door for them to step inside. Dixie was sitting at her desk, working at her computer.

"Jake and Roland are on their way here."

"Oh, good!" Dixie took off her reading glasses and laid them on the desk in front of her, and then stood.

Not quite an hour later the doorbell rang, and Hannah opened the door to Jake and Roland. Jake was holding a small box.

"This was sitting on the front porch, and it has your name on it." He held the box out to her.

She glanced at the shipping label. "It's my CDs!" She took the box and stepped aside, inviting the men to come inside.

Jake and Roland took a seat in the living room, Jake on the sofa and Roland in a side chair. Hannah settled onto the sofa and set the box on the floor in front of her.

When Dixie asked if anyone wanted coffee, everyone said yes. While she made the coffee, Hannah opened her box. Each CD was enclosed in a clear jewel case, and the printing on the front of the CD included the ten song titles, her name, and the album title, *Unchained Melodies*. She gave a CD to each of them, explaining that she had recorded the last song, "Unchained Melody," upstairs on her home studio equipment.

"I recorded it for your mother," she said to Roland. "Here's a CD for her too."

Roland wiped moisture from his eyes as he took the second CD from Hannah's hand. "I'm sorry," he said. "It has been an emotional day."

Dixie patted him on the arm. "It's been an emotional day for all of us."

Roland wiped his eyes again. "Thank you for your kindness, Hannah. My mother will appreciate your gesture. And it means more to me than you can ever know, especially considering what my son has—" Because he couldn't finish the sentence, he just shook his head.

"You're welcome," Hannah said, and turned to Jake. "What can you tell us about your meeting?"

"I think Roland would agree with me that we accomplished a lot."

Roland nodded.

"We cleared the air between all parties, and he gave my team information that may help the investigation."

"That's good," Dixie said.

"We talked about a lot of things, including some things that were not welcome news." Jake looked toward Roland. "Are you comfortable with my sharing everything with the ladies in your presence?"

Roland nodded.

Jake glanced around the room, finally turning to Hannah. "My team has confirmed that R. J. is involved in the business of human trafficking—and that Shannon Bridges is his business partner."

A collective gasp was followed by silence.

"Both R. J. and Shannon are missing, presumably on the run."

"Dixie, I would love a refill on my coffee," Jake said. "If you'll show me how to get it, I'll do it myself."

"Oh, no. You rest." She stood from where she had been sitting on the stuffed ottoman in front of Roland's chair. "Anyone else?"

"I'll take a refill, if you don't mind, honey." Roland handed her his cup.

Hannah jumped to her feet, took Jake's cup, and snagged hers from the coffee table. "Here, Dixie. I'll help. I'll get Jake's and mine."

Jake watched as the women walked into the kitchen. Everyone was tired. He could tell by the looks on their faces. But Roland had to be exhausted. The man was seventy years old, and his son had just been added to the TBI's most wanted list.

It wasn't easy for any of them. Dixie was caught between concern for Roland and worry about Hannah's safety. And Hannah, who had finally remembered the face of her attacker, was trying to stay strong for the sake of all of those around her.

With any luck, they would have all of this behind them soon. And without another innocent person being hurt. Although the odds in the case of the latter concerned him.

R. J. Davis and Shannon Bridges had a lot to lose. And when someone was pushed into a corner, they would come out swinging. Or bearing arms. If R. J. had been holding Shannon Bridges, his own partner, captive, there was no telling what he might do. He had already killed one woman.

Jake watched Roland as he played tug-of-war with the dog and wondered if he understood the gravity of his son's situation. If R. J. started a gunfight, law enforcement would mete out force with force. And the numbers were in their favor.

For Roland's sake, Jake could only hope that once R. J. was found—and he would be found—he would give up peaceably. If not, Roland could be burying his only son.

After Dixie and Hannah returned with the coffees, Jake told them that the TBI was looking into the possibility of R. J. and Shannon fleeing to Toledo, Ohio.

"What is R. J. and Shannon's relationship?" Hannah asked.

"That's something we haven't figured out." Jake said. "My boss, Frank Tolman, told us today that, based on the way they were living at R. J.'s house, R. J. was holding her hostage."

"I hope that's not true." Dixie put her hand on Roland's forearm. "Roland, is that even possible?"

He shook his head. "Dix, I don't even know what's possible anymore. None of this makes sense to me."

"I agree," Hannah said. "There's something we're missing."

"Many times criminal behavior is unexplainable," Jake said. "I learned years ago that you don't try to equate a criminal's actions with rational thinking. Nor do you try to second-guess them. Just as many victims of trafficking were often abused as children, their perpetrators may have been nurtured in an abusive environment."

He looked at Roland.

"Of course, that's not always the case. Sometimes biological dysfunction is to blame. Either that, or—and I think this may be the case with your son, Roland—they may have been manipulated by others."

"Do you think so?" Roland leaned forward.

"Why would you say that?" Hannah asked.

"What we know about Shannon Bridges tells us that she's manipulative, maybe even narcissistic. I'm not sure about the latter, although after meeting her, I wouldn't discount the idea."

"I'd love to hear more about that." Hannah spoke so quietly only Jake heard her words.

He smiled and repositioned himself in his seat. "One of my working theories is that, although R. J. may have been temporarily holding Shannon hostage physically, she had been holding him emotionally hostage for a lot longer."

"How awful." Dixie patted Roland on the arm again.

Jake looked at his watch. "Roland, are you ready for me to take you home?"

"Any time," the older man said.

"Thanks for the coffee, Dixie." He turned to Hannah. "What time do I need to pick you up to take you to the riding academy tomorrow?"

"Maybe twelve noon?"

"Are Brandon and Audrey meeting us there?"

"Yes, I confirmed that with Audrey earlier today."

"OK." He stood. "I think we all need a good night's sleep. It has been another stressful day."

"Yes, it has," Roland agreed.

"Everything will be OK," Dixie said. "I just know it will."

"From your lips to God's ears, Dixie," Jake said. "Although, I think you're right." He turned to Hannah. "We just have to stay vigilant and work smart, and that includes keeping Hannah safe."

"I'll be glad when it's not all about me anymore," Hannah said. "Someone else can have the spotlight for a while."

Jake smiled. "You can handle it," he said. "If anybody can."

233

"I'll take that as a compliment."

"It was meant as one. In all honesty, I would hate to be in R. J.'s and Shannon's shoes tonight. They are fugitives on the lam. That's not a good place to be. Not for them, and not for law enforcement."

"Thank you for the CDs," Roland said, getting up to leave. "I will probably take Mom's copy to her tomorrow or over the weekend."

"I hope she enjoys it," Hannah said.

Roland and Jake stood and walked to the front door. Dixie and Hannah followed, and while Dixie and Roland said their goodbyes, Jake and Hannah walked out on the front porch.

"You don't paint a very good picture for R. J.," Hannah said. "I feel sorry for Roland."

"You just take care of yourself," Jake said. "R. J.'s future is in his hands. He's now on the TBI Most Wanted list. So is Shannon. And law enforcement will use any means necessary to stop them if they resist. If they don't resist, this will, hopefully, end well."

Hannah reached for his hand. "Thank you for getting me through all of this."

He put his arm around her shoulders and drew her closer. "We're not through it yet, but we're a lot closer to the end than we were a week ago."

"It has been a long week." She looked up at him, and, only for a moment, Jake saw the scared little girl inside her.

He wanted to take her home with him and hold her. But he kissed her on the forehead instead.

That would have to be enough for now.

CHAPTER 44

Roland's townhome on Linden Avenue was only about five minutes away from Dixie's place.

"How long have you lived here?" Jake asked.

"About four years. I sold our family home in Williamson County because I wanted to live closer to downtown. And," he said, "I was tired of mowing grass."

"Can't say that I blame you for that," Jake told him. "I don't have much to mow at my house, and I'm not complaining. And you met Dixie—"

"Three years ago. Come to think of it, the anniversary of our first date is coming up." He looked over at Jake. "I'm glad you reminded me about that. I would have been in trouble if I'd forgotten." He laughed. "You know how the ladies can be about anniversaries."

Jake nodded. "Yes. That's a lesson you learn the hard way."

They both laughed.

"I'm glad you're feeling better," Jake said, glancing over to Roland while he waited for the stoplight. "This can't be easy for you."

"I wish he would call me right now and ask me for advice like he used to do." Roland tapped his fingers on the doorframe of Jake's truck. "I would tell him to turn himself in. Even if he has to go to prison, I want him to make it out of this alive."

Jake wanted to offer words of comfort, but he wasn't sure what he could say. The possibility of losing a child had to be unfathomable to a parent. He turned into Roland's driveway and stopped in front of his unit. The contemporary-style brick and steel townhome was one of twenty-five or thirty in the complex. And the complex was in a nice area of town, not far from where R. J. lived.

"Roland," Jake said. "I have one more question for you."

"Glad to help. What do you need to know?"

"Did you see your son on the morning of Hannah's attack?"

"No, I didn't. The last time I saw him before that was . . . maybe three days prior?" He stopped to think. "Yes, that sounds right. Why?"

"Are you sure?"

"Yes, I remember it well." Roland said. "R. J. stopped by my house on his way home that morning. He had just dropped his Jaguar off at the dealership to have it serviced, and he was driving a loaner car that the dealership had given him. He wanted me to see it."

"What was it, do you remember?"

"A Lexus SUV," he said. "A very nice vehicle, I remember."

"A Lexus? Do you remember what color it was?"

"Yes, it was gray. A silver gray. I remember telling him how much I liked it, and he let me drive it around the block."

"That's good to know," Jake said. "Because Hannah told us that her attacker was driving a light blue or silver Lexus SUV the morning that she was attacked."

Roland looked down at his hands. "I guess I just dug a deeper hole for my son, didn't I?"

"Unfortunately, yes. And I'm sorry for that," Jake told him. "But you may have just explained how the DNA transfer I've always suspected took place, and how your DNA showed up at the crime scene later that week. In hindsight, I wish I had thought to ask you earlier in the investigation." Jake paused. "But, then again, we never suspected that R. J. had anything to do with the crime, not until Hannah identified him."

"That's a scary thought, isn't it? That DNA transfer thing."

"I suppose it is. But new technology is helping solve more crimes and exonerating innocent people."

Roland nodded.

"I hope you have a good night. You certainly deserve it. I'll check in with you tomorrow. Or I may see you at Dixie's tomorrow when I drop Hannah off after her day at the riding academy."

"Goodnight." Roland opened the truck door and stepped out. "Thank you for making this mess a lot easier for me to handle."

Jake nodded.

A few minutes later, after making sure that Roland made it safely inside his house, Jake turned his truck toward his little cottage in Germantown. In fifteen minutes, he would be home. Nothing sounded better right now than a hot shower and a soft bed.

Before he did that, he would upload Hannah's new CD to his music library in the cloud. Then he would take a few minutes to download and save a few seconds of his favorite song she sang, "Unchained Melody," and use it as a ringtone for Hannah's calls.

Markham Davis turned his lamp out at ten o'clock. Tomorrow would be a busy day, and if he did everything right, Hannah Cassidy would be spending the night with them tomorrow night. After that, he would be free of Shannon.

He had listened to the woman babble on all day.

He opened the windows to his bedroom that overlooked the lake. There was something about being in this old house that calmed him. As a young boy he had spent the occasional weekend with his grandparents. Those had been the best days in his young life. He and Grandpa Max had walked to the lake and fished from sunup to sundown. Even if the fish weren't biting, and they rarely were, he would listen to stories from his grandfather's childhood. Then he would listen to the dreams Markham had for his own life.

Grandmother Harriet would cook his favorite meals, and in the evening they would play board games, watch TV, and stay up late. If he fell asleep on the sofa, he would wake up in his grandpa's arms being carried to bed, and then tucked in, at night.

There had never been a time when he felt more loved, or more accepted for who he was. Now, as he lay in bed, anticipating what he would do tomorrow to take his life back, he could almost bring those feelings back. He wondered why he had ever bought the big house in Green Hills, when he could have stayed in this old log house on the lake and been content for the rest of his life.

Maybe when he got his life back after tomorrow, he would sell the big house and do just that.

After Jake and Roland left, Hannah said goodnight to Dixie and went up to bed. The investigation was moving along quickly. Her attacker was on the run. And God was good all of the time. She knew these things as sure as she knew the sky was blue. And that the sunset tonight had been a promise of things to come.

She couldn't wait to have her life back. To have the freedom to leave the house again. To run the neighborhood without someone escorting her. And to work in her studio and make music the way she wanted to. But, even though all of that was still important, something had changed. Something she hadn't expected or planned for her life anytime soon.

And his name was Jake Matheson.

Just the little bit of time she'd had with him tonight had made her day better. Being held by him, comforted by him, and cared for by him had made her life better. And she didn't want to go back to the freedom she'd had before she met him. In her first twenty-seven years of existence, she'd always thought of love as for someday. Never now. But now had become an urgency she couldn't explain.

Despite that urgency, she knew she wasn't there yet. There was still an invisible wall, an undefinable obstacle in her path. And it was that unknown that allowed fear to settle all around her. There was something about the night, this night with its absolute darkness, that chilled her to the bone, just as it had at tonight's sunset. And, despite the darkness, or because of it, sleep would not take hold. She lay awake until three in the morning looking out her window at the absence of the stars that Jake had told her so much about. And she prayed for peace to come.

CHAPTER 45

Friday, September 10

Jake was in his office by nine o'clock on Friday morning, writing a report to document his conversation with Roland Davis the night before and following up on details.

He put a call in to Roland.

"How did you sleep last night?" Jake asked.

"Good morning, Jake. I did OK. You know, despite his troubles a man's got to sleep sometimes, even when he feels he needs to stay up and worry about the world. My father used to tell me, 'Roland, get your sleep and you'll be better equipped to handle whatever you face the next day.'"

Jake laughed. "Your father must have been one of those people who never had to fight insomnia."

"I think you're right." The older man chuckled. "I don't recall him ever talking about that."

"I'm calling to follow up about something I should have asked last night. Do you happen to know where your son got the loaner car you mentioned?"

"I sure do," Roland said. "It was the dealership in Franklin. Right down the street from the mall."

"I know the place you're talking about." Jake made a note. "I want to give them a call and verify a few things, maybe even take a look at the car for evidence. Thank you, sir, for your help."

"Glad to help," Roland said. "Maybe I'll see you at Dixie's later."

Jake hung up the phone, looked up the dealership's number, and gave them a call. When the operator answered, he asked to speak to the manager.

"Lee Rawlings, may I help you?"

"Mr. Rawlings, this is Jake Matheson. I'm a Special Agent with the Tennessee Bureau of Investigation."

"Yes, Agent Matheson."

"I'm calling about one of your clients. I understand that on or about August 25 you loaned a Lexus SUV to a man by the name of Roland Davis Jr. I believe he was having his Jaguar serviced that day."

Rawlings put Jake on hold but was back on the line within a few minutes. "Yes, I have the record right here. But our customer's name was Markham Davis, and he came in at eight o'clock that morning. He left his Jaguar for servicing, and we gave him a loaner car."

Jake made note of the timeline. "Can you also tell me what time Mr. Davis returned the Lexus?"

"Yes, sir. That would have been around two o'clock on August 28."

"Thank you. We have reason to believe that a woman may have been killed in the Lexus."

"That's not good news," Rawlings said.

'No, sir. And I need to take a look at the vehicle for any potential evidence. Is it available for inspection?'

"Let me look . . . yes. And, according to my records, it hasn't been loaned out or detailed since that day. When he dropped it off, Mr. Davis told us that it had a problem with one of the rear tires, and we haven't taken the time to check it yet."

"That's perfect," Jake said. "I will send a truck for it this afternoon."

"We'll have it ready, sir. But you will need to bring me the necessary paperwork when you pick it up."

"We will certainly do that, Mr. Rawlings. Someone from my office will be there this afternoon, and he will bring everything you need. We appreciate your cooperation."

After ending the call, Jake arranged to have the car picked up. With a plan in motion, he alerted Frank Tolman.

He was on his way out the door to meet Hannah when his phone played "Unchained Melody."

"Hey . . . just checking to see where you were."

"What do you mean? I thought we were meeting at noon?"

"We were. It's ten minutes past."

"It is?" He looked at his watch. "Oh, no. I must have lost track of time."

"Are you on your way?"

"I'll be there in twenty minutes. Don't go anywhere."

He hung up and ran out the door. Twenty minutes later he was pulling into Dixie's driveway. Hannah hurried down the steps and climbed into Jake's black TBI SUV.

"I'm sorry."

"It's OK. We're not that late. But I was getting worried about you. You're always on time. I called Audrey to let her know we were running behind."

"I've had a full morning. Roland gave me some interesting information last night, and I was following up. He confirmed that R. J. was driving a silver Lexus the morning he kidnapped and killed Ginny Williams."

"He did?"

"Yes, and I found the car. It's at a dealership in Franklin. I'm having it picked up today for forensic examination."

"More evidence to weigh in against R. J.," she said.

"Most likely. It's not looking good for him."

"I hate this for Roland's sake . . ."

"He's a strong man. I'm not sure I could be as strong if it were my son." He glanced toward her. "How was your night?"

"I think I slept all of three, maybe four hours. How about you?"

"I did OK. Were you worried about something?"

"I'm not sure what it is," she said. "But I was just on edge."

He reached across the console and took her hand. "It's going to be OK."

"I know," she said. "I know."

As soon as he saw them, Brandon ran to meet Hannah and Jake.

Hannah gave him a high five and asked him where Audrey was.

"Right over there," the six-year-old said, pointing toward the building entrance. Audrey was walking their way.

"Will you two be OK if I leave Brandon with you while I run a few errands in town?"

"Of course," Hannah said. "We have our usual routine."

Hannah led the way into the building, clocked in, and registered Brandon before Jake signed in.

"What's your routine with Brandon here?" Jake asked.

"It's not a lot different, except I will lead his horse around the arena when it's his turn to ride." She looked down at Brandon. "Why don't we go find Knickers and see how he's doing today?"

"OK!" The little boy took off running, making three circles around them before zipping around the corner.

"His horse is on the opposite side of the barn from where we worked last time," Hannah explained to Jake. "With Audrey away, we'll need to keep an eye on him while we muck out the stalls."

As soon as they turned the corner, they saw Brandon standing in front of a stall, talking to a tall, black horse.

"This is Knickers," Hannah said. "Knickers, this is Jake." She rubbed the horse's nose.

"Is this your horse, buddy?" Jake asked, and Brandon nodded.

"Now that we've seen him, do you want to help Jake and me clean the stalls before you ride?" She checked the time on her watch.

"Sure!" Brandon said.

She took the boy by the hand, and they made their way back around the stables to the front. "Do you and Jake want to start on that side? Or do you want to help me?"

"I'll help you," Brandon said, jumping up and down.

"OK. Let's go get our equipment from the equipment room."

After they returned, with Brandon riding in Jake's wheelbarrow, they started their work cleaning the stalls.

Hannah worked the right side, and Jake worked the left. Brandon mostly ran from one to the other, singing and hopping and skipping around the stable area. They were on their second stall, with Jake matching Hannah's progress this time instead of lagging behind, when Hannah noticed that Brandon was gone.

"Have you seen Brandon?" She walked into the stall where Jake was working.

"No. I thought he was with you."

"I lost track of him, because I thought he was with you."

"That's not good," Jake said.

"He's probably just hanging out with one of the staff members somewhere. Or he ran back to see Knickers. I just hope he's not gone into the arena without supervision."

"What can I do?" Jake asked.

"If you'll check Knickers's stall, I'll look outside," Hannah said, walking toward the back entrance of the barn.

Hannah hurried to the large back door that looked out into the back pastureland. She took a right at the door and walked to the far west side of the stable area, not seeing Brandon anywhere. Turning around, she retraced her steps and took off at a faster pace for the east side of the barn. As soon as she turned the corner, she saw Brandon standing there talking to a man.

"Brandon," she called out. "You know you're not supposed to be over here."

As soon as the man heard her, he picked Brandon up and started running.

"Stop! Stop that! What are you doing?" Hannah took off running after the man, screaming. "Brandon . . . Brandon!"

The little boy, now scared, started crying, and Hannah ran harder and faster. She caught up with the man just as he reached the parking lot, and he stopped and turned around.

It was Roland's son, R. J.

Jake hurried around the corner to the other set of stalls, expecting to find Brandon talking to Knickers. But the boy wasn't there. How could he have disappeared into thin air?

"Brandon? Buddy?" he called out. "You need to come back and help us. Hannah is looking for you."

When no one answered, Jake ran to the west entrance door and looked both ways. "Brandon?" He called out.

Still no answer.

Hoping that Hannah had found him, Jake hurried back to the east stall area. As soon as he turned the corner, he saw Brandon running toward him.

"Mr. Jake! Mr. Jake!"

"What's wrong, buddy?"

"He took her!"

Brandon turned around and started running toward the back pastures, but instead of going straight, he turned toward the east and the parking lot area. Jake sprinted after him, catching up as Brandon reached the side of the building. The boy pointed at the parking lot, screeching. "He took her! He took her!"

"Who?" Jake asked, his pulse racing, because he already knew the answer.

"Hannah! He took Hannah!"

CHAPTER 46

Markham's heart thudded as he spun off gravel, trying to gain traction and speed in the parking lot. When his tires finally took hold, he pushed the pedal to the floor, leaving a cloud of white haze behind him. At the end of the long driveway, he took a left, away from the main roads. His escape plan included the same back-roads he had driven on his way from the lake house. He knew he had just upped his chances for being seen—with new alerts being sent out for him as soon as Hannah Cassidy was missed—and that each minute he lost would be a minute that favored his adversaries.

In short, every cop in town would soon know his name and be looking for his red sports car. His only advantage was the time and miles he could put between him and that horse barn in the next few minutes.

Hannah Cassidy had fallen into his trap even more easily than he'd hoped. And, although she had recognized him immediately, she had put the boy's life in front of hers and allowed herself to be taken so he could run away. Her valor would be her downfall. She was now sedated, gagged, and lying in the trunk of his car, unaware of her destination.

Markham took a long breath. His freedom would soon be won. He looked at his watch and then back at the road ahead. In approximately thirty minutes, if he managed to avoid discovery, he would be delivering his package to Shannon.

"Brandon, do you want to help me find Hannah?"

The little boy nodded, drying his tears.

"Then let me carry you to the car. OK?"

"Yes."

Jake picked up the little boy, dialed Frank Tolman's number, and started running. He made the immediate decision to take Brandon with him, because Audrey wasn't due back for a couple of hours. He would work that out later, but first he had to call for backup.

Tolman answered.

"Frank, I need an immediate BOLO. Hannah Cassidy was just kidnapped."

Tolman cursed.

Jake winced. "I'll fill you in later how it happened. But first, we need all Williamson County officers positioned at every intersection in the area of the St. Francis Therapeutic Riding Academy." He looked at his watch. "The kidnapping happened about ten minutes ago. Maybe not that long."

"Were there any eyewitnesses?" Tolman asked.

"Yes, a six-year-old boy. He said it was a man who took Hannah, most likely Markham Davis." Jake unlocked his SUV, opened the rear passenger door, and buckled Brandon into the back seat. He ran around the front of the car, jumped inside, and started the engine.

"My best guess is that he's driving the 2020 red Jaguar coupe. You should have the license number on file."

"What's your ETA?" Tolman asked.

Jake glanced at his watch as he navigated the two-lane gravel drive toward the main highway. "About an hour. I need to drop the boy off at his grandmother's house."

Jake pressed end on the phone and glanced in the rearview at the boy, who seemed to be mesmerized by his present circumstances.

"Are you doing OK, buddy?" Jake asked.

Brandon nodded. His brown eyes were as big as half dollars.

"Great. Hang in there because we're going to see how fast this car will go. OK?"

The little boy nodded again and gave Jake a thumbs-up.

Jake dialed Dixie's number.

"Is everything all right?" Dixie asked.

"No," Jake said. "How did you know?"

"Because God has had me praying. What's going on?"

"Hannah has been kidnapped, Dixie."

"I knew it," Dixie said. "I knew something was wrong."

"I have Brandon with me, and I'm heading that way," Jake said. "I need to drop him off at your house. Can you call Audrey and let her know that's the plan?"

"Yes," Dixie said. "What else can I do?"

"Have Audrey call the riding academy and let them know I have Brandon. I want them to understand he's OK."

"OK. What else can I do?" She asked.

"Just pray, Dixie. Keep on praying, and I'll see you as soon as I can." Jake ended the call.

"Brandon," he said. "Get ready. We're going to turn on the siren now, OK?"

"OK!"

Jake engaged the car's blue emergency lights and siren before pushing the gas pedal closer to the floor. The little boy remained silent for the rest of the trip, leaning back in his seat with his arms straight beside him, as if he were held back by some invisible, high-speed G-force. It would most likely be the ride of Brandon's lifetime. Jake's only wish was that Hannah could be here with him to see it. He silently prayed that she would be sitting safely beside him again soon.

When Jake slid to a stop in front of the cottage, Dixie was already running toward them. He jumped out of the SUV, ran around to the passenger side, and unbuckled the six-year-old boy. He pulled Brandon into his arms. "Are you OK, buddy?"

"Yes," Brandon said, and then he wrapped his arms around Jake's neck, clinging tightly.

Dixie stopped in front of them and reached to take her grandson. "Hey, sweetie. You need to come with me."

Hearing his grandmother's voice, Brandon turned and crawled into her arms. "Call me when you know more," she said and then took two steps back.

"I will," Jake said. He hurried to the driver's side of the vehicle. "You can count on it."

Hannah stirred. What was that pounding in her head? She opened her eyes and saw nothing except pitch darkness. Closing them again, she reopened them slowly. This time there was a small slit of light to one side of her forward field of vision. But what was it, and where was it coming from?

She refocused on the steady vibration beneath her. It felt as if she were moving through space, but she had no concept of how. Or why. The air around her smelled of rubber. And hot asphalt. An almost toxic fume.

Her intuition told her to cover her face with her hands. But they wouldn't move. A strange sensation. They were bound together. And her knees were bent awkwardly in an uncomfortable space. Hard, plastic . . . unforgiving.

She twisted and bumped her head.

Ouch. She tried to say the word, but it didn't register in her ears. There was a tight band covering her mouth!

Panic set in. She couldn't speak. She couldn't breathe. She couldn't scream.

CHAPTER 47

When Jake reached Ellington Parkway, he pushed the gas pedal to the floor. Now that Brandon was safe in his grandmother's arms, Jake would really see how fast this car could go.

Within ten minutes he was pulling into the long driveway that wrapped around the back of the TBI. He parked and ran inside, making one step out of two, despite his recent injuries. He climbed the stairs instead of waiting for the elevator and rushed into Frank Tolman's office. He had already been on the phone with his boss twice since leaving Brandon with Dixie. He didn't bother to knock at the open door.

"Any word?" He was out of breath from the stairs, but he barely noticed.

"Sit down, Matheson," Tolman said. "I want to know how this happened."

"I hardly think this is the time, sir—"

"Sit."

Jake lowered himself onto the edge of the small blue sofa that anchored the corner of Tolman's tiny office.

"How did you let this happen on your watch?"

Jake shook his head and focused on the coffee stain on the rug. "I can't even believe it happened," he said. He replayed the few minutes between Brandon's disappearance and then Hannah's kidnapping. The time between then and now was almost a blur.

"It happened so quickly." He refocused on his boss, who was staring intently in his direction. "Hannah and I were in the stables, and she noticed that Brandon had wandered off." Jake realized the need to explain. "Brandon is the six-year-old autistic boy who is the grandchild of Hannah's friend Dixie, so losing sight of him could have been life-threatening."

He thought about the irony of his last statement.

"Hannah told me to run one way, and she ran the other." He thought about those few minutes. "I took off for one side of the barn, and she ran the other way. When I didn't find Brandon, I immediately turned around and ran back to where Hannah and I had been standing and then out the back door of the barn and around to the side. That's when I saw Brandon, crying and running toward me."

He paused.

"And that's when I knew Hannah was gone."

Tolman nodded.

"Brandon substantiated that for me, saying a man had taken Hannah." Jake looked directly at his boss. "And that's when I called you."

Tolman expelled a long breath of air. "I'm not sure I would have done anything different," he said. "But unfortunately, we're now on the defensive instead of the offensive. We have BOLOs with every county in the state and part of the surrounding states. So far, there has been no sighting of the car." He stood and walked to the entrance of his office, closing his door. "I just hope we're looking for the right vehicle. Do you have any other ideas?"

Jake shook his head. "I don't, sir. It has to be Markham. And unless he was driving his truck, which doesn't make much sense as a getaway car, he would likely be driving his red Jag. Unless he stole a car—or he's in collaboration with someone else. A player we don't know about."

"Shannon Bridges's car has been impounded," Tolman said, returning to his seat. He picked up a pencil and rolled it between his fingers. "A red Jaguar sports car should be easy to spot."

"You would think so," Jake agreed.

"The problem is that we have no idea which way he was heading. For all we know, he could have taken off for Memphis."

"Or he may have a shed or a garage somewhere in Williamson County that would be an easy drive from the riding facility. I'm guessing he knows the area well. It's not far from where Ginny Williams's body was found."

Tolman acknowledged Jake's thesis. "All we can do is keep looking."

Jake rose from the sofa. "If you need me, I'll be at my desk. I'm going to take a good look at the roads in that area and see if I can map out every possible scenario." He walked to the door. "But first, I'm going to call St. Francis to ask them to turn over their video surveillance footage from this afternoon."

Markham pulled to a stop at the end of the long gravel road that led to his family lake house. His Ford truck was gone. Had Shannon pulled it into the garage in his absence? He hit the remote and opened the big door. The F-150 XLT had, indeed, been pulled into the garage.

Exhaling pent-up breath, Markham disengaged his car engine and gathered his thoughts. Life had become simple again. Or would be, as soon as he delivered Hannah to Shannon and they left for an unknown destination.

His work was now done, but his conscience pricked. Was this really the thing to do? Hannah Cassidy hadn't done anything wrong. The truth was it had been his mistake. When he had accidentally targeted her, he had pulled her into his own personal living hell. One he had shared with Ginny Williams, Candy Hayes, and the other girls Shannon had victimized.

It was not a circumstance to be envied. *Ginny and Candy were now dead.* Hannah's future was still to be determined. Markham drew in a deep breath. He had been lucky to get out of this with his life. But would Hannah?

He would think about it later. Right now, he had to get her inside. He picked up his key fob and stepped out of the car. Walking to the back of the Jaguar, he opened the trunk and then rolled back the privacy screen. Beneath it, Hannah was lying in a contorted position. She winced and squinted, turning her eyes away because of the early afternoon sun.

She wiggled and moaned and tried to talk. He would leave her gagged until he took her inside.

Markham pulled his knife from his pocket, and Hannah's blue eyes blinked with terror. "I'm not going to hurt you. I'm going to cut the ropes off your hands."

She didn't move. Nor did she acknowledge him. But then why should she trust him after what he had done to her? Twice.

Once her hands were free, he pulled her upright, her body barely able to move on its own. "I'm going to lift you out of here," he said. "Don't resist me, or you might get hurt."

She stared at him.

He slid his arms underneath her and wedged her slender body between his forearms and his chest. She couldn't weigh more than a hundred and fifteen pounds, despite her height of five-six or five-seven.

Setting her feet first on the gravel drive, he held tightly to her arm to keep her upright. She had been forced into an unmerciful position for the better part of two hours, almost twice as long it would have taken if he had driven the main highways. If not for the ketamine he had injected into her, she would likely have injured herself, trying to fight her way out of the cramped space.

"Hannah," he said. "I know you're having problems walking on your own. Would you let me carry you into the house?"

She shook her head.

"I won't hurt you. I promise." Again, she shook her head, but she was clearly still under the effects of the ketamine he had injected. He had seen it time and time again when he had used it to subdue one of Shannon's girls. "OK . . . I'm picking you up now."

Hannah relaxed into his arms, and he carried her into the house. Shannon was standing at the lakeside windows in the living room and turned around when she heard them come in the door.

She greeted them with a single sentence. "Well, hello, Hannah."

"She can't answer you," Markham said. "She's still out of it from the injection."

"Then put her in the bedroom for the night. We'll deal with her tomorrow." Shannon turned and walked down the hall.

Markham carried Hannah to the last room on the right and laid her on the bed.

CHAPTER 48

While waiting for a call back from someone at St. Francis Therapeutic Riding Academy, Jake continued his needle-in-the-haystack search of the roads surrounding the academy. Although it kept him busy, he wasn't fooling himself. He knew his efforts were little more than a way to satisfy his need to stay busy and keep searching.

On the other hand, asking the riding center for their video surveillance footage could move the search along. If they were lucky, they would not only have the kidnapping on tape, including the face of the man who snatched Hannah, but they could confirm that he had been driving his Jag. They might also know which direction the driver had turned when he exited the academy grounds.

About an hour after he placed the initial call, Lindy Wright from St. Francis called him back. "Agent Matheson," she said, "I've uploaded footage to the internet for you, and I sent you a link. I believe you will find the images we captured to be beneficial to you. If you need anything else, please let me know." Her voice cracked. "We all love Hannah, and we will do anything we can to help you find her."

"I appreciate it, Lindy." Jake hung up and checked his email. Lindy's message was at the top of his inbox. He opened the message and clicked on the link. There were four files, and all four of them were on his hard drive within a minute. The first file was a pristine capture of Hannah, dressed in her blue cotton blouse and blue jeans, being confronted by a tall man. Brandon was standing beside them. After a few seconds of what appeared to be a lively discussion, the man grabbed Hannah and started dragging her toward the parking lot. Almost immediately, Brandon took off running toward the back side of the barn.

Jake's heart fell to his stomach. He had just missed getting there in time to save her.

He clicked on the second file. It was the reverse view of the first camera shot, and this angle gave him a better look at Hannah's abductor's face. Jake was almost certain it was R. J. Davis, but video forensics would be able to verify that in a matter of minutes.

The third file was a wide shot of the riding academy parking lot. The footage started as a tall man was half dragging and half carrying a slender blonde woman to a red sports car. Almost simultaneously, the man opened his trunk and the woman crumbled into a motionless knot. Jake replayed the footage. The second time through, Jake could see that the man had a syringe in his hand, which he plunged into the woman's forearm.

Hannah had been drugged.

Jake watched as the man bound the hands of the woman and tied a gag around her mouth. And then he had lifted her into the car, pulled a cover screen across her, and closed the trunk lid. The man then looked both ways and behind him, most likely to see if anyone had been watching. Satisfied that no one had, he jumped into the driver's side of the car and took off. Gravel flew behind him as the car fought to maintain traction during acceleration. A few seconds later, the sports car shot forward, down the driveway toward the main road.

Jake clicked on the final file. It was a distance view of the gravel drive all the way to the main road. Jake's heart beat in double time as he waited to see which way the Jaguar turned. *Left.* Bingo. Now they had something to go on.

Jake forwarded the four files to video forensics, as well as Frank Tolman, and followed up with a call. Within an hour, the forensics team would have important details, as well as still shots, to circulate to every law enforcement agency in the area, from city police and county sheriff's offices to corporate security officers and parks and recreational security teams, who might be surveilling the streets and highways around their areas of interest.

Based on what Jake knew already, he quickly put together a report, detailing every bit of information that might be crucial in getting the word out to his coworkers, as well as to outside agencies. After reviewing his work, he put a call in to the Bureau's publicity officer and asked for the details to be serviced to all credible news outlets in the area, from the four major television networks to local and regional radio stations and print outlets. He also put in the request for a TDOT digital highway alert.

Thanks to the cameras at St. Francis, they were now playing offense again.

Jake shuffled papers while he waited for forensics to get back to him. In the meantime, he had a dozen agents on hold, waiting for word on where to move.

He picked up the phone and called Dixie.

"Please tell me you have good news."

"I wish I did," Jake said. "But we're still spinning our wheels, waiting for someone to call in a tip about R. J.'s whereabouts."

"Have you confirmed that it was him?" Dixie's voice sounded tired.

"I'm sure I'll have it soon. There's no doubt in my mind." He rechecked his email. "How is Brandon?"

"He's fine. Audrey picked him up from here about an hour after you left. He was asking about Hannah, and we told him that you had gone to get her."

"I sure wish I could—"

"You'll find her, Jake." Now it was her turn to cheer him up.

"Have you talked to Roland?" Jake asked. "How is he holding up?"

"He just left here to go home for the night. He's doing OK. He's a strong man, Jake," she said. "But it's breaking my heart watching what this is doing to him."

"I know, Dixie. Sometimes we're all stronger than we really want to be, but . . ." He paused to think about the past two years. "But somehow we get through it."

"What do you think they'll do with her?" Dixie's voice was thin.

"Do you really want to know?"

"I just want your honest answer."

"I don't really like to think about it, but if they don't kill her, they will involve her in trafficking."

"Until now, I didn't believe that really existed. You know," she said, "not in my world anyway."

"Hannah caught an unlucky break when R. J. accidentally targeted her—" He stopped himself. "But we're going to find Hannah soon. And Shannon Bridges and—I hate to say it for Roland's sake—and R. J. Davis will be served the justice they deserve."

"I'll be praying for you, Jake. I know you have a lot on you right now, but I will pray that God gives you the strength and the insight to do what needs to be done."

"Call me if you need me, Dixie." Jake saw the message he had been waiting for appear in his inbox. "I'll keep you updated as much as I can."

Jake opened the email from forensics and clicked on the first file. *Bingo!*

It was an enhanced closeup of Hannah's abductor. It was the face of R. J. Davis.

Jake printed all the files, and then put a call into Tolman. "I'm on my way to your office," he said.

He grabbed the stack of papers from his printer, picked up his badge and cell phone, and headed out the door. When he got to Tolman's office, the door was open. "Come in, Matheson."

Jake entered, took a seat beside his boss's desk, and slid papers across the top. "I have positively identified Hannah Cassidy's abductor as Roland Davis Jr."

Tolman looked through the papers and leaned back in his chair. "There's really nothing there that surprises me. What else do you have?"

"We've also confirmed, by way of the same video footage, that Davis took a left out of the riding academy driveway."

"Where does that put us?"

Jake exhaled. "It doesn't give us much."

Tolman picked up his pen and rolled it between his fingers. "Let's make a personal call to every sheriff in Tennessee and ask them for their best ideas. We want suggestions for where Bridges and Davis could be hiding, backroads we may be overlooking, and crime-network locals who may have information. Sometimes old-fashioned police work works best. Can you put that kind of team together and accomplish it in two hours?"

Jake calculated quickly. "That's ninety-five sheriffs. I'll need about a half-dozen agents to get it done." He made a mental note of his best six agents who could easily be reassigned.

"And then, I want you to pay a personal visit to the offices of every sheriff located in counties adjacent to Davidson. That would be Cheatham, Robertson, Sumner, Wilson, Rutherford, and Williamson." Tolman rattled off the list by memory. "Can you accomplish that by five o'clock?"

"I'll need help."

"I'll take care of Davidson County, why don't you ask two agents to help you with the other six."

Jake stood. "I'm on it."

Tolman looked at his watch. "Let's meet back here at six o'clock, along with all of the agents you're reassigning to the case. Then we'll share our findings."

Jake hurried back to his office. He would need a four-man supervisory team, including himself, to get the job done. As soon as he got back to his desk, he jotted down three names, and then made a note of assignments underneath their names.

Special Agent Beau Gardner would cover Williamson and Rutherford Counties. Special Agent Andrew Robb would take Cheatham and Robertson Counties. Jake would handle Sumner and Wilson Counties. He would ask Special Agent Lisa Waller to lead a temporary task force of six agents to cover the rest of the state.

His first call was to Lisa. Then, as he prepared to walk out the door on his way to Wilson and Sumner Counties, he put in calls to Beau Gardner and Andrew Robb, giving them their assignments.

CHAPTER 49

On his way out of Nashville, Jake called Roland Davis. He answered on the second ring.

"I'm—I'm so sorry, Jake."

"Dixie told you the news?"

"Yes. Is there an update on Hannah?"

"No. I'm calling to let you know that R. J. has been positively identified as the man who abducted her this afternoon."

"I'd been hoping otherwise, but I'm glad you know for sure. Maybe that will help you find her quickly."

"Thanks. I also wanted to check with you to see if you had heard anything from R. J."

"Nothing," Roland said. "I've tried to call him, but my calls go straight to voicemail."

"I'm not surprised," Jake said. "We've been pinging both his and Hannah's phones but so far nothing. I'm sure they've been turned off."

"I won't stop until I reach him, and I'll let you know as soon as I do." Roland said. "In case you need me, I'll be in Hendersonville this evening. I'm having dinner with my mother."

"You're a good man, Roland," Jake said. "Keep your spirits up. Let's hope, and pray, we will find them both soon."

Jake hung up. He knew the odds of finding R. J. were diminishing with every hour that passed. The odds were even worse for finding Hannah. Statistically, the more time her abductors had to carry out their plans, the less likely law enforcement teams would find her alive.

Hannah woke up inside an unfamiliar room, on an unfamiliar bed, with no memory of how she got there. It took all the effort she had to raise her arm and look at her watch.

Three thirty. In the morning? What had she done today?

Her head ached—her whole body ached—and she was too tired to think about getting out of bed. But she would have to if she was going to figure out where she was. It just didn't make sense. There was something she was forgetting.

Maybe if she checked her cell phone. She reached in her back pocket, but it wasn't there. She tried the other pocket. Nothing. Where had she left it? Pushing herself up on one elbow, she scanned the left side of the room. No phone.

She had to get up and look for it.

It took all the effort she had to sit upright, and she had just put her bare feet on the floor—where were her shoes?—when Shannon Bridges walked into the room.

That's when everything came rushing back. The riding academy . . . her attacker . . . and Brandon. Brandon! *Where was Brandon?*

And where was Jake?

Hannah stared at Shannon, her mind still a fog of confusion.

"Well, aren't you the sleeping beauty?" Shannon said. "Either you were behind on your sleep or Markham gave you too much ketamine."

"Ketamine?" Hannah said. "How long have I been here?"

Shannon looked at her watch. "Not long enough yet, so you might as well relax. You'll be here for few more hours before we leave."

"Leave . . . ?"

Shannon didn't answer. Instead, she turned and walked out the door, closing it behind her. Hannah heard the lock click, and then she collapsed back against the pillow before sleep overtook her again.

Jake pulled to a stop in front of the Wilson County Sherriff's

office. He secured his badge and gun and grabbed one of his prepared packets of paperwork. Inside each packet was a thumb drive
with digital images of R. J. Davis and Shannon Bridges, as well as
Hannah Cassidy. There were also enhanced screenshots of both
suspects and Hannah, including an image from St. Francis showing R. J.'s confrontation with Hannah. Finally, there were comp
photos of the red 2020 Jag F-type and the Ford F-150 XLT pickup
truck. Frank Tolman's secretary had also included high-resolu-
tion print copies of the same resources.

Jake looked at his watch. It was almost four o'clock. This would
need to be a quick meeting. He entered the building between the
two flagpoles and hurried up to the reception desk.

"May I help you?"

"Yes, ma'am. My name is Jake Matheson. I'm a Special Agent
with the TBI, and I have an appointment with Deputy Mark
Miller."

Tolman's secretary had advanced his meeting here, as well
as in Sumner County, and for the other county meetings as well.
Gardner in Williamson and Rutherford Counties, and Robb in
Cheatham and Robertson Counties.

"Yes, sir. They're ready for you," the receptionist said. "Someone will be right out. Have a seat if you would like. May I get you
a cup of coffee?"

"No, I'm fine. Thank you."

Of course, he wasn't fine. Not knowing where Hannah was.
And even if she was alive. He paced around the lobby, staring at
the photos on the wall but not seeing them. All he could see in his
mind's eye was Hannah being tossed into R. J. Davis's sports car
like a piece of insignificant trash. Or a piece of merchandise—

"Agent Matheson."

Jake turned.

"I'm Deputy Mark Miller." He stuck out his hand. "I'm the officer in charge. Sheriff Reynolds is on vacation this week"

"Nice to meet you, Mark. Please, call me Jake. Is there somewhere we can talk?"

"Yes. In my office. I've asked a couple of other people to meet with us."

Jake nodded and walked with Mark Miller down the hall and into the elevator. They exited onto the second floor.

"My office is here," Miller said, gesturing to a door on the right. "Jake, I want you to meet Alex Rodgers and Chris Conley. They're with the Mount Juliet and Lebanon PDs. Your secretary asked me to have someone here from each department, if possible. Alen and Chris were able to break free." He waited a beat and then added, "Gentleman, Jake Matheson."

Jake greeted both officers and then took a seat. "Thank you for being here. It's nice to meet you all. As Mark said, I'm Jake Matheson with the TBI. I'm here because we've had a major break-through in a Middle Tennessee sex trafficking investigation."

Jake hesitated and looked around the room. "The bad news is that the key players have abducted a twenty-seven-year-old woman." He opened the envelope he had carried with him and handed the contents to Deputy Miller. "Here's the information, IDs on the traffickers and the victim." The word victim almost refused to roll off his lips.

This was not just any victim, not to him. It was Hannah.

CHAPTER 50

It was almost four thirty when Hannah awoke for the second time. She was feeling much better physically, and her mental acuity had returned. But along with that was the very real knowledge of her situation and the fear that came with it. It was almost as paralyzing as the drug she'd been given. And not just fear for herself.

Please God, help Brandon to be safe.

Thoughts about Brandon also brought forth concern for Dixie, who had to be distraught about Hannah's disappearance. Did anyone know what had happened to her? That R. J. Davis had found her and whisked her off to . . . *to where?* She had to find out so she could somehow get a message to Jake.

She sat up on the bed. No dizziness. She stood and walked to the only window in the room. Pulling back the shades, she saw nothing but tall evergreen trees and pastureland. She was still in Tennessee, or at least it seemed so. She walked around the room, pulling out drawers and rifling through them. She opened the closet door and sorted through its contents. There were several cardboard boxes. In one, she found a book of matches from UT Knoxville, a shot glass from Tootsie's on Broadway downtown, and several pairs of men's faded blue jeans. She opened another box and found a diploma. *The Trustees of the University of Tennessee have conferred on Roland Markham Davis Jr. the degree of Master of Science in Civil Engineering.* Lying beside it was a tassel with the year 2007 dangling from it.

This couldn't be R. J.'s home in Green Hills. She thought back to what Roland had said about a family home in Hendersonville. Maybe this was it. Roland had told them it was a ranch house, although he hadn't mentioned a log construction. She was about to open another box when she heard voices outside her room. She shoved the boxes back into the closet and closed the door. Then she took a seat on the bed.

R. J. walked into the room first with Shannon behind him. He carried a tray of food, and she held a bottle of pills. One was welcome. The other was suspect.

Hannah put on her best fake smile. If she was going to make it through this alive, she would have a better chance if she could stay conscious, and being nonconfrontational would, hopefully, make them less likely to sedate her.

"We brought you food," R. J. said, before setting the tray on the bed in front of her. "You're looking better now."

"I feel better, thank you," Hannah said. "I'm not sure what you gave me, but I don't want any more, please."

Shannon laughed. "'Please' and 'thank you,' isn't that nice? You keep that up, sweetie, and we just might be able to work together."

"Maybe so," Hannah said, spooning a bite of canned fruit cocktail into her mouth. The sugar was exactly what she needed to reenergize. She scooped up another big bite.

Shannon set the pill bottle on the corner of the tray. "Markham said you might have a headache. I thought you might want some acetaminophen."

"Thank you, but I think I'm good," Hannah said, doubting that Shannon was telling the truth about the pills.

"Do you need anything you don't have?" R. J. asked.

Hannah studied him. He was much different than she remembered him to be two weeks ago—or earlier today. He now behaved like a gentle giant. More friend than enemy. But she wasn't about to let her guard down. After all, he had tried to kidnap her twice, succeeding the second time.

Shannon could apparently read her mind. "Markham, I think she likes you better than me. All of the girls seem to favor you."

R. J. frowned and walked to the other side of the room.

"I'm sorry, sweetie, but you can't have him. You're coming with me."

"What do you mean?" Hannah tried to keep her tone relaxed.

Shannon laughed. "Sorry, you're on a need-to-know basis, and you don't really need to know that. But, trust me, we'll be getting out of here soon. And Markham isn't going with us."

Hannah's stomach climbed into her throat. She probably shouldn't keep eating because her digestion was about to go south.

"Come on, Markham, let's get out of here. You and I have business to discuss."

"When will you and Hannah be leaving?" Markham asked, closing Hannah's door behind him but not locking it.

"Soon." Shannon followed him into his bedroom across the hall.

"What do we need to discuss?" he asked. "I've done everything I'm supposed to do. Now it's time for you to leave."

She turned her back and left the room, slamming the door behind her.

Markham locked his door and took a seat on his bed. He had waited for this day for what seemed like forever. He would have Shannon out of his life. But it wasn't working out the way he had planned.

He was certain the police were after him now, with or without Hannah's testimony. There had been cameras all over the riding academy grounds. And his house had been ransacked. They had to have found his files. Maybe if he turned himself in, he could save himself—and Hannah. If he allowed Shannon to take her, things would only be worse.

He took off his shoes and lay down, resting his head on the pillow and staring at the old, spackled ceiling. This house looked and smelled like his childhood. The log walls. The musty scent of the lake. The way the sun shone through the old-fashioned windowpanes fashioning little squares of light and dark on the wall. It all came back, as he drifted off.

"Markham Davis, you come out here right now."

"Mommy?" Markham slid off his bed, half asleep, padded

barefoot to his bedroom door, and opened it. His mother, a statuesque woman with dark brown eyes, stood in the hallway. She stared down at him.

"What is this?" she asked. She was holding a fork. "Wasn't it your turn to wash the dishes tonight?"

"Yes, ma'am." Markham looked down at the floor.

She grabbed his chin and forced him to look at her. Then, holding the fork right in front of his face, she said. "Do you see this?"

"Yes, ma'am."

"It's still dirty. I found it in the kitchen drawer. Do you know what that means?"

"Yes, ma'am." He followed her into the kitchen. All the dishes in all the cabinets had been pulled from the shelves and stacked on the counter in an unreal tower of disaster. Every utensil had been pulled from the drawers and thrown into the floor.

"You will not go to bed before you wash these. Do you understand me?"

"But . . ."

"What did you say?"

Markham looked up at the clock. "But it's almost midnight, and I have school tomor—"

"You should have thought about that when you were supposed to do your job earlier." She grabbed him by the shoulders and walked him to the sink.

"When I get up in the morning, these had better be clean."

"Markham! Markham! Open your door."

Someone was banging on the door. What time was it?

"Markham! Get out here . . ."

Markham got out of bed and padded across the room, half asleep.

"Mommy?" He opened the door.

"What's wrong with you?" Shannon stared at him. "You're as crazy as a loon."

"What?"

"I said you're crazy." She laughed. "I've always known that. Although I couldn't have done it without you."

He stared at her. "Shannon?"

"Who did you think it is?" She pulled his grandfather's old revolver from her pocket. The one he had stored in the guest bedroom closet, never expecting guests. "I'm sorry I have to do this. I really am. But I need to leave here without baggage. Someone to squeal." She laughed again. "And the truth is, I just don't trust you, Markham."

"You can trust me," he said, fully back in the moment now and backing away from her. "You're going to take Hannah and live your life . . . and I will live mine."

"I'm sorry," she said. "I can't take any chances."

She cocked the trigger.

"Please, Shannon, don't . . ."

The noise was deafening. And the pain . . . the pain in his arm was excruciating. He fell to the bed.

Shannon took aim again, but this time the gun was pointed squarely at his chest.

"No!"

Shannon cocked the trigger . . . and a shadow moved behind her.

Just as she was about to fire, Hannah shoved her from behind, and the gun went off. The shot went wild and thudded into the wall beside him as Shannon hit the floor.

Markham jumped up, grabbing his upper right arm. It was bleeding bad.

R. J. pushed past Hannah, looking back and screaming as he ran down the hall. "Come with me, and I'll get you out of—"

"Stop where you are." Shannon had recovered from her fall, rolled over on her back, and was pointing the gun directly at Hannah. "Do not run away. I will shoot you. Don't doubt me because I have nothing to lose."

Hannah didn't move. R. J.'s footsteps disappeared down the hallway. He'd left her to face Shannon alone. "Don't shoot me." She lifted her hands in the air. "I won't run."

Shannon pulled herself up and looked around. "There." She gestured to the bed. "Sit there."

Hannah kept her hands in the air and slowly walked to the bed, lowering her body onto it, watching Shannon as she moved. Praying she wouldn't pull the trigger.

Shannon shimmied sideways toward the far side of the bed, and Hannah felt a hard tug on the sheets. Two more tugs and the top sheet slid from underneath her.

Shannon walked around the bed, still pointing the gun at Hannah, and threw the sheet at her. "Tear this. I need something to tie your hands."

Hannah caught the sheet and, keeping her eyes partially trained on Shannon, she found a weak spot in the already threadbare sheet. She pushed her thumb through the loose threads, compromising the fabric. From there, it was easy to tear a long strip of cotton. She tossed the first strip of material aside and repeated what she had just done. Finally, after tearing three long strips of cotton, she waited for further instructions.

"Lie face-first on the bed and put your hands behind your back."

Hannah followed Shannon's orders and waited for her to bind her wrists. Once she had that accomplished, Shannon wound a second strip of fabric securely around Hannah's ankles.

"Sit up."

Hannah braced herself with her hands and sat up on the side of the bed. "These are too tight," she said.

"You'll be fine for now. Don't get too comfortable. As soon as I can pack, we will be out of here."

Markham heard Shannon shout as he ran through the kitchen.

There was no need to go back. Shannon still had three bullets in her chamber and chances were that the next shot would disable, if not kill.

He ran to the kitchen, snatching his car fob off the counter, and straight out the door to the garage. Hitting the button to open the garage door, he limboed beneath the half-ascended door and unlocked the Jag, sliding inside and turning on the engine.

Why did I let that happen? He had given Shannon the upper hand.

He looked down at his arm, which was bleeding profusely. He had never had a gunshot wound before, and his arm felt like a dead weight that had been attached to his shoulder. The wound both burned and felt numb at the same time. At this point, the pain was tolerable. Or he was in shock.

Markham opened the console and pulled out a leftover piece of fabric from what he had used to gag Hannah. Her cell phone lay beneath the cloth. Markham picked it up and tossed it on the passenger seat beside him, then he wrapped the strip of cloth around his arm and pulled it tight, securing it in a knot with his teeth and left hand. It was all he could do, and it would have to be enough.

He picked up Hannah's cell phone and turned it on. Did he have time? He got out of the sports car, already weakening from the loss of blood, and took two steps to the passenger side of his work truck. Opening the door, he tossed the phone into the passenger side pocket and partially covered it with an old chamois cloth, hoping Hannah—and not Shannon—would see it. It might give her a chance to call for help on her own.

Hurrying back to the Jag, he fell into the driver's seat and engaged the engine. Putting the sports car in reverse, he kicked the gas pedal to the floor. The car roared backwards about fifty yards through the gravel, then he released the accelerator and hit the brake simultaneously, while twisting the steering wheel to the far left and throwing the car into a spin. Markham accelerated just enough at the one hundred eighty mark and shot forward down the driveway on his way to the main road. He drove as fast as he could and still maintain control around the sharp turn in the middle of the break of fir trees that hid the house from the road, and he accelerated again once he could see the main road. With only a slight hesitation to look for oncoming traffic from the left, he spun out to the right on the main road and put as much distance as he could between himself and the lake house.

When he was finally on Nashville Pike, the main thoroughfare that ran through Hendersonville and into Gallatin, he used his crippled right hand to reach into his pocket for his cell phone. Engaging CarPlay, he voice-dialed his father.

Roland Davis Sr. answered on the second ring. "Son!"

"Where are you?" Markham asked.

"I'm visiting your grandmother in Hendersonville."

A surge of emotion ran through Markham's chest. *Family.*

"I will meet you there."

"Where are you?" Roland asked. But Markham ended the call.

Jake's meeting had gone well, and he was now en route, via Highway 109, to the Sumner County seat in Gallatin. He glanced at his watch. He should be there in plenty of time for his five o'clock appointment with a gathering of law enforcement officials in the county, which included officers from the Portland, Gallatin, and Hendersonville police departments.

He was hopeful that Sumner County's law enforcement officers would lend their full support, as the Wilson County men had done. Miller, Rodgers, and Conley had promised to increase the number of resources they had assigned to the investigation. No one wanted to miss the chance to bring down a trafficking ring.

It was a beautiful drive between Lebanon and Gallatin, and Jake had just crossed the Cumberland River when his phone rang.

CHAPTER 51

It was Roland's number in the Caller ID. "What's going—"

"R. J. called."

Jake's heart plunged to his stomach, but he didn't speak.

"He's on his way here."

"Where are you?"

"At my mother's senior center."

"What's that address again?"

Roland rattled off the address, and Jake engaged his emergency lights and sirens. "Don't let him leave. I'm in Gallatin, and I'll be there in fifteen minutes." After ending the call, Jake dialed Tolman. "We just heard from R. J. Davis."

"Where is he?" Tolman's tone held a sense of urgency.

"On his way to meet his dad in Hendersonville. I'm in Gallatin, about fifteen minutes away. Can you call in backup?" Jake gave his boss the address.

"Is Shannon Bridges with him?"

"I don't know."

"And . . . how about Hannah Cassidy?"

"I don't know." Jake's voice cracked.

"Good luck, Matheson."

"Thank you, sir."

Jake placed a call to the Sumner County Sheriff's Office, identified himself, and asked to be redirected to the conference room where the team he was to meet was waiting for him. Sumner County Deputy Sheriff Darrin Jones picked up the phone. "Deputy, this is Jake Matheson with the TBI. I've just received a call from the father of one of our suspects. His son called him, and he is meeting his dad at the Angels Unaware Senior Center on the east side of Hendersonville."

"I know exactly where it is," Jones said. "We'll reconvene our meeting in the parking lot."

"Stand by, please," Jake said. "Please position your cars outside of a two-mile perimeter and stay off the main road. I don't want to spook this guy. He may have a hostage with him."

"Ten-four on that, but I'd like to dispatch unmarked units to the scene, if that works for you," Jones said.

"That works. I'll see you there."

Jake ended the call, sent up another silent prayer, and formulated a plan of action. Thankful he had been to the senior center about a week before, he was familiar enough with the area to approach the facility from the rear. He would park his vehicle a block away and travel the rest of the way on foot. If R. J. had Hannah with him, anything else would risk her life.

Hannah sat on the edge of R. J.'s bed, while Shannon gathered her belongings from another room. Hannah could hear cursing and shuffling noises from up the hall. Finally, she heard the sound of a suitcase being zipped, and momentarily Shannon appeared in her doorway.

"Let's go!"

"I can't walk," Hannah reminded her, looking down at her leg bindings.

"I'll be back."

Shannon disappeared, and for a brief moment, Hannah celebrated the possibility that she might have left without her. No more than five minutes later, the petite blonde returned. She untied Hannah's leg bindings and urged her out the door, holding the gun to her back. Hannah took her breaths in shallow bursts until she was confident that Shannon intended to take her with her and not shoot her on the spot.

R. J.'s red sports car was missing from the driveway, giving Hannah some hope that he might solicit help for her, even though she would be gone. But did he know where Shannon was taking her?

272

Shannon opened the passenger side door of the big work truck and yelled at Hannah to get inside. Hannah stumbled on the stirrup-like step, bringing back memories of climbing inside Jake's big truck. He wasn't here to help her this time. She was on her own.

She looked at Shannon. "I can't get in this monstrosity with my hands tied." She held them out.

Shannon glared at her, defiant.

"I'm not going to try anything while you have a gun on me. I'm not stupid." She held out her arms, wrists facing up.

With a growl, Shannon untied Hannah's hands. Once Hannah was inside the truck, Shannon slammed the door behind her and ran around the back of the vehicle. Climbing inside, she engaged the engine, opened the garage door, and backed up slowly before putting the truck in drive and making a wide circle around the front yard, connecting again with the driveway on their way out. The garage door closed behind them.

Once they had cleared the tree line, Hannah could see that civilization hadn't been far from them, although the houses in the area looked to be few in number and were set back from the main road. The chances of anyone hearing the gunshots twenty minutes before would have been slim, and most likely dismissed as someone who was hunting.

Shannon took a right at the end of the driveway. For miles, the narrow but well-paved road in front of them wound around the countryside with houses, mini-farms, and even subdivisions populating each side of the road, becoming even more frequent the farther they drove. Although she hadn't seen anything that looked familiar, Hannah was certain they were still in Tennessee.

Four or five miles up the road, Shannon stopped at a traffic light and seemed to be assessing her options. "Do you know your way around this place?" she asked Hannah.

I wouldn't tell you if I did. "I have no clue. Sorry." Hannah shrugged and looked up. A sign hanging above the crossroad read Nashville Pike, and Hannah knew exactly where she was. They were almost midway between Hendersonville and Gallatin. Harriett Davis's senior living center was a few miles to the right, and the old Sumner County Drive-In was to the left.

"Don't you know where you are?" Hannah asked.

Shannon shot her an angry look. "Of course, I know where I am. I'm just trying to decide which way I want to go."

"Depends on where you're heading," Hannah said, risking the ire of her captor.

"Why don't you just shut up?"? Shannon snapped at her. "If you think I'm telling you where we're going, you're wrong. Although I will tell you it's a long way from here. I hate this place."

"There's a surprise," Hannah mumbled under her breath, but Shannon heard her.

She pointed her finger in Hannah's face. "*You* had better shut up unless you want another dose of ketamine."

Hannah nodded and stayed silent. She would need to be vigilant if she was going to break free from this woman and staying vigilant meant staying lucid.

Jake drove past the senior center so he could get a visual before making his approach on foot. Nothing appeared to be out of order, which meant that R. J. had not yet arrived. Jake parked in a church lot about a hundred yards away, checked his pistol, secured it in his shoulder holster, and grabbed his cell phone. After locking his vehicle, he dialed Tolman.

"I'm a block behind the senior center where Davis will be meeting his father. Has backup arrived yet?"

"You're the first on the scene," Tolman said. "But they're on the way."

"Good. I'll be back in touch." Jake ended the call and dialed Deputy Sheriff Jones. "Do you have the unmarked cars on site yet?"

"Yes, two uniformed officers are sitting in a vehicle on the west side of the building with a view of the front parking lot."

"That's what I needed to know. Let them know that I'm here, approaching from the rear. Thanks."

"We also have about eight vehicles from various local agencies standing by outside of your requested two-mile radius."

"OK. I'm going in now on foot. I'll keep you informed."

"Good luck," the deputy sheriff said.

CHAPTER 52

Shannon spat out a curse and took a left, heading into Hendersonville. Almost immediately, Hannah saw a police car backing into a driveway ahead. Apparently, Shannon saw it too, because she cursed again and made a quick left turn into a business parking lot, turned around, and headed back in the direction they had come. She drove through the intersection they had just navigated and kept driving toward the city of Gallatin. Less than a mile up the road, they saw another police car, one that Hannah recognized as a Sumner County Sheriff's vehicle. Shannon made another immediate turn, this time into a church lot. She drove around the back of the church building and then took a right turn onto the main highway.

They had one option left. Hannah prayed for God's provision and scanned the truck for something to defend herself in case Shannon threatened her. In the pocket of the passenger side door, she saw a small metal gray object lying beneath a chamois cloth. Her heart jumped. Was it what she thought it was?

She dropped her right arm to her side and gently tugged at the cloth, exposing more of the object. It was her cell phone. But how—?

R. J. He had left it for her. There was no other explanation.

Thank you, Lord! Be with him.

When Shannon returned to the intersection where they had originally entered the highway, she took her remaining option, which was a right turn. Hannah knew they would eventually wend their way around to Long Hollow Pike. Hannah leaned back in her seat and prayed. She needed a chance to call Jake.

Jake watched as R. J.'s red Jaguar sports coupe pulled into the Angels Unaware parking lot. Roland, who was outside the building standing beside his own car, waited for his son. As soon as the Jag stopped, he ran to it.

R. J. powered down the driver's window, giving Jake a good opportunity to look past him. Hannah wasn't with him, unless she was in the truck. That meant she was probably with Shannon.

While Roland engaged R. J., Jake slipped around to the passenger side of the car. He could only understand Roland's part of the conversation. Something R. J. said elicited a frenzied response from his father.

"Son, we need to get you to a hospital!" There was panic in Roland's voice.

If R. J. was injured, it was time for Jake to step in, but he couldn't take the chance of having him drive away. Or worse, discharging a weapon in a public parking lot.

Come on, Roland, get him out of the car.

Almost on cue, Roland insisted that his son get out of the car, and the driver's side door of the Jag opened. R. J. tried to stand and walk, but immediately fell backwards into the car.

"Help him! Help him!" Roland screamed.

Jake pulled his gun from his holster and ran around to the driver's side of the car. Roland was almost completely bearing the weight of his son.

Jake reholstered his gun and helped Roland lower R. J. back into the seat. Then he grabbed the key fob from the front seat and made a quick visual search of the vehicle for weapons.

"Mommy shot me," R. J. mumbled.

"That's not right, son. Wake up . . ." Roland leaned in close to his son's ear. "Who shot you?"

"Shannon."

Roland turned to look at Jake.

"Where's Hannah?" Jake leaned into the vehicle.

"With Shannon. You have to help her."

"Where are they, R. J.?"

"At the lake house."

Jake turned to Roland, and the older man nodded with understanding.

Jake motioned to the driver of the ambulance that had been on hold near the side of the senior center. "The ambulance is coming," he assured Roland. "Can you give me an address for the lake house?"

"You'll never find it," Roland said. "I need to go with you."

"You need to stay with R. J."

"The ambulance is here. Hannah needs us."

"Let's go!" Jake started running for his SUV and shouted over his shoulder. "I'll be right back to pick you up."

Hannah glanced at her watch. It was almost five thirty in the afternoon. They would have daylight for another couple of hours.

When they reached Long Hollow Pike, Shannon made a quick left, heading almost due west, although Hannah suspected she was flying by the seat of her pants. Less than ten miles ahead they would be back in the Nashville Metropolitan area. If the police vehicles they had spotted earlier were there for them—and Hannah prayed they were—there would be a lot more of the same when Shannon drove into Davidson County. But . . . if Shannon was successful in getting them out of Nashville tonight, Hannah feared they might never be found.

I'm out here, Jake. Don't give up.

By the time Jake returned to the senior center to pick up Roland, R. J. was being loaded into an ambulance. Roland said goodbye to his son and jumped into the SUV.

"Is he going to make it?" Jake asked.

"He's lost a lot of blood, but the EMT thought he had a good chance."

"I'll be praying for him," Jake said. "Let's hope for the best.

Now, which way am I going?"

"Take a right up here and head straight for Gallatin." Roland pointed to the main road.

"How far?"

"About five miles, and then we'll take another right. The house will be back toward the lake."

Jake turned on his emergency lights. "Buckle up, Roland. You're in for a ride." In less than ten minutes, Jake was turning onto the side road that led to Roland's family home.

"This was my mother and father's house," Roland told him. "I'm not sure why I didn't think about it earlier. R. J. lived there for a couple of years after he returned from college, but he never liked the place. It wasn't high-end enough for him." Roland shook his head. "I hope I'm not the cause of Hannah getting hurt."

"Go easy on yourself," Jake said. "Do you see the row of police cars behind me?"

Roland looked in his side mirror.

"I hope we don't need them." He pointed to the right. "Up there. That's the gravel driveway. The house is almost a half mile down the road on the other side of those fir trees. Are you going in with the car or on foot?"

"For the sake of time," Jake said, "I'm going to drive in and leave our backup back here out of sight."

Jake phoned the driver of the lead car in the caravan, Marty Warren with the Sumner County Sheriff's Office, and passed along those orders. The marked and unmarked cars pulled over and waited as Jake drove on. Once he'd driven past the row of fir trees, he could see the old ranch-style log cabin. He scanned the property and scrutinized the windows. All the blinds and curtains appeared to be in place, which helped to convince him that they were still unnoticed.

"Any security cameras?"

"Not that I'm aware," Roland said, "but I've not kept up with what R. J. has done out here."

"Is there any chance we can peek inside the garage to see if there's a vehicle inside?"

"There's a window on the north." Roland pointed to the left. "And I have a key." He pulled his keyring from his pocket and dangled it in midair. "I keep it on here, so I don't lose it."

"God bless you, man."

Jake pulled his vehicle to a stop and held out his hand. "Give me the key. You stay here." Roland nodded. Jake got out, silently closing his doors, then ran to the north side of the garage. There was no window covering, and it was easy to see that the garage was empty. Returning to the door into the garage, Jake used Roland's key to enter and stepped silently to the back door, listening for someone in the house. When he heard nothing, he opened the door and walked inside with his gun drawn. Jake phoned Sheriff's Deputy Warren. "You can send cars up the drive now. It appears they've already gone."

Indeed they were. After a thorough search of every room in the house, they found no sign of anyone having been here, except for the full trash can.

Shannon and Hannah had just passed Beech High School when Hannah spotted a Metro Police car up ahead. "Do you see that?"

Shannon nodded and braked, taking a hard left into a small parking lot. "Do you know this area?"

Hannah nodded. "I grew up close to here."

"What's the best way out of here to avoid seeing a cop?"

"I don't think it matters," Hannah said. "Look. There's another police car."

"I'm not going down this easy." Shannon turned the truck around and headed east again. "We're going to find a place for the night."

About a mile down the road, she made a left into a large subdivision, avoiding yet another police car.

Shannon turned to Hannah. "Help me find an empty house."

"We're going to stay in somebody's house?" Hannah cringed. *Was she going to take a family hostage?* Hannah prayed that didn't happen.

"Look!" Shannon said. "That house is empty."

"How do you know that?

"There are always little signs." Shannon took a hard right into the driveway and pulled the truck behind the house, hidden from the road. "That was close," she said. "There was a police car behind us. Stay in the car. I'm going to look for a hidden key." She glared at Hannah. "Do not tempt me to shoot you."

Shannon pocketed her keys, got out of the truck, and closed the door.

Hannah watched as she looked around the back patio, checking under the mat, flowerpots, and nearby rocks. This was Hannah's chance. She fetched her cell phone from the side door panel pocket and speed dialed Jake's number. As soon as she was sure it was ringing, she slipped it into her pocket.

Within seconds Shannon returned holding a key. "Let's go inside. Quickly!"

Hannah opened the truck door and slid to the ground, pushing her cell phone deeper into her pocket and pulling her blouse over it. She followed Shannon to the back door and watched her slip the key into the lock cylinder and turn it. The door opened, and within a few minutes they were standing inside the kitchen.

Shannon spotted a note on the counter addressed to a woman named Susan.

Thanks for taking care of the plants. We'll be back in two weeks. It was signed *The McMurtrys.*

"Well, it looks like we have plenty of time to relax here." Shannon smiled, a look of "I told you so" in her eyes.

"How do you know that?"

She pointed to the note, then at a large heartleaf philodendron near the breakfast table. "There's fresh water in the tray beneath the pot. Apparently, Susan was here recently to water the plants. I doubt she'll return for another week."

Hannah's heart sank. But at least they were still in the Nashville area.

"Let's check out the bedrooms." Shannon had the pistol in her hand and was pointing it at Hannah. "Just a reminder."

Jake turned around in the lake house driveway, disappointment dousing the adrenalin he'd mustered on their twenty-minute trip.

"What do we do now?" Roland asked.

"We wait," Jake said. "And we hope R. J. knows something that will help us find them. Why don't you call and check on him?"

Roland dialed R. J.'s number, but no one answered.

"Do you know what hospital they were taking him to?"

"Tri-Star Hendersonville is the closest."

"Give them a call," Jake said.

Roland searched for the main hospital number and placed the call. "My son just arrived there by ambulance." He looked at his watch. "Maybe thirty minutes ago. His name is Roland Markham Davis Jr. Can you tell me how he's doing?"

Roland turned to Jake. "They said I need a code to verify my identity."

"Give me the phone," Jake said.

Roland handed him the phone. "This is Jake Matheson. I'm with the Tennessee Bureau of Investigation. Please put me on hold and call the main switchboard there and ask for Frank Tolman to verify my identity. Yes, I'll wait."

Jake gave Roland the thumbs-up, and a few minutes later the woman returned. "Yes, sir. Thank you, Agent Matheson. Roland Davis Jr. is in surgery. We won't have an update on him for another hour. In the meantime, let me give you the code so you won't have a problem the next time you call."

"Please give it to his father." Jake handed the phone back to Roland.

"Yes, ma'am," Roland said, reciting the numbers. "I have it. I'll call back in about an hour." He ended the call and looked at Jake. "Thank you," Roland said. "That was handy."

"Usually is."

Jake's mobile phone vibrated, and then the first few bars of

Hannah singing "Unchained Melody" began to play. He engaged the SUV's Bluetooth system and answered, but no one seemed to be on the other end. He was about to hang up and call his office to have the signal tracked when he heard a faint conversation in the background.

Jake placed his own phone on mute. "It's Hannah," he told Roland. "She's turned on her phone so we can track her. Give me your phone, Roland. I need to call my office." As soon as he reached Tolman, he filled him in and asked him to order call tracing. "Call me back on this number."

CHAPTER 53

After Shannon had checked the bedrooms, she stashed her gun in her pocket. "I'm hungry. Do you cook?" she asked.

Hannah did her best not to laugh. Thanks to Dixie she could bluff her way through this. "Oh, yes. I love to cook."

Please God, forgive the white lie.

Shannon checked her watch. "Let's eat first, and then we can rest. We will travel early tomorrow."

Hannah led the way back down the stairs and into the kitchen. Shannon settled at the kitchen table. "I'll be right here, while you work."

Hannah gathered her thoughts and opened the refrigerator. Nothing. She tried the freezer. Frozen hamburger patties, frozen hamburger buns, french fries . . .

She closed the freezer door and walked to the pantry. There were a lot of canned vegetables and staples. Broth. Fruit. Flour. Rice. She closed the pantry door and went back to the refrigerator. There was sliced cheese in the dairy drawer and a halfway decent looking-tomato in the corner of the veggie drawer—even she knew you weren't supposed to keep tomatoes in the refrigerator.

She turned to Shannon. "How about cheeseburgers and fries?"

"Great!" Shannon said. "How long?"

Hannah froze. *How long?* Hmmm. "Oh, I don't know. I need to see what appliances they have. Probably thirty minutes."

"Sounds good."

Hannah turned and started looking through cabinets. Bingo! There was an air fryer, a pressure cooker thingy, similar to the one Dixie had used. She pulled it out of the cabinet, set it on the countertop, and plugged it in. Then she started going through the cabinets again. There was also a cast iron skillet. Dixie had told her those were the best.

Did she have cooking oil?

She found it in one of the top cabinets, along with salt, pepper, and other spices. *This might actually work.* And it gave her time to think.

"Why are you looking through all of the drawers? Just start cooking!"

Hannah went back to the refrigerator for the tomato. Then she pulled the frozen hamburger patties, the fries, and the buns out of the freezer. She set the food on the counter next to the sink.

Utensils?

Hannah shot Shannon a grumpy look and started opening drawers again. She found forks, knives, and spoons. In the next drawer were napkins and plastic baggies. And in the drawer next to that, she found paring knives, vegetable peelers, a garlic press, a potato masher, and a large chef's knife.

A chef's knife? No way. She had seen television shows where people used those things to chop, dice, and mince with ease. But she wasn't about to try it. She would probably lose a finger, if not two. She gingerly picked out a paring knife.

A few minutes later Hannah had the oven heating up, the air fryer heating up, and the cast iron skillet sizzling hot. She dumped the frozen fries into the air fryer. She put two hamburger buns in the oven to warm. And she plopped two hamburger patties into the hot skillet. They sizzled and smoked immediately, so she turned down the heat.

What next?

The tomato. And maybe they had onions.

"Do you want onion on your burger if I can find one?"

Shannon shook her head. "No. I'm good."

Hannah went to the refrigerator and retrieved the sliced cheese, along with ketchup, mustard, mayo, and a jar of pickles. She walked to the table and set the condiments down.

Shannon's eyes were closed. Had she fallen asleep?

Hannah went back to the cabinets and found plates and glasses, pulling two of each out and setting them on the countertop. Then she walked to the silverware drawer and picked out two knives and two forks, plus serving forks. She set those on the plates and went back for napkins. She carried the plates, napkins, and serving forks to the table and set them down. Shannon was still sleeping.

This might be her chance to get away!

Hannah tiptoed to the back door and opened it. There was no creak or pop. She might make it. She had her hand on the screen door, took a deep breath, and—

"Where do you think you're going?"

Shannon was standing beside her with her gun in her hand. Hannah calculated her chances. If she could get a head start, she could run to the street, or to a neighbor's house, and ask for help. She took a step forward, pretending to give in to Shannon's authority. Then she headbutted her. Ouch! That hurt. But it hurt Shannon too, who screeched, stumbling backward.

Hannah slung her arm out, knocking the pistol out of Shannon's hand, and it bounced, then slid across the floor. Both women looked at it, and then at each other. Before Shannon could make a move, Hannah reached again for the door.

Shannon pulled her back, and Hannah resisted. The two wrestled, neither besting the other, neither going down for the count. Hannah struggled to keep her footing. She remained standing but lost ground. Shannon shoved her away, throwing her into the cabinetry near the prep area.

Hannah could hear the hum of the air fryer next to her ears. She was near the utensil drawer . . . the chef's knife! Hannah yanked open the drawer and grabbed it.

Shannon backed off, eyes wary, darting between the knife and Hannah's face.

Hannah moved forward, gripping the knife, and holding it midair between them. "Don't come closer!"

Shannon's eyes widened. She wiped blood from her mouth with the back of her hand. "You fight like a girl." She lunged forward.

Hannah stepped backwards, her heart pounding. It was enough to set the other woman off-balance, and Shannon stumbled as

Hannah moved away again.

"I promise you," Hannah said. "I will hurt you."

The professor quickly regained her footing and lunged again.

This time Hannah jumped sideways, a few feet closer to the door.

The wild-eyed professor charged her again, grabbing for the knife. Hannah fell backwards against the back of a chair. Shannon grabbed Hannah's knife-wielding arm, pulling the blade down toward Hannah's chest.

Dear God. Help me.

CHAPTER 54

She's OK. The words kept replaying in Jake's mind as he led a caravan of law enforcement officers back to the main road. Shortly before they reached Nashville Pike, his phone rang.

"We have a rough triangulation on Hannah Cassidy's cell phone." Jake engaged the speaker on Roland's phone so they could both hear. "She's somewhere off Long Hollow Pike near Newman's Trail."

"Can you pinpoint it closer?"

"Not yet, sir."

"OK, please keep me updated."

Jake glanced to Roland, who gave him directions. "Stay on this road and take Lower Station Camp Creek Road straight through to Long Hollow Pike. It's probably your quickest route this time of day."

Jake did as he was instructed, and the caravan of police cars followed him.

But where were they headed? Long Hollow Road was a long stretch of highway between Hendersonville and Gallatin.

"Somewhere close to Newman's Trail. Do you know where that is, Roland?"

"Roughly. Keep going the way you're headed."

It took only about ten minutes to drive from Nashville Pike to Long Hollow Pike, but it felt like an hour to Jake. Once they'd reached Long Hollow, he asked Roland where to turn.

"Left, if you want to go toward Newman's Trail," he said.

Jake took a left. The road and related subdivision were on the right.

Hannah summoned all the strength she had, pushing Shannon away and regaining her footing. But it was impossible to run before Shannon charged again.

This time Hannah stood her ground, calculating the distance between them in inches.

Shannon reached for the knife, and Hannah plunged it downward. The blade only grazed Shannon's arm, but it was enough to give her pause.

And enough to give Hannah time to run.

She was halfway across the room to the door when a cat darted in front of her, throwing her forward. Hannah felt herself falling. The carpet rushed toward her in slow motion. She threw the knife away to avoid falling on it and landed facedown on the floor, her torso hitting first and knocking the breath out of her. She couldn't breathe. She couldn't move. A hard lump pressed into her chest. *Think, Hannah.*

She was only thirteen. Casey's older brother, Roger, had gone with them to the horse barn and dared them to shimmy down the hay rope. It was her turn, but the rope had stung her hands. She let go . . . too soon. Down she fell. The ground came quickly. And hard.

I can't breathe. I can't breathe—

"You can breathe." Casey was saying. "Look . . . you're breathing. Get up!"

Hannah rolled over, steadying against the wall, her hand closing around the metallic lump that had been beneath her, a lump that had a distinctive barrel and grip.

But where was the knife?

She looked up and saw it in the other woman's hand.

"I hope you and your man have been enjoying each other," Shannon said as she closed the distance. "He was interested in me first, you know."

"How dare you!" Hannah said, as she slowly raised the gun, aiming at Shannon's chest. "Don't move!" she said. "I will shoot you. I promise you! I will do it."

And then the door opened.

It was Jake.

"Shannon, it's nice to see you again," Jake said. "Although under quite different circumstances."

"I'm sure it is," she said, fluffing her hair and tilting her chin. Her clothing was bloodied and torn, and she was still taking her breath in gulps. "What's this party about?" She gestured to the law enforcement officers in the room.

Frank Tolman, who had met up with them in front of the house, answered for them all. "Ms. Bridges, I'm Agent-in-Charge Frank Tolman with the Tennessee Bureau of Investigation. You are under arrest for human trafficking, kidnapping, conspiracy, and felony murder. You have the right to remain silent . . ."

"Murder? I didn't kill anyone. I'm afraid you need to see Markham Davis about that. In fact, he's the problem." She grimaced and the tears began. "I was being manipulated by him to—"

"Ms. Bridges, anything you say can be used against you in a court of law. You have the right to talk to an attorney for advice before we ask you any questions. You have the right to have an attorney with you during questioning. If you cannot afford an attorney, one will be appointed for you before any questioning if you wish. Do you understand these rights?"

Tolman nodded, and a short blonde policewoman, wearing the dark-blue uniform of the Hendersonville Police department, stepped up to Shannon Bridges and closed handcuffs around her wrists.

"Yes—ouch!" Shannon snapped at her. "That hurt."

The policewoman shook her head, took Shannon by the arm, and led her toward the door. As Shannon walked past Jake, she gave him a seductive smile. "You have no idea what you missed, honey."

"Take her out of here." Jake turned his head in disgust.

Shannon continued to complain as she was led out of the room, the sound of her voice diminishing once the door closed behind them. Jake turned around, and Hannah smiled, disheveled but beautiful. "I'm glad you got here when you did." Her eyes filled with tears, then she seemed to collapse.

He pulled her into his arms and held her while she cried.

He knew her journey of fear was now over, and he prayed she could have peace in her life again. And that the vicious, angry woman, who had held so many women captive, had been taken off the street.

Jake walked Hannah out the back door, and Roland walked over to them. "Hannah," he said, "I'm so sorry."

She pulled away from Jake and reached to hug the older man. "It's OK, Roland. Everything is OK now."

"What will happen to R. J.?" Roland asked Jake.

"He can get some help now," Jake said. "But he will also answer to justice."

Roland nodded.

Jake looked from Roland to Hannah. "Why don't we all go to Dixie's place and see if she has any of that brisket left in her refrigerator? I don't know about the rest of you, but I'm hungry."

Hannah laughed. And everything was okay in the world.

EPILOGUE

One year later

Jake laughed until he hurt. He had fallen into a family of comedians. A family who, although diverse, had welcomed him with open arms. A family who had reminded him that love is still alive and well. Not only in his life, but in the lives of others who have had to start over again.

Picking up the pieces was a lot easier when somebody helped. He looked across the table at Hannah and thought about the scared little girl who still lived somewhere deep inside of her. But right now, he saw a strong woman. One of the strongest he had ever known. She was not only strong and resilient but also beautiful. And she said she loved him.

He loved her too.

For years, he had asked himself if he could really move on. He knew now that he could. He would never forget the past and the foundation it had laid for him. In fact, he could now embrace it. The hardest part of grieving was accepting. And letting go. But since the day he met them in late August, Hannah and her family—Dixie, Roland, Brandon, Audrey, and Roland's daughter, Rebecca—had rocked his world. In a good way.

Roland's family had been through a lot in the last twelve months. But they had pulled together. They had been pulling for R. J. too.

Because of the extenuating circumstances, the judge had been fair to R. J. Once the facts were on the table, it was obvious that Shannon had manipulated him into committing acts he would never have committed on his own. He was almost as much a victim as Shannon's girls had been. In fact, two of the girls, who were now free and living in a halfway house, had testified on R. J.'s behalf.

On the other hand, justice had thrown the book at Shannon. She had been convicted of murder and attempted murder, among other things. But the facts about her cruel and inhuman treatment of her girls had been terrifying to the mothers and fathers on the jury who had children of their own. Children who could one day be manipulated and victimized by someone like Shannon.

It was also Shannon's attitude during the trial that had helped seal her fate. No one can talk back to the judge or stare daggers at jury members and expect to receive mercy—the mercy of the court system specifically.

Of course, the mercy of God was always ready and available. Even to people like Shannon. Even to people like him.

Jake knew because he had discovered it afresh in his life. He had even made his amends with Rylie's dad and attended a few church services there. But he had also introduced him to Hannah and explained that he had decided to attend church with her, Dixie, and Roland at another church across town, where Hannah was trying to convince him to join the choir with her. That wasn't about to happen, but he was considering the idea of a special needs children's martial arts class. Something that had been brewing in him since he had been working with Brandon.

"Jake! Jake!" It was Brandon's voice that brought Jake back to the moment, sitting around Dixie's table waiting for dessert to be served. Audrey was helping Dixie in the kitchen, and Brandon was sitting at the head of the table, with Jake and Hannah on each side of him. That kid thought Hannah hung the moon.

That made two of them.

A few minutes later, Dixie and Audrey came back into the room with a big cake and a tray of assorted flavors of sparkling water, along with glasses of iced tea for those who wanted it.

Dixie took a seat and looked around the table, stopping at Jake. He nodded.

"Everybody," Dixie said. "Jake wants to make an announcement." She took her knife and clanged the water glass in front of her.

Could he do this? Was he blushing? He suddenly felt like a teenage boy with a crush. His stomach was in knots. But he could— and he would—do it. He took a deep breath.

"Hannah," he said. "Will you marry me?"

Hannah gasped. Then started crying.

Did that mean "no"? Maybe he had gotten it all wrong.

She wiped the moisture from her eyes and hiccupped out a laugh. "Yes. A thousand times yes! I love you, Jake Matheson."

Jake looked around the table. Everyone in the room had tears in their eyes. Everyone except Brandon, who was grinning from ear to ear.

"Way to go, Mr. Jake," he said.

And the tears turned to laughter.

# # #

THANK YOUS & CREDITS

One of the best parts of writing is meeting inspiring people, who are not only willing to share their time and expertise—but their passion. There are a lot of passionate people who helped with this book.

Many thanks to—
Dr. Tim Adair
Marco Conelli
Hendersonville Citizens Police Academy Association
Josh DeVine, Tennessee Bureau of Investigation
Jennifer Dornbush
Stacy Elliott, End Slavery Tennessee
Katherine M. Skiba
Denise Combs Ward, American Therapeutic Riding Center
Lindsey Wood, SaddleUp

Thank you to friends, family, and encouragers—
Carol Bell
JoAnn Bennett
Joe Bonsall
Terry & Sheri Calonge
Priscilla Cothran
Tom & Letha Edwards
Mable Hall
Patti Harris
Jeraldine Heflin
Carolyn Johnston
Phyl Kisshauer
Jon Mir
Erma Smith
Andrea Stray

Linda Veath
Rebecca Whittington

In memory of Avagene Moore and Debbie Copeland

Special thanks to—
Ed Laneville, for being an important part of this story from the beginning to the end.

Debbye Scroggins, a major cheerleader and an "honorary writing coach" for this story.

Julie Gwinn of The Seymour Agency, a woman who is an incredible force in the lives of every author who is fortunate enough to work with her.

Ramona Richards, who is not only my editor but a mentor and my real-life writing hero.

My hope is that this story will reflect the Word, Jesus Christ, who was, is and will be forever. I write to the rhythm of His song.
—*Kathy*

The Story Behind the Story
I knew very little about human trafficking when I first started writing this book. I knew that it was more prevalent than most people think. But I didn't know that it "occurs in every city, every county and every zip code in Middle Tennessee" (https://www.endslaverytn.org).

I also didn't realize that the Tennessee Bureau of Investigation has four dedicated anti-trafficking agents to help stop the problem in our state. However, despite being proactive, human trafficking is "the second-fastest growing criminal industry, just behind drug trafficking" in Tennessee (https://www.tn.gov/tbi/crime-issues/crime-issues/human-trafficking.html). On the positive side, Tennessee is one of the highest-ranking states in the US for effective human trafficking laws, law enforcement training, and victim outreach. In fact, our state has been a leader in this area.

And more good news. Contrary to the fictional story presented in this book, no human trafficking incidents have been reported on college campuses in Tennessee in recent years (https://www.tn.gov/content/dam/tn/tbi/documents/2019CrimeOnCampus.pdf).

Yet human trafficking does occur in all fifty states, and it is on the rise. It affects every age group, every income bracket, every social status, and every ethnicity. It affects men, women, boys, and girls. It affects citizens and noncitizens. And it happens in small towns, big cities, and rural areas. It can be found in almost every social setting—from foster homes to churches. And it may be as close as your next-door neighbor or the family living around the block. Money is always the bottom line. Trafficking exists to provide income for the perpetrator.

Online is now the primary method of communicating with and targeting victims, but don't forget the familial connection. Most victims of human trafficking are from an abusive past and have an expectation of being treated in this way. Most victims have a missing piece in their lives, leaving them vulnerable to being manipulated through compliments, intimidation, etc. Some victims were born into unloving families or have relatively no family.

The Truth Will Set You Free
There are a lot of misconceptions about human trafficking. Here are three of the most common myths provided by the Polaris Project.

Myth #1: Traffickers target victims they don't know.
The Reality: Many victims have been trafficked by romantic partners, including spouses, and by family members, including parents.

Myth #2: All human trafficking involves commercial sex.
The Reality: By definition, human trafficking is the use of force, fraud, or coercion to get another person to provide labor or commercial sex. Worldwide, experts believe there are more

situations of labor trafficking than of sex trafficking, but there is much wider awareness of sex trafficking in the US than of labor trafficking.

Myth #3: Human trafficking is always or usually a violent crime.

The Reality: The most pervasive myth about human trafficking is that it often involves kidnapping or physically forcing someone into a situation. In reality, most traffickers use psychological means such as tricking, defrauding, manipulating, or threatening victims into providing commercial sex or exploitative labor.

For additional information and statistics about human trafficking, visit https://polarisproject.org.

Action Points

- Stay alert to human trafficking for the sake of your loved ones and friends. Prevention is much easier than aftercare and rehabilitation.

- Stay vigilant in your home, school, business, and community and report any suspicion of human trafficking to your local law enforcement agency.

- Consider donating your time, talent, and/or financial resources to a qualified anti-trafficking organization in your area.

Most of all, remember the power of love and our biblical charge: "So now faith, hope, and love abide, these three; but the greatest of these is love" (1 Corinthians 13:13 ESV).

For additional information about what you can do in the fight against human trafficking in your community, log on to my website resources page, https://kathyharrisbooks.com/resources/.